THE FINAL FLING

break.
free.

JH SIMON

Copyright © 2022 by JH Simon & Miki Clarke.

Written by JH Simon. Story by JH Simon & Miki Clarke. Edit by Miki Clarke.

All rights reserved. No part of this publication may be reproduced, distributed, or transmitted in any form or by any means, including photocopying, recording, or other electronic or mechanical methods, without the prior written permission of the author, except in the case of brief quotations embodied in critical reviews and certain other noncommercial uses permitted by copyright law.

Special thanks goes to Katinka Noack for her deep editing. This book would not be the same without her tireless work.

Illustrations by Jennifer Addens (@juicy__jane_tattooart).

ISBN: 9798846408760

*

This book is dedicated to the serenely beautiful Andalusian countryside, where I rediscovered my humanity, learned what it was to be a good man, and fell in love with the woman who would help me become one.

THE FINAL FLING

1

MEET ME IN BERLIN

JASMIN

THIS ISN'T WORKING. Those were the most honest words Thomas had ever uttered. First, he sat me down at his apartment to talk. Next came a burdened sigh. His hazel eyes, which had inspired my love for a decade, were everywhere but on me. Those lips, which had caressed and danced with mine thousands of times, made the frown of a defeated man. He was ending it. Again.

"Jaz? You agree with me, right?" he said with a trembling voice.

This time I did. We had been dancing near the abyss for too long. Years of long distance only drove us closer to the edge. Me in my dream city, Amsterdam, him in Stockholm living his own Scandinavian dream. Until that moment, I would have immediately folded. Would have come over to him, kissed his hair, and asked him how he could say such a thing. Sure, things were not perfect, but we could have worked through it. We had always found a solution before. For some reason, that day felt different — despite still loving him. As I quietly looked over this man I adored, I felt the ice melting over me, revealing the warm, inviting glow of something I never expected to experience in such a situation...

"Relief!?" said Michaela, putting her cocktail down and shifting her entire body in my direction, giving me her full attention and focus.

"I know it's weird," I said after sipping on my old fashioned, the two of us deep in our breakup-discussion bubble. "But that's how I feel."

"Sure," said Michaela. "But you're turning thirty next week. I'm glad you're not devastated, but how do you feel about the timing?"

The question aroused that same unsettling feeling I got when I turned twenty-nine. The surrounding chatter barely registered while I searched myself. I felt a world away from my friends, who were gathered around me for my early birthday drinks at our favourite rooftop bar. Behind us were the night lights of Amsterdam-Noord. In the corner were my work colleagues, busy with office gossip. Meanwhile, I sat there looking ahead to a life without Thomas. I took another sip of my drink to wash the lingering uncertainty away before answering.

"Better now than later," I said with a shrug.

"True," said Michaela. "I'm proud of you. I'm just surprised you're not freaking out."

I barely gave her words a chance to sink in before looking across for a diversion.

"So, where's Kate?" I said.

Michaela was on it. She scanned our congregation.

"There she is," said Michaela, sitting up. "Kate!" she commanded over the chatter.

Kate turned her head suddenly to catch who called her, then walked over to us looking like a vision.

"Hello, my gorgeous ones," she said in her sweet and loving voice.

Kate was stunning. She had men and women throwing themselves at her, but never blinked. She was happily married to her high school sweetheart. Her life was seemingly perfect, as was she, which made me feel the exact opposite. I was about to spill the breakup details to her at work when she was interrupted by our boss, who called her in for an emergency client call — leaving me hanging and reminded who the favourite was.

"So babe, Jaz is relieved about Thomas," Michaela said with a twinkle in her eyes which had me noticing.

"I guess that's better than being devastated," said Kate.

"That's what I said," replied Michaela.

I melted. From the crown of my head to my feet. There was nothing more reassuring than seeing my girls on matching wavelengths. It was *because* I was turning thirty that I was relieved. A part of me missed Thomas, and was terrified of going it alone, but at least I still had time to make the most of the situation. Europe was on the cusp of spring, and I had dodged the winter phase of the breakup. No nostalgia when hearing certain songs. No stuffing my face with salted caramel ice cream. No makeovers or soul-searching trips to India. Only my own company, and me open for anything. I counted myself lucky.

Michaela shifted in her chair and leaned her head to the side.

"So when you say you're relieved, does that mean you're ready to date, or do you want something physical only?"

"Don't know," I said. "I'm off work until the end of next week. I want to get out of Amsterdam and figure everything out before going to my parent's. See what comes up."

"That's good," said Kate. "Take your time. You could always pop into Vondel Cafe for some eye candy when you're back. All the hot guys in Amsterdam go there."

I observed Kate's bright, innocent gaze and royal posture, her hands carefully placed on her lap. The thought of her lusting over some random guy popped into my head. Did she ever stray from her perfect life and into naughtier places? Even in her imagination?

"I guess I could," I said, not really moved by the idea of window shopping.

Kate's smile turned to a satisfied grin.

"You totally should," said Michaela, piggy-backing on the idea. "Use next week as an opportunity."

My Michi-radar went off. She was up to something.

"Opportunity, huh?" I said, taking her bait the way she was clearly hoping.

"Yeah," said Michaela. "See what's around."

"Oh, spill it!" I said. "What's up your sleeve?"

Kate rolled her eyes and shook her head with a chuckle. Like me, she knew what Michaela was like.

"Right, guys," said Michaela, flicking her hair back, her chest coming forward.

Here we go. I braced myself for another of Michaela's wild and wonderful ideas. That woman was the life of the party for a reason. My mind went to her annual bottomless house party — no pants, skirts or underwear allowed inside. Thomas had flipped when I suggested going.

"Hear me out," continued Michaela. "I've got the perfect palette cleanser to prepare you for single life, Jaz."

My senses brightened as Michaela searched through her phone then handed it to me. On it I found an image of a party invitation. Two intersecting handcuff chains decorated a black canvas, with the following text underneath:

Passion Parade
Sex-positive dance party in Berlin
Midnight until late
(un)dress to impress
Lingerie // shirt but naked // black leather // NO streetwear

The event was on Saturday. In two days. I scoffed and shook my head, handing the phone back to Michaela.

"A sex party?" I said.

"Why not?" said Michaela. "You loved hearing my stories about Berlin. All the kinky stuff I got up to."

"Sure," I said, twirling my straw in circles. "I liked hearing about it. I never saw myself doing it."

"Never? All I know is that—" Michaela leaned forward and lowered her voice. "You always spoke about how shit the sex with Thomas became. How quickly he finished, and how in his head he was. How you wanted more."

Yep. My sex life with Thomas had been nauseating me for years. I missed what we had. My reflection in his pupils as he thrust his fiery love into me. The careful attention he paid with his mouth to the entirety of my body. The feeling that I was the only woman on the planet. We went from pure, unbridled love-making, to something bordering on mechanical, soulless sex, all in a couple of years. As the fights piled up, and the insults and accusations grew harsher, my heart tightened shut. I felt constantly worn out. Without the fuel of youthful devotion, the sex grew empty. We had been spluttering on fumes since. We went from missionary to doggy style and back, and when we had been drinking, I sometimes got to ride on top — when he could keep it up. *Joy.*

"Right," I said. "But not more dicks. Just better sex."

"You'll get both in Berlin," said Michaela, steepling her fingers, her sales persona coming out.

"Michi, she's just come out of a nine-year relationship," said Kate. "Give the girl a break. Maybe a date or two in a few months, not a sex party this weekend."

"It's a sex-*positive* party," said Michaela. "Kinky dress and dancing. Sex is optional. The underground parties are something else entirely. I wouldn't do that to her. She's not ready for that."

"Don't do it, Jaz," said Kate, sensing my temptation. "I wouldn't."

Good old Kate. Of course it made sense to get back in the dating game the proper way. Yet to my surprise, a fuzzy sensation formed in my lower belly and caused a quiver between my legs. Michaela's devilish stare was unrelenting. She had waited until my third cocktail before bringing up her insane plan for me. Now she was going in, knowing how much of a push-over I was when tipsy. The girl was good. She was also my best friend for a reason.

I considered the idea further, refusing to look Kate in the eyes.

"That's where I check out," said Kate finally.

She walked off, looking me dead in the eye as she passed. She finished with a wink and floated off to grace the others with her presence. It seemed she had better things to do than getting involved in sex adventures. I was fine with that.

"She's a terrible help," said Michaela, poking her tongue out at Kate.

"Maybe in this case," I said, sitting up. "So. Are you going to this thing?"

Michaela sighed and shook her head, surprising me with her reaction.

"I wish," she said. "Hendrick and I are driving to his parent's place in Enschede. We haven't been to a kink party in ages. I didn't tell anyone this, so keep it between you and me. We're thinking of starting a family."

I twitched and leaned forward suddenly, my face brightening up.

"Michi, that's wonderf—"

"Shh," she cut in, her eyes swelling open.

"That's so exciting," I whispered.

"To be honest, I'm terrified," said Michaela with vulnerable eyes.

I felt her slipping, and held her up with a reassuring smile.

"But we're ready," she said. "I think." She shook her head to regather her wits. "Anyway, we're not talking about me right now."

This was not part of her strategy to sell me the party, I realised. It was real. My best friend was going to try for a baby. The same teenage girl who would drag me to the shops to get a look at her latest crush. The same woman who at one stage was attending weekly sex orgies, and who once had an open relationship with a fifty-year-old painter, was looking to be a mother. How times had changed. What had I done in my twenties? What reckless abandon had I experienced during my relationship with Thomas? A lot less than I wanted. Was I ready to be a mother now like Michaela, and accept the regrets of a life barely lived? It was something I needed to put some thought into. And soon.

"Jaz, this is perfect for you," said Michaela. "I wasn't going to say anything until you were ready, but clearly you're fine."

"This weekend is too soon," I said. "Plus, I want to go with you."

"You moved to Amsterdam with a suitcase and no friends," said Michaela. "You can handle this."

"I had you," I said.

"You still do," said Michaela. "But you've also got yourself. Don't forget that."

Alone. In Berlin. The city of debauchery and sin. The thought had my insides in a spin cycle. No way.

Michaela studied my hesitation. What would a salesperson do in such a situation? Go for the kill. Naturally. She reached into her handbag and took out a present wrapped in shiny gold paper, with a card on top that read *Jazzy Jaz* — her nickname for me.

"For you, my darling," she said.

I received my early birthday present without a word. Opened the gift carefully from the sides and slid the cardboard box out without creasing the paper. Lifted the flap, and found two items. The first was an erotic novel called 'Lover of Prey.' I caught myself lingering on the cover. It showed a tanned, muscle-bound man with perfect abs stalking a dreamy-eyed, black woman through her bedroom door as she lay on her bed, reading in lingerie with the light reflecting off her curvaceous body. I turned to the back and caught the first couple of lines of the blurb. I never read romance, let alone erotica. *Cheesy.* And worse still — written by a man.

I turned my eye to the other present. A black 'vibrating bullet.' I shook my head, looking up at Michaela with a bemused smile. She was something else, that girl.

"This was to help you cope," she said. "Obviously you don't need that. But read the book on the train, and the vibr—" She lowered her voice. "Take it with you to Passion Parade."

"I don't know," I said with a sigh. "Thank you. Really. This is great. But I can't do this."

Michaela placed her eternally warm hand over my cold fingers.

"You can," she said, holding me in her worldly eyes, giving me the melting feeling that everything would be fine. "There's no right time."

I shook my head to break her spell, but could still feel its pull inside me. I thought back on all the times Thomas had dangled the breakup stick over me. I could have taken the untraveled road many times, risking losing a flawed love for something more fulfilling. Instead, I looked down what felt like a dark, treacherous path and chickened out, staying with the same boyfriend and cushy job because it felt safer. Now I was standing out in the open again, with only a party invitation for a map, and an overwhelming sense that the clock was ticking. Michaela's sharp, watchful eyes steered me where I needed to go.

"Ok. *Maybe*, I'll go," I said.

"That's my Jazzy Jaz!" yelled Michaela too loudly, forcing me to instantly regret opening my mouth.

"I said maybe!" I hissed.

"Let's say you do go," said Michaela, lowering her voice again. "You need to be clear about a couple of things. What space do you want to play in?"

I broke eye contact, caught off guard by the question. *Sub. Brat. Dom. Switch.* Michaela had experimented with all of the BDSM roles. She even had sex with a guy who let her slap his face and called her 'mistress.' So ultimately, she was a switch. I had zero experience and zero idea what I was.

"Uh..." I said. "A sub, I guess?"

"Babe," said Michaela bluntly. "Every woman assumes she's a sub. It feels great to let go and let the dom control things. Do lots of that. But I know you. There's more. The least you can do is make him work for it."

Teasing and provoking a man did sound fun. But was I a brat?

"I'll think about it," I said. "I don't know yet."

"Fine," said Michaela. "Next thing. Do you know your hard boundaries? Do you want to do group stuff? If so, guys or girls, or both?"

Uh, what? I had no clue what to do with one guy, let alone two, let alone a girl. I had tickled the idea of a three-way once before shutting it down. Too out there.

I rubbed my wrist for a second, then stopped myself. To be fair, Michaela's wild stories over the years had widened my sexual lens. Lately I had even considered an open relationship with Thomas; an idea I had labelled insane and never uttered to anyone. I wondered if I should tell her about that now? Or the disturbing fantasies I had been having recently. The scenarios I had dreamt up. The punishments I wanted.

"I've never done anything like that," I said. "How am I supposed to know what I like?"

Don't worry, you'll know, came a voice from inside, sending shivers through me. I shifted in my seat. *Where did that come from?*

"You'll know when the time comes," said Michaela, echoing my thoughts. "Go easy. One step at a time, and always trust your body. You've got this." She smirked suddenly. "Basically my advice for anyone trying anal for the first time."

Jesus.

"Oh," she added, sitting up suddenly. "I never told you that story, did I?"

"Michi!" I said with a slap of her hand.

Michaela could barely keep it together. That woman loved to take it a step too far. I watched my best friend laughing to herself and could see she was really getting into the idea of me going to this party. She was also making me feel a little more comfortable with the whole thing. *Holy crap.* I needed to give her something.

"Do you think Thomas could have handled an open relationship?" I said.

Michaela lowered her glass and stared at me, holding her sip before swallowing.

"You're kidding," she said. "Thomas?"

"It could've worked. A relationship with a nice guy, and exploring the other stuff with someone else."

"The *right* guy will give you both," said Michaela. "Thomas was never it."

I nodded, but could not stomach her words. Thomas was the right and wrong guy rolled into one. Our early years proved that we were a sexual fit. But too many times I stood naked in front of the mirror with that tight longing in my chest, wishing he would come up from behind with an open heart and a raging hard dick and just... well... fuck me the hell open! How else could I have put it? The thought of it caused me to shudder as I sat there in my chair watching Michaela plotting my hypothetical orgy. If only Thomas could have found a way to transcend the faults in our relationship, to overpower the pain with some masculine might. Eventually, I lost hope in that. But not in my desire for passion that would break me out of my prison. I carried it like a raging fire between my legs. The fantasies drifted out of our relationship and into the public realm. Musicians. Yoga instructors. Married men. Being caught between Thomas and that fire was suffocating me — until he set me free last week.

"Right, everyone," we heard Kate say to our friends, turning our attention outwards. "As Jasmin won't be around, we need to sing loud enough for her to still hear us on her big day. So get your lovely singing voices ready. Haaappy Birthday to you," she began, and was joined by a chorus of our friends, followed by the other strangers drinking around us.

My face almost exploded with embarrassment, and I covered it for the entire song with both hands. A big applause broke out at the end, and I was forced to look up and smile at my beaming friends. If I was in denial about it before, I had to let that go now. I was turning thirty next weekend. Single. Alone.

Two cocktails later, everyone had left except for Michaela and me. Michaela was busy typing a long text into her phone, before she looked up at me with the same crazed expression she used to have back in high school before we went off on another adventure.

"Hendrick wanted to leave early for Enschede tomorrow," said Michaela. "But I just told him I had important business to take care of. Let's go back to yours and get you packed and ready."

"What? I didn't say yes, Mich-"

"Your eyes did," she cut in.

Someone help me.

Michaela paid our tab and we left, wandering down the narrow, charmingly-lit Amsterdam streets. With doubts circling my mind like vultures, we crossed over one of the city's many canals, leaving behind the warm orange hue and entering the red light district. Michaela's attention was straight ahead, while mine drifted to the side. I locked eyes with one of the beautiful women in the windows, who was wearing a bright-white bikini. She perked her lips and blew me a kiss, the power and serenity in her eyes putting me on a cloud that carried me all the way home and through my doorway.

As Michaela started tearing into my wardrobe, rejecting anything that was not remarkably sexy, the whole thing started to feel real. Too real. Panic shot through me.

"Michi," I said. "Seriously, I don't know about this."

Wrinkles appeared above Michaela's eyes, and her expression darkened.

"Do you remember our trip to Barcelona when we were seventeen?" she said. "Juan Jose and Roberto?"

I thought back before a smile found its way to the corners of my mouth. *Of course.* The two middle-aged men we met at the beach while on holiday, which our parents somehow agreed to let us go on alone. We ended up at some random apartment with the two of them. With the Spanish music on blast and wine flowing, the sexual tension quickly followed. The age difference made us conscious of acting 'grown up,' so Michaela and I started making out in front of them. Surprise, surprise, they loved it. Roberto grabbed Michaela's wrist and they disappeared inside. Juan Jose put his sights on me, and eventually had me on the sofa with two fingers deep inside me while sucking on my neck. I opened my eyes briefly and looked at his free hand, freaking when I caught the bright-white tan mark where his wedding ring should have been. I ended up storming in on Roberto's bare-white butt in my face while he thrust into Michaela in missionary. At first she was furious with me for dragging her out like that. Later we laughed about it. Our bond as sisters was forged in the fires of dangerous, young passion. A fire that continued for Michaela, and stopped for me when Thomas came into my life.

"What about it?" I said.

"I want you to remember who you were before Thomas."

"A reckless teenager?"

Michaela made a disappointed face.

"A *wild woman* ready for anything," she said.

The windows were closed, but I felt a cool breeze pass over me. Her words had stirred up the spirit of the past, but that was all it was — the past. There was an emptiness inside me now, and I knew I had to fill it. For that, I needed a new adventure. I finally understood what Michaela was getting at.

I went over to the drawer and fetched my white, see-through 'datenight string.' Stood in front of the full-body mirror, pulled off my jeans and underwear and slid it on. Michaela seemed to struggle to process what was happening. Her eyes darted up and down, and her mouth slowly went slack. She had seen me naked before, but never like this. I pushed my butt in her direction.

"How do I look?" I said.

"Are you serious?" she responded, finally meeting my eyes. "Sexy as hell. What else?"

"Good," I said. "So let's do this."

Her face brightened.

"We're doing this?" she said.

"We're doing this!" I cried with a firm nod.

"Right," said Michaela with a broad smile, rubbing her hands together and beginning what in sales would be called the paperwork. "Outfit."

I shrugged slowly with a pout while changing back into my usual underwear.

"Leather pants?" I said. "Whip?"

"Hey, don't joke around," said Michaela. "If you bring a whip, be prepared to use it. Do you have something sexy and black? Like a lingerie set you put on for a special date?"

"I have this," I said, pulling on the lace thread of the white datenight string. "But I only wore it for Thomas."

"Not anymore," said Michaela, taking it from me and tossing it in my luggage.

I put on an electronic set from some Berlin DJ to set the mood, and we continued scouring my stuff for more clothes to pack. We rocked our heads to the beat while creating a pile of discarded clothes in the middle of my bedroom floor. I started dancing over the mess, and got a bewildered stare from Michaela.

"Look at you!" she said. "Little Miss Clean Freak has lost her mind."

"Your fault," I said, moving my hips side to side.

"Man, I wish I was going with you," she said, joining me above the pile of clothes and play-grinding against me.

"If only," I said, practising a little twerk in my mirror.

The two of us collapsed onto my bed and lay side by side, looking up at the ceiling while my drunken head spun in circles.

"Did you ever get judged for the things you did in Berlin?" I said.

"Sure," said Michaela. "Most people didn't say anything, but there was always this underlying judgement. Like their brains were ticking. Not that I ever hid it. I'm sick of the taboo, you know?"

"I get it," I said. "I just want to see a guy I like and have him take me then and there. No guilt, no questions asked."

"Jaz!" yelled out Michaela with a deafening cackle that trembled the mattress beneath us and probably woke the neighbours.

"I don't care anymore," I said with a shrug. "It's been a rough nine years."

"Apparently not rough enough," said Michaela, spanking the side of my ass. "Oh, that gives me an idea. Get your laptop out."

I did as she said, lifting the lid and entering my password. Michaela took over immediately and opened a website for a luxury hotel resort in Berlin.

"What's this?" I said.

"Äden," said Michaela with a squint, engrossed by the screen's contents. "You'll love it. Gorgeous place with gorgeous people in the centre of Berlin. Perfect for you."

I scanned the photos. It looked like it belonged in a movie.

"And it's got the darkrooms," said Michaela, looking up at me again with that scheming smile.

"Darkrooms?" I said, freezing up. Things were starting to get weird.

"It's a hidden maze inside the resort. Absolute darkness for anything you want to do. *Anything*. You get total discretion. Hendrick and I had a four-way there with a couple who we never met — or saw."

"You did what?" I said with a gasp. "I still can't believe mama orgy wants a baby," I added, shaking my head.

"Don't remind me," said Michaela. "Shit," she then blurted. "It's almost 4. I have to go, babe. I promised Hendrick. Practising being good mother material."

Hello, reality. Michaela's demeanour changed instantly, one moment living vicariously through me, the next fretting over her trip to see the in-laws. She looked at me once over.

"This is a good thing," she followed up.

"I hope so," I said, getting up with her.

"Have fun for me, lovely."

"Thanks, Michi."

One long, last hug and she was gone, leaving me with terror in my veins and gratitude in my belly. A tornado had torn through my apartment and blown out all my doubts. With fun time over, I switched my phone from aeroplane mode to normal, and a text from my mother immediately came through:

What time do you land next Friday, sweetie? Looking forward to seeing you!

At the end was a flirt emoji. Why could she not be normal? No matter how many times I told her, she kept using it. I checked my flight booking and texted her the time. It was six months since I had been home to London, so naturally she was excited I would be there for my birthday. I was too. Even though I was fine with the breakup, I still craved the love and attention that I only got at home. Having my clothes washed, ironed and folded. The sweet meringue and strawberry taste of the Eaton Mess awaiting me when I arrived. My mother and I dressing up on Sunday for afternoon tea at the Huxley Grand Hotel. The morning cuppa and chats on the terrace. A whole weekend being pampered and taken care of. Daddy would be in his workroom fiddling with some new gadget of his. When he was in a good mood, he would join us for a while. Ask me some awkward questions about drugs in Amsterdam. My mother would have a laugh at his expense, he would escape to his room, and the cycle would repeat.

I only recently became aware of how much they hid for the sake of our 'happy' family. I was at the shops with daddy last year when he ran into a beautiful woman from his past who I had never seen. His jittery body language and the way his eyes lit up told me she meant something to him, as did her wistful look while they bid each other farewell. I complimented him on his charm with the lady, and noted that I had never seen it with my mother. When he said to me "There are some things your mum and I don't share," it struck me with full force. He had regrets and unfulfilled desires like any other married person. He was only human. Reaching the end of my twenties had taken off the rose-coloured glasses and force-fed me a bitter pill. After that, I saw my future with Thomas differently, and it looked dim.

That outlook was improving quickly as I focussed back on the party. I made an online reservation at Äden and set my alarm for 10:00 am. Booked the 12:00 pm fast train, which would get me to Berlin by the late afternoon. Got into my PJs, brushed my teeth and washed off my makeup. I was wiped, but the excitement kept me awake. I flicked through the pages of Lover of Prey and tested my new bullet vibrator against my cheek before stuffing them both into my handbag. Slipped into bed, and took another look at the party invitation. *(Un)dress to impress.* I crawled out of my skin at the thought of having sex in front of a group of people. Then my phone vibrated again. My heart clamped up and skipped a beat when I saw the message.

Jaz, I'm sorry. I made a terrible mistake. Can we talk?

I remained mesmerised for a long time before lowering the phone. *Dammit, Thomas.* Why did he have to text now? Could he not have waited until Monday? Let me have my fun and *then* pull on my heartstrings? I left it. I could write him back on Sunday after the party. With that I put the phone down on the bedside table and stared at the ceiling, my mind circling. Michaela and a week of freedom had shown me that I was hungry to explore, to reach dizzying heights before even thinking of settling down. That need was not going anywhere now. The horny genie was out of the bottle.

But I could not deny the impact that Thomas' message was having on me. I lay there powerless as the familiar shadow of the past descended on me. Was one text all it took? I let my body sink into the mattress and grew acutely conscious of the paint colour of the wall. My only company now was Amsterdam's night sounds and an empty apartment. I could hear and feel my breath rise and fall. Could see my chest follow its rhythm. And for the first time since he left me, I felt it. *I was alone.* Relief was not going to save me now. I should have known it was too good to be true. Michaela had seen it all over my face.

At that second a strange idea hit me, bringing with it a shooting star of hope which immediately soothed my heartache. A compromise. An olive branch. I sat up and fetched my phone. It was too late to go back. I was certain of it. But that did not mean all hope between us was lost. I thought about my earlier idea, having Thomas by my side, and the 'right' guy behind me, satisfying me the way Thomas never could. Was it crazy to ask such a thing? Definitely. Was it right? Questionable. But if Thomas wanted back in, he would need to deal with a new reality. It was time to roll the dice, all the way down into the Berlin underground, and see where they landed. The deeper they travelled, the better. Thomas swore he would never return to Berlin. I knew that. But my instinct told me to do it anyway. I hit reply:

Meet me in Berlin.

2
SAME OLD

MICHAELA

A hand rocked me side to side.

"Michi," came an irritated Hendrick's voice. "Wake up."

I groaned and rolled away from him.

"Sweetheart," he said. "It's 11:30. We're leaving in an hour."

"Go without me," I moaned into the pillow.

"Michi," he said with a determined voice.

Dammit. I felt like a boxer down for the count. In a daze, my entire body aching, I rolled back in Hendrick's direction, and he reached over and cuddled me, pulling me into his warm, firm embrace. I groaned my frustration and exhaustion into his chest. It helped. Soon my eyes were open.

"Big night?" he said, resting his head on his fist and looking lovingly at me with amusement in his eyes.

I nodded. Six cocktails big.

"How's Jasmin doing?" he said.

I smiled wearily, the sleep on my face lifting with it.

"She's going," I said.

Hendrick's mouth came open.

"You convinced her?"

I nodded and smiled proudly, forcing myself upright.

"Yup," I said.

Hendrick shook his head.

"Darling, you could sell oil to a Saudi king," he said.

I grasped my phone from the side table.

"And she's doing fine with the breakup?" said Hendrick.

"More than fine," I said with a yawn, switching off aeroplane mode and looking at my husband. "She took it way better than I expected. Makes sense. Nine years of his bullshit."

"Good," said Hendrick. "That guy was always wrong for her. About time she saw that."

"I'm just glad it's finally over," I said.

My morning notifications came vibrating through. A message from Kate asking for her hair straightener back. All the likes flowing in from my photo post from Jasmin's birthday celebration. Lastly, a message from Jasmin. Probably her writing from the train wanting to share her excitement. I opened it. Read it carefully. Then froze. My shoulders dropped, and I covered my face.

"Fuuuck!" I yelled.

"What?" said Hendrick, moving closer to me.

"She invited him to Berlin."

"Huh? Who?"

"Jasmin," I said. "She invited Thomas to join her in Berlin."

"I thought they were broken up?"

I pinched my nose and closed my eyes.

"Why does she keep doing this!?" I groaned. "Where's her self-respect?"

I was wide awake now, the hangover making this news more unbearable than it needed to be.

"Seriously. That girl is never going to learn," said Hendrick, shaking his head and leaving the room.

I sighed, re-reading her message in disbelief. The guy dumped her God knew how many times. Made her twenties an absolute misery. And now, just when she was free, she backpedalled and let him back in.

I forced myself up and opened my cupboard to pick my outfit for the day, but my mind was kept distracted by Jasmin's stupidity. I always held out hope that she would find her way. Leave the dysfunctional bullshit behind and settle into something healthier. That hope was being tested now. Majorly. I had been through it with her every step of the way. Drama after drama. The never-ending cycle of breakup and makeup. All the times she called me in tears. What could I say? She always took the difficult route. I had heard it all from her. *I like to be challenged. That's not for me. But I love him. If only he could just...* There was no other way to look at it anymore. The girl was a masochist. She loved the pain. And she clearly needed more of it before she woke up. A lot more. Would she *ever* learn?

JASMIN

Forty-five minutes late and counting. All I had been doing for the last nine years was wait on Thomas to show up. Sitting in a Berlin cafe with him on the way felt ominous, considering his history in this city. The tables around me had the odd person focussed on their laptop screen, others chatted excitedly over a colourful brunch. Meanwhile, I chewed on my nail, my mind going back to those three months Thomas spent in Berlin. The constant drinking and partying. The cocaine-and-ecstasy-fueled session that stretched out to forty-eight hours and left him in the hospital with a chronic stabbing pain in his stomach. Berlin had tested him, and he had failed. Years of Michaela's underground stories had painted me an intriguing picture of a city that promised severe punishment if you hurried its madness. When Michaela paced herself, she found an intrinsic sense of self on its erotic carousel. Berlin favoured those who tossed aside their agendas and prejudices. It had its own plan for you, and only cushioned your fall if you surrendered fully. When its infinite nights lulled you in and spat you out, the purple clouds the morning after would be a dream. In any other city it would be a nightmare. Where a city like Paris inspired romance and sophistication, Berlin exuded hedonism. It commanded an innocent darkness, the purest form of freedom. But if you lost yourself in the high, it became a meat grinder. Berlin had turned Thomas to mince, taking him months to recover. Now I had invited him here for a party, of all things.

I stopped biting my nails and sat up straight. No, this was exactly what Thomas needed. He had to face his demons and get back on the carousel if he was to have another chance with me. I was not getting any younger.

Last night's birthday binge in Amsterdam had me feeling raw and testy. I put on my headphones and played some jazz to soothe myself, and started scrolling through our photo history. Reminiscing, trying to make sense of how we got here. First came the photos from Thailand the previous year. I opened the selfie he took of us at the beach in Koh Samui. He was beaming cheek to cheek. I was a pale-looking, premenstrual grump. Sometimes he just had no clue.

I flicked further back in time. There was that photo of me at brunch in Stockholm. I had just given in my thesis after months of high-level stress and then flown in late. I was a wreck the next morning. God, my skin. And that deathly stare I gave him and the camera. At least the food was delicious, I thought, looking at a perfectly angled, succulent photo of my meal — smashed mint, pea and avocado on sourdough with the perfect poached egg, topped off with a drizzle of chimichurri. That was the picture which got me to one-hundred-thousand followers on my food blog. My love of cuisine could save any miserable day.

Maybe I was being too harsh on Thomas. It had not all been bad. There was that naked photo I took of him fresh out of the sauna. He was raising his arms and yelling victoriously over the snowy Alps. So embarrassing. At least his little round butt looked sexy.

I played a morning video he shot for me from his apartment in Stockholm, and grinned at the beautiful and witty things he said. I scrolled further and seized up when 'the' dick pic came up, checking around instinctively to make sure nobody saw it. I lingered on the photo of our torsos for a moment longer than the others. We had just finished a half-decent session of sex. My leg was crossed over the other, his upright dick was in my hand. He did have a great cock. Straight and proud with a smooth head. Stole my attention when it was out. If only he used it the right way.

There was a photo of us from a few years back at a Halloween party. We went together as Gomez and Morticia Addams. Him in that pinstripe suit and fake moustache, me in that sexy black dress with the slit across the leg. The scary makeup. I smiled and melted as I remembered the moment he told me I would make a good wife, scary or otherwise. That had been such a fun night.

I went back another few years. To university in London, where Thomas and I met. I cringed at my fringe. Horrid mistake. It was the longest year of my life waiting for it to grow out. For Thomas and me, it was our first and best year. I had my hand over my mouth while recalling the first time I saw him. The infamous elevator incident. He came in staring at his phone, barely noticing me and Michaela standing in the corner. He glanced at the buttons then left them, apparently also going to the top floor. Then he lowered his phone and turned towards us. His eyes swelled when he saw me. My heart expanded at the sight of him too. We both froze, entering into a serene, timeless space, until he resumed the clock by moving to the button panel. He glanced back at me with a cheeky grin, and did something that changed our fates forever, pressing all the buttons for the elevator. I thought he was a weirdo. My skin crawled with fear at what he might do next. But then, with a shrug and a cheeky smile, he saved it.

"More time with you," he said.

Amazing how fine the line between creepy and charming was. His gaze was so magnetic, I was hooked. Well, almost.

"What makes you think I want to spend time with you?" I hit back.

"Because you're smiling," he said.

My smile widened more. He had me there.

Now here we were. In Berlin. I was no longer hooked. He had lured me, and spent nine years reeling me in, until abruptly letting me go. Things had changed. It was time for him to jump into the deep end.

A text message from him popped up:

The train still hasn't moved, babe. It's driving me crazy x

I sighed and tossed my phone onto the table. Was I really still his babe? His *babe* wanted to roam free. It was his choice if he wanted to swim alongside me, or with other fish, for that matter.

I grabbed Lover Of Prey out of my handbag. It took little for me to get back into the flow of the story. The warmth in my lower belly came quickly as Lorenzo made his move on Larissa at the gym. He had on his short shorts, and his dark, curly locks were glistening. After a hundred pages of tension-building drama, they finally broke through, going into an empty exercise room and locking the door. Their sexual eruption escalated rapidly. Lorenzo took charge of Larissa while she was on all fours on a bench press. He gripped her hair tight and drove all the way inside her, his pelvis slapping against her behind while she watched him fucking her in the mirror. He threw her on her back onto the mat and penetrated her with a tight grip around her neck. Larissa, stubborn to the end, pulled his arm away and spat on his chest. A statement. That was the moment I really started liking her. Yet Lorenzo held firm, cementing his domination over her. Larissa knew the gym-goers outside could probably hear, and made sure of it by moaning at the top of her lungs, bordering on screaming. *So fucking hot.* As Lorenzo pinned her arms down and ravished her into submission, I noticed my leg was tightly crossed over the other. My skin was simmering, and I quickly put the book down to check if anybody had seen me.

Someone had. The man at the counter who had just placed his order was smiling with amusement in his gentle eyes. I flinched when I saw him and lowered my head, finding him again from the corner of my eye. He was a handsome, middle-aged silver fox with tanned, leathery skin. Dressed in a white hemp shirt, hemp loafers and chino shorts. A Dutchman, if my guess was correct, which after years of me living in Amsterdam, likely was. His attention shifted suddenly, as a young girl no older than ten embraced him around the hip. Their matching opal blue eyes told me it was his daughter. After he thanked the cashier and received his two cups of coffee and juice, he smiled again at me in goodwill and joined his wife at their table.

A lightning bolt struck me. The father, comfortable in his role as a family man, had easily noticed my aroused state. Not only that, he managed to make me feel good about it. He was secure enough in his sexuality to acknowledge me and flirt with ease. He had no agenda, posed no threat. I had enjoyed his presence, had been comfortable in it, and at once knew that Thomas could never measure up to him. Not even close.

I drifted off, picturing what sex with the Dutchman would be like. I saw myself going to the bathroom. Him stealing a look at me while his wife was busy with their daughter, me flicking my hair and holding his eye contact for an extra second as I strolled by. I would get inside the empty ladies bathroom and start touching up my lipstick. A minute later the door would open, and there he would be with a dark hunger in his eyes. No more Mr. Nice Guy. The lipstick would fall out of my hand, and he would look towards the cubicle. I would walk into my trap, turn to him, and stare deeply into his eyes. As he calmly joined me inside and locked the door, my pulse would spike and drive me into a frenzy of claustrophobic excitement. His musky scent intoxicated me, and gave me a high which spun my head backwards. He would push me up against the wall, take me by the throat and suck on my lip. Pull my top up and thrust my bra out of the way. Grasp my breast in his powerful grip and suck hungrily on my neck while I moaned from the spike of adrenaline coming through his mouth. He would demand me to get on my knees and unbutton his trousers. His pleasure would become mine as my pulse now went berserk and his breathing turned erratic from what I was doing to him. And best of all — his wife calling for him from outside, thinking he was in the men's.

Mmm. How I loved the hot stranger in the bathroom fantasy. But that was what it would remain. As I looked over at the Dutchman lovingly hugging his daughter, a warm feeling entered my heart, and made me question the whole thing.

I checked the time. One and a half hours late. I read a couple more pages of Lover of Prey before a shadow appeared over the book. I looked up and met with Thomas' weary, hesitant eyes.

"Hey," he said. "Sorry I'm late."

He reached over and hugged me, holding me close for a long time as though filling up his empty tank, taking from what little I still had in mine. When he was satisfied, he took a seat beside me, where I managed to see him clearly. His face appeared ten years older. Sleep-deprived. His mouth was turned down, and wrinkles had shown up on his forehead. Maybe not the brightest idea inviting him after all.

He spent a moment studying the cafe, then gazed out at the street, his eyes tracking the passers-by.

"I'm in Berlin," he said with a reluctant smile, shaking his head. "Jesus."

I watched him without saying a word. We both knew what it meant for him to be back. I allowed him the chance to absorb the situation, before he turned back to me.

"How are you?" he said.

The question twisted my heart like a sponge, but only resistance came out.

"I'm fine," was all I could manage. "You?"

"I'm ok," he said.

The pain of the breakup had arrived with Thomas, and was sitting beside us in the room like a fat, stinky elephant. I was not ready to look at it.

"Where the hell do I start?" he said, throwing up his hands.

"With a coffee?" I said.

"Right," he said. "Can you get me a flat white with oat milk?"

"They don't do oat," I said.

"Who doesn't do oat?" said Thomas, squeezing his nose up.

My jaw tightened at hearing his whiney voice. Two minutes and he had already gotten on my nerves. I was hungover. I did not need this.

"I'll get us espressos," I said abruptly and marched to the counter before he could answer.

As I ordered, I could have waited like that ten times over. Thomas smiled at me from his seat, and I reciprocated as warmly as I could. I returned, and we drank in silence. After a long sigh, he opened up.

"Jaz, that was the hardest week of my life."

Damn. You would think he would at least see it from my side. Nope. It was always about him. I was curious to know what he had gone through. But even more, I wanted to see him grovel for what he had done. So I said nothing, and waited for the apology. He cleared his throat and looked expectantly back at me. We remained in that tense, confusing space which had dominated our relationship over the years. Suddenly, plates smashed on the floor somewhere in the kitchen and stole our attention. I turned immediately back to Thomas. He was busying himself looking towards the source of the sound, as though that mattered more than our conversation.

"Was it then?" I said with a firm voice, leaning back.

"Was what?" he replied, turning his head back towards me slowly and deliberately.

"The hardest week of your life."

He sniffled and shrugged while looking down.

"Of course," he said. "I had this horrible ache in my chest the whole time."

I exhaled my frustration and looked outside to the street for some reprieve. He had a uniquely maddening way of sidestepping the point.

"But you were right," I said, not giving him a millimetre. "Things were never great between us."

He started scratching above his heart.

"Never?" he said, suddenly grinning. "I remember a lot of good stuff."

His defiance nibbled at my resolve and had me second-guessing. Then he picked up his spoon, and began mindlessly rubbing it against the tip of his espresso cup. The squeal of porcelain and metal scraping together became sandpaper against my hangover. I grabbed his hand.

"Stop that," I said.

He reached over with his other arm and took my hand in his, and began to stroke it.

"Jaz, you're my soulmate," he said.

How original.

"And I know I'm yours," he continued. "The fire went out between us, that's all. We just need to work out how to light it again."

His beautiful use of imagery lit a spark in me, which I put out immediately. I pulled away, tidied up our cups and stacked them together.

"You broke up with me, Thomas," I said. "We need to face that."

"I know, " he said. "It was a mistake".

I slumped back in my chair. So much for grovelling. Did he think because he had an ouchy in his heart and a sudden change of mind he could have it his way?

"Why was it a mistake?" I said.

"Because I never got the chance to tell you *why* I wanted to break it off."

"That's not a reason, Thomas," I said, folding my arms. "Answer my question."

He cleared his throat.

"I was surprised you didn't ask at the time," he said. "You just went cold and agreed straight away."

Pressure closed in on me from all sides. His voice rang true in a way I knew I could never admit. I could feel every droplet of oxygen struggling to work its way in and out of my throat.

"You wanted to break up, and I believed you," I said, shifting impatiently in my chair. "So I walked."

"It wasn't just me. We both did things wrong."

He was pinning this on me? This time a calming breath only amplified my irritation. The pressure had nowhere to vent.

"So why was it a mistake then?!" I yelled.

My outburst heralded silence in the cafe. A few eavesdroppers gave us sideways glances, trying to remain inconspicuous. Thomas grinned at me with a wide-eyed, satisfied stare while biting down on his lower lip. My face burnt bright with embarrassment. *Dammit. He got me.*

"Calm down, babe," he said.

"Don't tell me to cal—"

"At the time I wasn't sure," he cut in, forcing me to squeeze my jaw shut to avoid snapping again. "But you inviting me here proved it was a mistake."

I blinked hard. *What?*

"But you texted *me first*, wanting me back *before* I invited you," I corrected him.

Why was I falling for his game, when it was him who needed to prove himself? This time I knew better. I shook my head and looked away, relaxing my mouth again, thinking of the coming storm I was about to pitch to him. Whatever he was playing, I wanted nothing to do with it. I let go and let him stew in the stink of his creation. He waited, and I gave him nothing. He looked deeper into my eyes. I glared back.

"I..." he finally said, scratching the top of his head. "It's just that..." He hesitated.

"What, Thomas?" I said with force.

"That," he shot back. "What you're doing now. It's hard to deal with sometimes. It makes me feel... inadequate."

He uncrossed his legs and changed sides. A sadness appeared in his eyes, powerful enough to soften me. His act was losing steam. There was that defeated frown again. His shoulders slowly hunched before my eyes. I sensed us going into heavy territory. It was going to prematurely spoil the entire weekend if he slipped into that place. And it would have — if I finished the moment off by telling him about wanting to open our relationship.

No way I was going to let that happen. At least not for the next couple of hours. It was best to keep him on point, otherwise I would never convince him of my plan. I was going to give him this battle so I could win the war. How sad that we needed these games. What was wrong with us?

"I don't want to dwell on the past," I said, touching his hand. "Let's use this as an opportunity."

"For what?" he said, another two wrinkles appearing between his brows.

"To start fresh."

Hope found its way to his face, and then jumped over to me. *God, that look.* That innocent smirk of his, paired with the sparkling squint. It made everything feel right, even when it was clearly not. We were so dysfunctional.

"I'd like that," he said, leaning forward and resting his hand on my hip.

In truth I had so much else I wanted to say. The week off had given me incredible clarity on our relationship. How he could never find a way to make me feel remotely sexy. How guilty he made me feel anytime I wanted to travel without him, or have a drink with a guy friend. How every time I wanted to change something with us, he convinced me it could not be done. That since the moment we broke up, I was hell-bent on leaving all of that behind. There was something, or *someone*, deep inside me who could never come out. That he had held *her* back. Had extinguished her fire with his negativity and cynicism. He might have been my soulmate, but he would not use that to control me anymore. I was not going to let him. *Her* voice was growing louder by the day. She was returning, and there would be no stopping her.

I clocked one last look at the Dutchman. He caught me yet again, gifting me another of his candy smiles. An anxious emptiness came over me when he left with his family. Instead, I had Thomas; full of potential, but unable to use it to save his life.

I knew one way to help him. Reading Lover of Prey the entire morning had made me want to feel some potential inside me. Now I was suddenly in the mood for some makeup sex. Plus I had to soften Thomas up to the idea of an open relationship. I rubbed the inside of his thigh and kissed him, softly biting his lip for a second.

"Let's check into our room," I said, stuffing Lover of Prey into my handbag. "Get these clothes off."

Neither of us said another word. We left the cafe with our bags and walked the short distance to Äden. The hotel resort was directly by the Spree River. The dark timber facade and Japanese-style gable roofs were at once striking and inviting in their elegance. We stepped into the lobby, and with that left the 'real' Berlin behind. In a place that was always going somewhere but never quite arriving, Äden gave the impression that you had reached your destination. Orange hues lit the space from the corners, while the brown and velvet-purple interior was a sophisticated slap in the face to the city's concrete grey socialist past.

A man in a black suit at reception gave us a pleasant greeting as we approached. I put on my civilised, good girl act, wondering if the guy could sense the situation between my legs. I took possession of our room cards, and we caught the elevator upstairs. Left our stuff by the door, our clothes by the bed, and our problems in the past. Collapsed onto the plush king-size mattress while kissing.

There was an urgency to our foreplay, a sense of rebirth in our eye gazing. The hurried touch of Thomas' hands reminded me of our first months at university, both of us equally infatuated, experimenting with our imagination and our senses. Back then there was a willingness to submit to and learn from each other. The energy between us was magnetic. I had been enthusiastic about the future, idealistic even. He was pragmatic and steady, with a boyish charm. The perfect yin and yang fusion caused an explosion between us. Every caress of his breath over my body transmitted the entire realm of possibility between us.

It was not long before Thomas' charm began to wear off, however. The fights began, and the sex was the first casualty. I tried to talk to him about it, but he blew up each time. We never spoke about sex again. I accepted my role in the status quo.

That same shadow descended now over our furious exchange. I was on top, feeling into and offering myself to him, until he abruptly turned me over and around. Fumbled with the condom for a full minute, hesitated, then entered. I felt something inside me, but nothing in him. *Where are you, Thomas?* Something left me. *She* left. I accepted my place again. He put his thumb over my anus, and I seized up.

"What are you doing?" I whispered.

"Sorry," he said, and continued to pump away, his energy retreating even further into his head.

Where did he get that move from? Another idea from a porn video? Like that time he had wanted to finish on my face? Nothing had changed. Why did I assume it would? After some minutes he began to convulse and groan, before the room fell into a haunting stillness. He pulled out and collapsed next to me, inviting me with a hand on my shoulder to lie with him. Duty done, that same old feeling arrived. Emptiness. He had taken what he needed, and left me nothing but my unfulfilled desires.

He kissed me passionately and disappeared into the bathroom. After all that, all I could taste was the bitterness of the lingering coffee in his mouth. I lay there the way I always had, unsatisfied, pressing my face into the pillow. Every affirmation I had made since the breakup was rendered zero. I had let him back in. I was the only one to blame. The same me that let him lead me down that miserable nine-year path was the one with her face buried away.

I looked ahead to the party tomorrow. Some flickers of hope returned, sending bright ripples through the dark, deep waters of my sadness. No, coming here had been a good idea. Maybe we would find what we needed at Passion Parade. Maybe, just maybe, tomorrow would bring something into my life that would save me from this misery — if I could convince Thomas to come.

I kept that hope alive until after we had ordered room service and were done binge-watching some online series about American football. Eventually, night fell and Thomas dozed off. His heavy breathing came like clockwork, followed by his snoring. He seemed to be sleeping well. Not me. I was wide awake in the pitch black.

I found myself thinking about the next phase of my life. Turning thirty. Quitting my job and monetising my blog. Travelling the world, then getting married and having children. I wanted those things. But what would that look like? Who knew. The road ahead was as dark as the room I was in, and in that darkness, I landed somewhere I could only feel in my imagination. The darkrooms of Äden. I nibbled on my fingertip while wondering about Michaela's four-way. I was only half sure that I could handle going inside this maze of filthy deeds. In my imagination I went there anyway, taking one cautious step after the other. Then I came out abruptly, having forgotten something important. I reached over to my handbag and took out the lubricant and bullet vibrator.

I had been playing with myself since I was sixteen, but it was my first time with a toy. Late to the game, yet again. I inhaled deeply in anticipation. *What have you done to me, Michaela?* The thing was compact, and felt solid in my hand. I rubbed on a tiny bit of lubricant and switched it on, hoping it would be quiet enough. No luck. The thing needed a silencer. But whatever. Thomas was a heavy sleeper. Besides, if he had done his job right, there would be no need to do it myself. I took a deep breath and touched the tip against my— *Oh*. What was going on? It felt like my electric toothbrush. Except this thing was making my pelvis swell and toes curl. Thomas shuffled and turned to his side, his dead, half-open eyes pointed directly at me. I gasped and held my breath. Pulled the vibrator away while carefully watching him. Some part of me wanted him to wake up and see. But I let that go, and went where the vibrator took me instead.

I closed my eyes and dove headfirst back in. Beyond the surface were the darkrooms, where I could only sense with my ears, nose and skin — and tongue. Thomas was with me, his soft hands digging into my buttocks, his lips caressing my nipple. He took me by the waist and pulled me in, the excitement in his breath oozing onto me. Our tongues danced, before his dick invaded me. I moaned while my head fell back. His hips collided with mine like a wrecking ball, pushing harder inside than I knew was possible. He fucked me with force, each thrust erupting within me and throwing me into a spin.

As the tension between my legs built and built from the constant vibration, I sensed someone else in the darkroom. A stranger. Suddenly, I was unsure if Thomas was there at all. Was he the one penetrating me, or had he been standing behind me the whole time? Was he even in the room? The swelling of mechanical pleasure peaked, and I tossed Thomas out of the fantasy altogether. The Dutchman took his place inside me instead, spiking my excitement ten-fold. The stranger's hand then touched my shoulder from behind, and his foreign lips kissed my neck. I spread my legs all the way, and the Dutchman's thrusting grew harder and deeper. The man fondling me from behind steadied my body against the force of the Dutchman, his thick chest hair pressed against my back while my mind ceded to the pleasure high coursing through me. I rolled over quickly and bit down on the pillow, suffocating my moan while shaking from the immensity of my orgasm, which spread through my entire body.

"Fuck. Oh fuck," I whispered.

It was like nothing I had experienced before, making my fingers seem outdated like a horse-drawn carriage compared to this compact, dick-shaped Ferrari. Gasping for air and sweating all over, I checked up quickly on Thomas, and found him dead asleep. I sighed and melted into the mattress. The relief of the afterglow had me feeling better about everything, and I was able to leave the day behind. I stuffed the lubricant and my trusty bullet vibrator back into my handbag, making a note in my head to clean it when I had the chance. Yes, tomorrow would bring something wonderful. I was sure of it. With that, I rolled into a foetal position and drifted into sleep, filled with tingles. It seemed the optimistic Jasmin never said die. And for that, I was glad.

3
J&A

JASMIN

I felt safe underwater. The tranquillity within the depths calmed my senses and brought me into my body. The world went on pause, and I was free to roam the abyss. Each stroke took me further from reality, and deeper into myself, until the pressure in my lungs reminded me that I was on borrowed time. I turned upwards to the surface, where life awaited me. My doubts. My regrets. My past and future.

Time resumed just as I emerged into the sunlight, sucking in a huge breath. Äden unpaused itself, and the current of nude people at our hotel resort flowed once again. In the middle of it all was a grumpy Thomas. He was reclined on his sun lounger at the other side of the outdoor heated pool while staring into the distance, one leg crossed over the other and a cigarette in hand. I rose my head slowly over the edge, stalking him and that stinking death stick. I placed my hands on the edge and lifted myself out with a mouthful of water. Just as he took another puff, I spat on his face, making sure to hit the smoke as well. He twisted his body away in shock, and the cigarette fell out of his hand.

"Jaz!" he yelled. "What the fuck?"

I brought my tiny frame over him, placing a hand on his chest and moving to kiss his cheek.

"You're wet," he said, frowning and turning his face away.

His reaction was a blunt reminder that the old days were over. The shadow of the breakup loomed over us, even when we lay in paradise. I kissed his shoulder instead and shifted over to my chair. Not the smartest way to get him out of his funk, but worth a try. He had been in a state since breakfast, after I had brought up the party, along with the idea of opening our relationship.

"Are we going to talk about this?" I said.

"About what?" snapped Thomas without looking at me. "You in an orgy of guys while I watch on like a loser?"

I sighed and shook my head.

"Jesus, Thomas. It's not like that."

"What happened to you last week?" he said with an unsightly look.

"Nothing," I said. "Anyway, even if tonight was an orgy, you'd be among those guys."

Thomas' legs hit the ground suddenly, and he almost knocked the table over. His face turned bright red, and he stood and marched off.

Whoops. The hot knife cutting through my chest told me I had gone too far, and that I should go after him. *Her* voice inside told me to relax and order a bottle of Rheingau riesling; my and Thomas' favourite white wine, and go-to celebration drink. He might not have been in the mood to celebrate, but I sure was. We were here for a party, after all.

The wine arrived, and Thomas came back over half an hour later and retook his position beside me. He poured himself a glass, and seemed to have calmed down. I melted into my chair and enjoyed a moment of reprieve. It was so surreal. We were attending a sex party. Well, sex-*positive*. It was a chance to dress down, dance, and see where things led. Dip our toes in the kink scene. Let our inhibitions free and see what happened. I was not going to join an orgy of guys, thank you very much.

Well, actually... Why would I hold myself back for him? He was the one who broke it off last week. If he wanted to be a child about it, he would get no say in the matter. So what did I want exactly? An orgy, or not? I looked around at the surrounding scenery. It was nice to be in a gorgeous resort, but if asked to blow the candles on my birthday cake, I would not be wishing for paradise. I had no fixed expectations for this weekend — except one. It had to be hot as hell. I wanted passion. Wild, indescribable experiences. I wanted to melt into an ocean of bliss, to be devoured by a wild beast.

Wild beast. I looked at Thomas again, his dishevelled brown locks, his tense shoulders and lanky frame. He had lit another cigarette and was biting his nails while staring into space with his sad eyes, his baby-smooth body limp on the sun lounger. I sighed and finished my glass. For once I wanted him to let go and enjoy the moment. Maybe even forget himself in it like during our university days. There was no sign of that cheeky, vibrant Thomas who pressed all the buttons on the elevator and made his move. In his place was a pale and anxious shell of a man, lost in his head. Seeing him that way made me nervous. Not to mention my worry about how he would act at Passion Parade. Now I was overthinking.

"Babe," I said. "Do you know what you're wearing tonight?"

Thomas maintained his gaze into the distance. For a time it seemed he had not heard me, until he shrugged.

"Have we decided we're going to this thing?" he said.

My fingers and shoulders went tight.

"I've decided," I said with force.

"I've heard there are better sex parties in Berlin. Classier ones."

"And where did you hear that?" I shot back. "An online forum?"

He seemed hurt by my remark, and turned away while sucking in what remained of his cigarette. It was happening again. *The Thomas effect.* My jaw was stiff, my mind was ticking at a hundred miles. I took a few calming breaths and came out of it. Turned away from him and focussed on the environment. Tried to appreciate where I was. I was not going to let him ruin this weekend.

The outdoor heaters at Äden were burning bright while smoke rose from the heated pool. Berlin had been blessed with one of the few clear, sunny April days. *April does what it wants*, the Germans would say about the unpredictable weather this time of year. Äden really was the perfect choice. It had a sophisticated blend of white leather upholstery, dark timber facades and lush trees. The vibe was dream-like. Nobody was rushing or causing a fuss. Looking good and passing time were the only priorities. There were no clocks. The surfaces were spotless, the lighting impeccable. Outside was radiant, the ambience inside relaxed you instantly. Nudity was compulsory in all areas, but the mood remained civilised. There was the odd raised voice or muffled laughter, otherwise people politely made way with charming smiles and floated by. It was like someone had incensed the air with opium, establishing a womb that nurtured you as you went about your pleasure.

I felt like a carefree child on the beach; I loved having an excuse to be naked. On the other hand, there was nowhere to hide from prying eyes. Thomas had no issues with it at all. Being from East Germany, he was a natural nudist. I turned my head to check on him and found an empty chair. The surrounding area showed nothing. He was gone. I paused, then found myself drawn to his towel, where I spotted a business card poking out from underneath. I looked behind me first, then pulled it out. 'J&A' was embossed on the top in black. In the middle was the name 'Ana Nemati.' Her mobile was on the bottom. Nothing else. *Strange*, I thought, feeling a papercut of jealousy. Thomas had disappeared twice now. Where the hell had he gone? The darkrooms? *No way.* Panic zapped me, and I was forced to my feet. After another glance at Thomas' empty chair, I was overcome by an unsettling urge to go find him.

I strolled along the pool, made self-conscious by the glimpses from the sunbathing men and women. Most eyes were on me, but I felt my sight drawn towards a calm, steady presence sitting by the edge of the pool with his legs dangling in the shimmering water. From my position I could see he was a big guy who took care of himself. The rest I learned from the people around him. He was typing something into his phone, and only paused to wave back to the random, passing person greeting him. An athletic-looking guy crouched next to him with a wide smile and fist-bumped him, exchanging some pleasantries before humbly leaving him to it. Women wandered by, flicking their hair and stealing a look. One of them playfully caressed his neck as she passed, exaggerating her hip movements and looking back. He must have been interrupted a half dozen times while I stood there, but gave every single person his attention, appearing unfazed by the whole thing.

It took me some time to remember the man I was looking for. I blinked a couple of times and moved to the indoor pool, which immediately consumed me. The domed ceiling above was a portal to elsewhere, the shimmering blue beneath an invitation into the deep. The building was three stories high, with pathways on each level lined by arches overlooking the water, covered by majestic see-through white curtains that ran from the ceiling to the floor. I found yet more people lounging with their skin on display. There was no Thomas among them, so I went inside the sauna area.

Upon approaching the floor-to-ceiling pane of glass, the light reflected off the surface and revealed my exposed body. I focussed on my pear-shaped breasts, which hung too far to the sides for my liking, and my oversized, pink-brown nipples which covered way too much of the surface. My lips and mouth were too small. People constantly told me my blue eyes and high cheekbones looked elegant, but I thought they only made me look like a little girl. Why did everyone in this place have to be so damn beautiful?

I turned away, towards a separation wall offset by a human-sized gap. Intrigued, I left my reflection behind to take a closer look. There was no sign to indicate what it was. I could easily slip inside, but it was pitch black. I looked around. Everyone seemed happy in their own world. A woman got off her chair and entered the sauna, closing the door behind her. I focussed again into the black. Took a breath and slipped through. It was deeper than I expected. Then it hit me. *The darkrooms*. The light from outside illuminated a corridor which bent right. I followed it, taking slow, cautious steps until I reached the corner.

Rhythmic, hot-blooded breathing came from inside. Each exhalation was more urgent than the last. I hugged the wall, my breathing barely making it past my throat. The unmistakable and sudden sound of a spank ricocheted off the walls, making me jump. I froze like a statue, my naked skin pushed up against the cold concrete, my lips parted, my ears like radars. I stared intently behind me, where only dim orange light shone through from the sauna area. I waited for a long time, but nobody came. *All clear*. For now.

The rasping seized my attention again. It grew louder. Faster. Like a runner on the final stretch. My pulse quickened to match, and I momentarily forgot where I was. A moan slipped out from the black. Then a grunt, as though a wild animal had joined in on the action. The pace accelerated, forcing me out of my body. Grunt after grunt was paired with an ecstatic moan, before another hard smack almost made me yell out. The man cursed in German. I pushed off the wall, half my body urging me to flee, the other half mesmerised, my heart banging like a jackhammer.

No chickening out, I told myself, stepping forward while placing my feet stealthily on the floor one at a time. I hugged the wall and stretched my neck around the next corner, hoping to get closer for the moment of climax.

The thrusting stopped.

I froze again, holding my breath and listening into the black.

"Don't be shy," came a high-pitched, playful voice from inside.

My head spun, and I stumbled backwards. I stopped again at the corner and listened, hearing the laughter of the two men. Then came a pause, before the heavy panting resumed at a slower pace. I pressed my palm to my heart and exhaled. My legs were trembling. I tip-toed towards the exit, slipping out of the darkness and back into the safety of the sauna lounge.

A woman on a deck chair looked up from her book and directed her judging eyes at me while I hurried through the dimly-lit brown and gold room. *Yes. Look at the naughty girl.* At the same time, an older man emerged naked from the sauna. His cheeks were flushed red, and he rubbed a hand over his face while looking me up and down with serious eyes.

His stare was like dozens of spiders crawling on me, and it forced me out of the room and through the locker area. Outside I squeezed my eyes shut to protect them from the sting of the sunlight reflecting off the bright blue water. It took a moment to acclimatise, and to remember that I was at a hotel resort, not some seedy sex dungeon.

At the corner of the pool, I stood looking out. People were lounging, drinking, laughing. The creepy man walked by me and stole one last look, gifting me a final, unwanted shiver. Thomas' sun lounger was still empty. I turned and found him in the distance, gliding through the water with his head up. He reached the end and turned back, kicking off and veering to the edge before lifting himself out. He ran a hand through his soaking hair and returned to our spot. His boyish glow and cold expression created a picture of a male model owning the runway.

The unpleasant feelings from our fight instantly ceded. There was the man I invited to Berlin. I smiled to myself, wanting to feel the sensation of his body close to mine. To pull my head into his chest and let him fondle my back the way he always did; with the gentle strokes of a harp player creating music inside me. This time he would also be wet, so he had nothing to moan about. I stepped forward to go over and reclaim him.

"He's such a dish," I overheard a woman's voice from the right, causing me to stop. She continued speaking to someone. "Darling, if you're the main course, he's dessert. I'm going to lick him clean."

I turned and found a couple in their mid-to-late thirties on a pair of sun loungers. The woman hungry for Thomas struck me immediately, appearing like a vixen goddess. She had a tall shapely body, lush firm breasts and vanilla skin. Her sharp, intense eyes, hawkish nose and dark features matched her predatory words. Her face was like a porcelain doll's, and her rose-coloured lips were plump, giving her a girlish pout. Jet-black, dead-straight hair gleamed while running down to her waist.

"I didn't know you were into teenagers," said the boyfriend with a gravelly voice that reverberated inside me.

My face immediately burned up at the sight of him. *The guy by the pool.* I could see every detail now. He was a hulk, brutish and chiselled. His trained chest protruded through the thick brown hair covering it. His abs were cut, and his shoulders were like pillows. His jawline drew me to his torso, which was angled with perfect symmetry. Rough, well-groomed brown hair gave him a movie-star look of quiet dominance. There was a force behind his presence which told me he could handle himself in a crowd, in business, and especially in bed. He was smiling proudly at his own joke, his teeth sparkling, his lips like candy, his ocean-grey eyes cunningly beautiful.

Then those eyes looked at me.

I twitched, and my skin lit up. His smile faded, and his eyes sharpened. His stare incinerated my oxygen like a wildfire raging through a fragile village, wiping out everything it touched. His eyes sharpened further and cut deeper, unwavering in their intensity. Then he smiled that gorgeous, devious smile again, and my power returned to me. I remembered what he had said about Thomas. I crossed my arms and pursed my lips, looking him up and down.

"That little thing looks like it belongs on a teenager," I said, signalling between his legs and waving my pinky finger.

Where did that come from?

His mouth fell open, and I could see his face go slowly red. Even his demeanour changed, and for a second I thought I was looking at a little boy.

"Excuse me?" said the vixen goddess, sitting up and looking at me.

There was a split moment where I was sure she recognised me. Yet I had no idea who this woman was.

"Thomas isn't a teenager," I said, my heart pounding.

"Of course," said the woman, now smiling. "Thomas is your boyfriend."

I did a double-take.

"You know Thomas?" I said.

She looked over at Thomas, who was staring curiously in our direction. She twinkled her fingers seductively at him, to which he lifted his head even further to get a better look.

"Yes, we met earlier. He didn't tell you?"

Ana Nemati. The papercut of jealousy became a knife.

"No," I said, looking at the hulk again, still radiating from his stare. The little boy was gone, and the man smirked, having collected himself. My vision followed his massive arms hanging at the side.

"What's your name?" he demanded to know with his booming voice while lying comfortably on his sun lounger.

"Jasmin," I said, my eyes snapping up when I realised I had lingered too long.

"Jasmin," he repeated, trying my name on for size. It fit him perfectly.

I shifted my weight from one leg to the other. I could barely feel my body now, the tension too much. I blushed, putting my hand over my mouth.

"I'm sorry," I said. "I didn't mean to say that. It just came out."

"No, it's fine, sweetie," said Ana. "You had a right to speak up. Jordan can be juvenile sometimes," she added while turning to her boyfriend, who ignored her.

"Jordan," I said, trying him on as well.

"Do you live in Berlin, Jasmin?" said Ana.

"No, I'm only here for the weekend. It's kind of a celebration for my thirtieth."

"How lovely," Ana said with a warm, feminine smile.

Wow. Did Thomas tell them nothing about me?

"You're Ana," I said.

"Yes," she replied, bending forward and shaking my hand with a firm grip. "I thought you said Thomas didn't mention me?"

"I found your card," I said. "Nice to meet you."

"I see," said Ana, appearing to be thinking before relaxing again. "So, how do you two plan to celebrate?"

"Um," I said, hesitating, wondering if I should admit where I was going. They seemed like they could handle it. "Well... It's called 'Passion Parade.' A friend told me about it."

Ana and Jordan locked eyes briefly.

"We know it," she said. "It's a kink party."

"That's right," I said.

"Fetish dress code. Dance floor, and a private area for whoever wants to do naughty stuff."

"Right. How do you know about it?"

"We know the couple who run it. Good friends of ours. Interesting way to spend a birthday. It's tonight, right?"

I stole a glance of Jordan, who was quietly taking me in like a lemonade on a warm day.

"My birthday is next Saturday. But the party is tonight, yes," I said, blinking twice and turning back to Ana.

"Are you a regular in the scene?" said Ana. "I don't think I've seen you at any of the parties."

"No, it's our first time. A friend told me about it," I said, turning hot when I realised I had already mentioned my friend.

"Aha," said Ana, smiling smugly. "I'm sure you'll have lots of fun," she added with a hint of sarcasm.

"What?" I said, scrunching my face, which burnt even hotter.

"It's just that..." Ana shook her head dismissively. "It's probably not for you."

"What's not for me?"

"I'm just thinking, if it's your first time, you might want to do something more memorable."

"Tonight's going to be memorable," I said, straightening up.

"Passion Parade's fun. But your thirtieth only happens once. You might want to go to a real party."

I took a step back and crossed my arms.

"And which party is that exactly?"

"Do you have experience with group stuff?" said Ana.

"You mean..."

"Orgies, dear. Underground parties."

"Oh," I said, flinching when I realised what she was talking about. I heard Michaela's words again. *She's not ready for that.* I brushed them off. Maybe I was. "Well, I've done threesomes," I lied.

Ana smiled amusedly and looked towards Jordan. The tension hung thick as she seemed to be waiting on him. He studied me carefully, lingering for a long time. My throat hardened into a rock. Finally, he shrugged.

"We host ours once a month," said Ana. "At a secret location. You'll find most of the Äden regulars there, among others. The vibe will blow you away. Lucky for you, the next one is tonight."

"Hey, babe," said Thomas, appearing from nowhere and placing a hand on my back. "Hey, Ana," he said with a lift of his chin as though she were an old friend. He ignored Jordan.

"Hello again, handsome," said Ana with a sparkle in her eyes.

Jordan looked Thomas up and down with a blank expression.

"Are you talking about tonight?" said Thomas, looking at me.

"Yes," said Ana. "I was just discussing it with Jasmin."

"I was going to tell you about it," said Thomas.

Were you? I thought, giving him a long stare.

"We can't change our plans," I blurted, turning back to Ana. "But thanks anyway."

Ana reached over and handed me the same business card she had given Thomas.

"This one's for you. If you change your mind, give me a call," she said. "I can share the details with you then. It starts at midnight."

"Sure," I said, now feeling restless, uncomfortable having the four of us together. "Nice to meet you both," I said.

"It was an absolute pleasure, Jasmin," said Ana, smiling courteously.

"Bye," I said, giving Jordan one last look.

"See you, Thomas," said Ana with music in her voice.

Thomas jutted his chin at her again and put his arm around me as we walked off. I could not shake the feeling that he was acting differently in front of Ana, so I shook his arm off instead.

"What did you guys talk about?" said Thomas as we made it back to our sun loungers.

I looked across at Jordan and Ana again, and caught Jordan staring in my direction. Ana then stood, sauntered over to him and got on his lap. She wrapped her arms around him and stole his attention back with a deep kiss. My face burnt at the sight of them. The idea of going to Ana's party put my stomach in knots and made my hands clammy. I could never compare to her. Their picture-perfect naked bodies looked stunning merged together like that. Plus it was an underground party. Neither Thomas nor I were ready for hardcore orgies.

"Babe?" said Thomas.

Something about finding Ana's card hidden under Thomas' towel felt off. And she wanted to lick him clean? What did that mean?

"Are you listening?" said Thomas.

"I heard you!" I said, scowling at him. "Why didn't you tell me you met them?"

"I don't know," he replied with a shrug. "I was going to."

I glared at him like an angry mother. It was his fault for being so thick-headed. I turned away and fell back onto my lounger, staring into the distance.

"I want to go to Ana's party," said Thomas.

I froze, disoriented by his statement. I turned towards him.

"No," I said slowly. "We're going to Passion Parade."

"If we're going ahead with this open thing, I want to go to J&A."

"Well, go by yourself," I said reflexively.

"Fine," he shot back.

I paused, waiting for him to crack. He lit up a cigarette instead. Meanwhile, Jordan's ocean-grey eyes remained burnt in my imagination, and just the thought of them made my skin glow warm again. Sure, he was incredibly hot. But there was something else about him I could not put my finger on. Something to do with those little boy vibes fused with a grown man's presence. I had seen only a glimpse of his vulnerable side, but it was enough. His gaze penetrated me like nothing before. With others I felt confident in my natural boundaries. I had an inner space free of outer influence. Jordan stepped right through as though no door existed. Combined, Thomas' nonchalance and Jordan's fire eroded what little resistance I could put up. I huffed and gave in. *Suit yourself.* If Thomas wanted hardcore, he would get it.

"Fine," I said. "Let's go to J&A."

4

THE PARTY

JASMIN

I tossed my bullet vibrator onto the mattress for packing, along with a box of condoms and lubricant, all on Ana's advice. The party had supplies, but it was best to use what you preferred. The 'right fit and feel' were her words in the text she sent to Thomas.

Thomas stared at the vibrator for a long time before going off to the mirror to put on his tie. After a while, I noticed him struggling and came over. Already in his thirties and still could not manage.

"Here," I said. "Let me."

"I'm good," he said firmly, not letting me pull his arms away from the tie.

"Suit yourself," I said, shaking my head.

I left him to it and continued getting ready. Thomas had not been himself since meeting Ana. He was stand-offish. His mind was in other places. The questions and doubts about opening our relationship had dried up. I wanted to be relieved that he had cooled off, but that business card continued to cut at me. The way he u-turned so suddenly did not sit well. *Shut up, Jasmin. This is what you wanted.* Jordan's ocean-grey eyes then appeared. His meaty frame hovered over me, his shadow menaced me.

I wondered what was going on in Thomas' mind. Was he still in panic mode? Was he fantasising about what we could do together at the J&A party? Was he thinking about Ana? We had to lay out the ground rules for the evening. Instead, he was in his world, and I was in mine. But whatever. Better than him grumbling and moping.

We finished getting packed and ready and left our room. Inside the elevator, Thomas pushed the ground floor button then adjusted his cuffs in the mirror. His Windsor knot was immaculate. His shoes were spotless. *Good job, babe.* Maybe I had been too harsh before. I looked him up and down and melted at the sight of the man before me. He looked dramatically different in his grey tweed suit. Its slim fit together with his textured locks of hair and soft features gave him a quiet confidence, with the wandering eyes of the blonde standing next to us in the elevator confirming it. How could I stay mad at those charms? I moved closer to my man and rested a hand on his shoulder while admiring our reflection, blocking the blonde's line of sight in the process. My slinky, long-sleeved ribbed dress and stilettos gave us an air of prominence, with my hair loosely-curled to complete the transformation. The elevator opened to the lobby, and we walked through the rolling glass door and came out of Äden like a power couple.

Not that I felt the part. I had been trying to shake off my impostor syndrome since meeting Ana and Jordan. Judging by her and Jordan, there were going to be some exquisite people attending. After just one look, they would probably laugh us out of the party. Or me, at least. I held Thomas' hand tighter while standing on the sidewalk waiting for the taxi. He kissed my neck and pulled me close, the warmth of his body and the smell of his skin pacifying me. He had stepped into his stride, and I was struggling to land in his footsteps.

A chill in the air gave me goosebumps. The cold front had arrived in Berlin. Even snow was forecast. April doing what it wanted again. The taxi arrived, and we slid into the warmth of the backseat, where I found the time and space to settle my nerves as I watched the Berlin streets flicker by. I imagined the possibilities which going to Jordan and Ana's party might bring. The conversations I might have, the wild things I would see. The only thing bothering me was Ana. I was almost sure I disliked her. The way she acted all sweet towards Thomas got under my skin. But then again, so did Jordan's gaze. I wanted him, *and* I wished Ana would back off from Thomas. I wanted Ana's cake but did not want to share mine. The hypocrisy of it did not escape me; I just did not care. I felt how I felt.

Soon we reached the intersection where Ana had advised us to stand and wait. The city felt like it would eat us up and spit us out without even noticing something in its teeth. The grey cobblestone path was ugly and harsh, cruel even, and I almost tripped over when the tip of my stiletto cracked into the corner of an uneven stone. Passersby barely glanced at us. The ordinary world remained in relative harmony. All was as it should be. I clutched my handbag tight with a wildfire in my stomach. The normality of it all was killing me. I wanted to dive in already.

A tram crossed the intersection and stopped in front of us. The doors opened, and a crowd poured out. I was distracted trying to recognise any party people among the new arrivals when a hand touched my shoulder. I turned to find a fake-tanned guy with platinum blonde hair, black jeans and sweater. His face melted like ice cream in the sun when he smiled, and I liked him instantly.

"J&A?" he said.

"That's right," I said, glancing at Thomas.

"This way," said the guy, and marched off.

We followed him down the road through the crowd of pedestrians before he turned left at the first street. As we came around the corner, we stopped at an inconspicuous door with a pin pad next to it. While our chaperone punched in the code, cars wooshed by behind us. He pulled the door open.

Thomas walked in first, and I followed him, leaving the common world behind. We entered a musky-smelling cellar entrance with little headspace and only a dim light against the wall.

"Down the stairs," came our chaperone's voice. "Get changed in the foyer, hand over your stuff at the cloakroom, and have fun."

"Thanks," said Thomas, and the guy's face melted into that smile one last time from outside before he closed the door after us.

Thomas inspected with doubt in his eyes the stairs which led into the dim underground. I nudged his shoulder to go ahead of me, and we descended with slow steps, careful not to hit our heads on the concrete above. In the distance came the muted sound of jazz, which grew louder when we entered the foyer, finding it congested with naked skin. While the entrance above was left neglected, downstairs had been polished and cleaned to party. Luxurious carpet covered the floor, and crystal light fittings warmed the space. The air was infused with pheromones and anticipation. People were undressing while chatting and chuckling amongst each other. The look on Thomas' face said it all. He seemed to be struggling to soak it all up. I, for one, had never seen anything like it. I immediately scanned the women in the room and compared myself to them. I seemed to be the only one. Everyone else looked content, standing around in their naughty outfits as though it were the most normal thing in the world. I felt the tension of the drive over dissipate into the electrified space. Soon after, a surge of possibility came shooting out of me.

"What the hell?" whispered Thomas into my ear before walking forward.

What the hell indeed.

A guy wearing only a bow-tie and black thong placed a gentle hand on my shoulder to encourage me to move as he reached to give his bag over to the cloakroom. A long-legged girl with the coolest afro rocked up and down in her white kicks, looking stunning in a pink and orange one-piece bathing suit while waiting for her boyfriend to finish his conversation with a topless guy in latex pants. When our eyes met I smiled, to which her face softened. *First contact.*

Another girl with a head of fiery auburn hair stormed in from inside, cackling loudly.

"I knew he was all talk!" she said, catching the room's attention.

She pushed by me and leaned over the cloakroom counter, spreading her arms and fingers while pushing her ass out.

"Sweetie, can I have my bag again, please? I forgot my butt plug," she said to the cloakroom girl.

"I'll be in the massage room, April!" came a voice from the doorway.

"Ok!" yelled April with a wave of the hand.

I marvelled at the new arrival. It was more than her abrasiveness which stole the limelight. April's energy oozed out like a thick perfume. Her breasts put a strain on her silver, bedazzled bra, her voluptuous frame was a warning to any feeble-bodied man — or woman — who might dare step forward.

With a slack expression, Thomas admired April's round, tanned backside separated through the middle by her matching silver thong. I could barely blame him, I was smitten as well. April finally received her bag, and with butt plug in hand, marched out the way she had entered.

Thomas and I exchanged a knowing look, almost giggling to each other, then moved aside to strip down in the open with everyone else. The communal undressing added to the buzz of anticipation. People smiled and laughed in their outfits, ready to get frisky, impatient even. Or maybe that was just my feeling. I neatly folded my dress, and stood waiting in my favourite black lingerie set; a see-through bra with floral lace and matching g-string. The material revealed my nipples, and the way it held my breasts in place made them look firm and luscious. To keep my feet warm I had on my white socks printed with kitten faces. While removing his trousers, Thomas noticed the socks and locked eyes with me, to which I smiled and shrugged.

In minutes we had handed over our bags and clothes and were standing in the middle of the foyer like the first day of school. We were ready to follow April's blazing trail into the party. Thomas approached the doorway in his white Calvin Klein boxer shorts and scruffy hair. He stretched his hand behind him without looking back, and I quickly grasped it while reaching around and clutching his arm. As we entered the bar my senses flared, being inundated by colour, vibration and excitement. I took a belly breath to steady myself. I had arrived.

The doorway was only wide enough for Thomas and me. I left the imposter in the foyer.

"Woah," said Thomas. Apparently he too had arrived.

The bar spanned the entire length of the room. There were two male bartenders wearing nothing but bow ties, and a female bartender wearing a black bra and nothing underneath. A collection of burgundy leather sofas housed over fifty people scattered throughout, holding drinks and cocktail glasses. On each side were doorways. The bare concrete walls had various erotic art deco paintings, with close-ups of genitalia and people performing sexual acts. There was girl on girl, man on man, animal on animal. One piece in particular caught my eye. It had a smiling monkey with its head raised and arms spread across the sofa like a human, with the top of another monkey's head at the bottom of the canvas.

"Do you want a drink, babe?" said Thomas.

"In a minute," I said, my voice trailing off as I let his arm go and made for the left doorway.

I felt Thomas' presence behind me in the hall. The music transitioned seamlessly from jazz to house, and the sound of giggling came from the first room. I approached and found a king-size bed with no blankets and two naked girls on it; a petit, ruby-haired bundle of joy, and a sharp-eyed, olive-skinned brunette.

I watched in awe as the divine scene unfolded and Thomas pulled up beside me. The plush white mattress supported the two girls like a cloud. Surrounding them were a dozen people watching the show from the floor as though observing the heavens. The ruby-haired girl's curves were like the mattress, inviting in their softness. The antique bed frame matched the brunette's drum-tight figure, and could have come from the Victorian era. It had a rusted-gold frame with vertical bars, and a charm that demanded good manners and civility.

There was nothing civil about what was taking place.

The brunette had invaded heaven and taken the ruby-haired angel hostage. Hands tied firmly to the bars with pink rope, the angel lay at the brunette's mercy with her legs spread. The brunette had on a black bodysuit and was covered in tattoos. Her ponytail was as tight as her outfit. She had her fingers between the ruby angel's legs and her mouth on one of the nipples. She moved her hand as though playing the accordion, tilting her wrist in various directions, with the ruby angel moving and adapting in response, her moans becoming a melody. The ruby angel's body was like the surface of the ocean, rising and falling and rising again, suspended for a time before crashing in a state of bliss. As another wave came, she let out an ear-piercing shriek. Muffled laughter broke out among the audience.

"Do it again," said the ruby angel, lifting her head to reveal a cheeky grin while licking her upper lip.

The cunning brunette invader drove her hand deeper between the ruby angel's legs and sucked on the nipple while cupping the breast with her other hand. She took the nipple between her teeth. The two girls exchanged gorgeous, knowing smiles, the kind that revealed pure synchronicity and connection. Meanwhile, the ruby angel watched on in anticipation, then squealed when the brunette clenched her teeth.

"Ah!" she yelled and giggled.

The brunette swiftly moved her head down between her victim's legs, and the ruby angel's giggle turned into a deep, resonant moan.

Thomas went a long time without blinking. His lips were parted, his face twitched in random places. His chest and stomach were barely moving. He watched the scene intently, his gaze unfamiliar to me. He swallowed to clear his throat, and his pupils dilated as the brunette invader feasted on the ruby angel. His pleasure suddenly became mine, and I wondered what it would be like to invite another woman to join us. The touch of her lips on mine, the arousal in Thomas' eyes while he watched. It seemed my hypocrisy went a step even further. The idea of Ana lathering her charms on Thomas the same way made my knuckles turn white.

A butt-naked guy inside the room rose from the floor and came onto the cloud while holding his penis, watching the two girls intently. The sharp-eyed brunette was quick to notice. She lifted her head and scowled at him, before pushing him away. The crowd broke out in laughter, and the guy sheepishly resumed his position on the sidelines with a good-natured laugh. Meanwhile, the brunette went back to her sinful business.

I felt the impact of every ripple of the ruby angel's pleasure. My thighs, my belly, even my throat had been inundated. I wrung my wrist with a hard twist and stole a look down the hallway, where the promise of more indecency awaited. Thomas remained utterly entranced, never once clearing his throat. Seeing him so taken by the girls, I sensed relief, as though the leash binding us together now had limitless length. Feeling the slack, I slipped away to explore, sure to be back in no time.

I ambled through the bare-concrete hallway. The slow beat and harmonies from above accompanied me, lulling me deeper down the bunny hole.

It was oddly quiet in the first room, but not for a lack of people. Six massage beds contained six oiled-up bodies. Everyone was naked, including the people massaging. Raindrops and Indian sitar melodies vibrated from the speakers above, creating an oasis effect. The masseuses were sensual in their movements, as though spirits were working through them. The quietness of this space was no mistake. It created a blissful tension that had everyone in a kind of sensuality-induced trip.

My eyes tracked to the back. There was a shadow on the wall, a silhouette of a man holding some kind of rope, gently and purposely measuring it between his hands. I tip-toed inside, imagining myself in an invisibility cloak, watching to see if the masseuses noticed. One of them glanced at me, smiled warmly, then closed his eyes and fed his energy back into his partner. I reached the wall, and found the room bent into an L-shape hidden from the doorway.

Her bright pupils struck me immediately like two massive diamonds. She was on her knees with her hands tied behind her back. The rest of the room then stole me away, the surrealness of it causing my vision to blur. Never had I witnessed a scene so provocative and arousingly beautiful at the same time. Two gorgeous women were suspended from the ceiling by rope which surrounded their bodies. They had nothing on apart from black lacy underwear. One woman had her back curved outwards while her feet and hands were extended up to the ceiling. Her man admired her with fragility and focus while spinning her slowly in a circle. He seemed honoured by this woman presented to him in goddess form.

The other woman was hung the opposite way by her torso, her body curved towards itself, her pussy on show. Her man admired her for a time, then slowly pried her legs further open. He moved her thong to the side and gently penetrated her while she hung there in absolute surrender, moaning and heavily breathing.

I returned to the woman on her knees. The shadow on the wall was her male partner, admiring the intricate star shape he had meticulously drawn around her breasts with rope. *How beautiful.* He had paid careful attention to her unique form in a way that celebrated and accentuated its majesty.

Shibari was always on my radar, and I suspected that I would love it. Now as I saw it up close, my arousal confirmed it. The expression on this woman's face was serene and invigorating, like looking out over the sea on a summer day. The look in her eyes spoke to me silently. She was blissed out, having finally unburdened herself. Her captor was her saviour. By now he was looking at me. He had a gentle presence embodied by a masculine build. Held himself well. One of those guys that you want to get to know. He delicately held the rope out, inviting me to do just that. Get to know him. I smiled and extended my arm, rubbing my finger over the threads before grasping on. The tension in the rope felt safe, transmitting his energy through the rope and into me.

"How does it feel?" he said with rigour in his voice, keeping the rope tight.

I froze, hoping the patch in my knickers would not drip all over the floor. There was something in the rope that made me want to try it. To let my life fall into absolute surrender. But only with the right man. I let the rope go.

"Not this time," I said.

He smiled warmly and nodded, and I got out of there, rushing out of the massage room without my invisible cloak.

Wow, was all I could think as I came out of my hypnosis and continued down the hallway. The scent of perfume summoned me to the next room, and I took a second to focus on the floor, hoping to bring myself back to reality. No chance of that, I realised, as I peered inside. Two more Victorian-looking king-size beds were squeaking from the movement caused by a pretzel of body parts. A mouth devoured a penis, before another one entered from behind, and the mouth found its way to yet another dick. Two women embraced, then turned their bodies around in a sixty-nine position to consume each other. The last free woman had climbed onto her man, while two more ready cocks awaited her on each side. One remaining man lay grinning with penis in hand, seemingly satisfied with his own company, before the two women snatched him out of his solitude.

My jaw had tightened. One of the girls looked in my direction while being taken from behind. She smiled at me and licked her lip, her body rocking back and forth from the penetration. I held her gaze, allowing her to transmit her pleasure into me. Finally, she could no longer hold on. I lost her as her eyes rolled to the back of her head and she began moaning to the heavens. I turned my attention outside for some reprieve. A butt-naked guy came out of the next room and walked in my direction. I turned towards him, but he only paused for a split second, looked me up and down, then walked by me into the room.

"May I join?" he asked the group.

One of the women looked up briefly, then held her hand out with a mischievous smile. Their lips met as I continued to the room he had come from, shaking my head in disbelief.

Heavy breathing foreshadowed the solitary couple laying in missionary, with the woman's nails dug into her partner's wide back, her legs fully open in surrender to his loving breach. I welcomed seeing some normality amid all the debauchery. Rested in it. Took solace in the bubble of tradition within the chaos, before a wild scream came from the last room and made me flinch. The couple carried on happily with their vanilla love-making, and I watched on while resting my head on the door frame. After some time, I began to feel like a foreigner on intimate soil, and left the pair to their bliss.

The hallway bent right. The dance floor in the next room was warming up. Electronic music blasted inside, and flashing lights revealed a dozen or so dancing bodies. I now felt I was at the limit of my leash, and longed for Thomas. It was high time to reel him back in. What if some ditsy girl had gotten her hands on him? Worse still, what if Ana had dug her manicured nails into him? I recalled his facial expression while watching the girl-on-girl action. He might even be open to inviting someone to join us. But first, I had one room left to explore.

It was behind me. It had its own narrow hallway with a low ceiling. Candlelight flickered inside, where the lighting was far dimmer than in the other rooms. I felt a knot developing in my chest as I approached, getting tighter with each step. The hard, dark techno behind me made it impossible to hear what was going on. A shadow flickered inside. As I neared the doorway, my throat closed up. When I saw it, I seized up like an antelope that had run into a pack of lions.

I looked on. Mesmerised. Numb. Jordan choreographed the act like a dance, directing his three girls with ease using various moves. A hand on top of a head, a rotation of the hips, a whisper, a nudge. He knew where, when and how he wanted them. At one stage he had one of the girls bent forward while he thrust in and out of her with an athletic, natural rhythm. Another girl was on her knees at his side french kissing him. The third was on her back with her legs spread while the girl Jordan was penetrating ate her out. All three women looked to be in their late twenties. Any of them could have been me.

Jordan, his hair soaking wet, sweat dripping from his face, clutched his partner's hips and continued to pump away. Meanwhile, he choked the girl at his side, and her eyes rolled back. She croaked and groaned before he sucked on her tongue, the rhythm of his fucking remaining unaffected. He then pulled out and revealed his condom-covered dick. Now that I saw it fully erect, I noticed how abnormally thick and long it was. *Not a teenager's.* He released the girl's neck and grabbed a handful of her hair instead. Ripped off the condom and guided her down, pushing deep inside her throat. She gladly received him, placing both hands on his buttocks and taking him deeper still. Without Jordan's penis in the mix, the other two girls lost interest in each other. They rose and moved immediately to his side. One of them moved behind him and pressed her face between his buttocks. The other sucked on his nipple.

He looked up.

I gasped and pulled my head back behind the door. It was pointless. He had long seen me. I might as well have been an ostrich with its head in the sand. When I leaned forward again, he was waiting. His grin, at first barely perceptible, grew sinister as his eyes narrowed. The girl continued to face fuck his dick while he maintained absolute eye contact with me. My breathing was erratic, close to hyperventilation. The other two girls had stopped what they were doing and turned their attention to me, flanking Jordan on either side. They were possessed. Their eyes glowed with an intensity I had never seen. Jordan stared deeper into my eyes, the pleasure of the blowjob transmitting through his face. My skin radiated with terror yet again, and now I understood why. I needed him. All of me did. I needed him from the second our eyes met. It was not his muscles, or his arrogant charm. His handsome features and angular frame had nothing to do with it. It went far deeper, as though life itself were somehow conspiring to bring us together. I was terrified of my desire for him, and I had zero choice in the matter. For one reason or another, we were destined to meet. I knew it.

But he was not getting me. Not tonight. Not like this. Even as his erotic mastery had me quivering, I was not going to be his plaything. Not like those girls. I left, going back by the dance floor and returning the way I had come while exhaling slowly, trying to shake off his spell. I felt my lust for Thomas flicker, fighting to stay alight like a candle above an ocean cliff. I wandered into the next room to see if he was still going gaga over the two girls. More people were watching now, but Thomas was gone. The ruby-haired angel had broken free, and was on her knees on the mattress with a black strap-on penis around her waist. The tattooed brunette waited on all fours. The ruby angel was giggling and spinning her silicon penis in circles, to which I quietly approved. It would be the first thing I would do if I were a man. I pulled my head back out of the room and entered the bar area.

The absurdity of it finally hit me. I was in my lingerie among dozens of near-naked people. A woman was being eaten out metres away from me on the sofa. Jordan was inside having his way with three girls. *Three!* What the hell was this place? Glances came at me from all directions. Some had an unsettling thirst in their eyes, others seemed curious. I took a deep calming breath, and reminded myself that this was what I wanted. Anything was possible. The thought resonated throughout my body and lit my cells up like Christmas lights.

Then I saw Ana and Thomas, and my temperature rose. Thomas was on a stool with his back to the bar and his arms spread out. Ana was facing him while caressing a cocktail. She had on an intricate emerald-green one-piece lingerie set and matching feather on her head. Her ass looked geometric. Her skin was flawlessly even, her posture like a monarch. It was clear she was the queen of the party. She could have any man she wanted. And she was talking to my man.

"There you are," said Ana as I approached. "You look amazing!"

"Hi," I said, half-heartedly accepting her embrace.

"Are you ok?" she said, carefully studying me. "You seem flustered."

"I'm fine," I said, fluttering my eyes and pushing out a smile.

Ana continued staring intently at me, then smiled while her eyes remained unchanged.

"Thomas and I were just talking about you," she said.

"Oh, yeah?" I replied.

"Where were you?" said Thomas with grave eyes and tight lips, nursing a glass of riesling.

I shrugged.

"Just looking around."

Thomas pushed his eyebrows together and frowned.

"What were you saying about me?" I said to Ana.

"How beautiful you look," said Ana. "People have been asking about you."

"Oh," I said.

"Well, about both of you. I'm glad you made it tonight."

"Yes, me too," I said, itching to take Thomas away from her.

"It's fine," said Ana. "You can say it. It's a lot, right?"

I shifted from one foot to the other.

"Yeah," I said with a shrug and a reluctant smile.

"Don't worry, you'll get used to it. I've already introduced Thomas to some people, and he's fitting right in."

"That's great," I said, glancing at Thomas.

"So, what are you having?" said Ana. "Tonight's your first time, so you don't pay for drinks, ok?"

"That's sweet," I said. "Thanks."

"She'll have a riesling," said Thomas.

"No, actually, I'll have an old fashioned," I said.

Ana tilted her head.

"Old fashioned?" she said.

I looked at Thomas.

"Yes, please."

Ana shrugged and leaned over the bar. She summoned the bartender by making a come here motion with her index finger. Thomas sipped his riesling and looked away.

"Hey," I said, moving closer to him.

He gave me a blank stare and looked away again.

"Hey."

"Sorry I walked off. I wanted to check the place out."

"It's fine. Did you see anything interesting?" he said.

Again I imagined Jordan gripping the girl's hair tightly while she pushed her face onto his dick. I squeezed my eyes shut briefly to get the image out of my head.

"There's a dance floor if you want to start there?" I said.

"Yeah, I saw it."

My body tensed up. Had he also seen me looking in on Jordan?

"Aha," said Ana, turning back abruptly as two guys approached. "Thomas, sweetie, could you fetch Jasmin's drink when it's ready?"

Sweetie?

"Jasmin, these charming young lads wanted to meet you," said Ana. "This is Kaspar, and this is Tim."

Kaspar came forward and hugged me, the flesh of his body pressed firmly against mine, his strong arms gripping me tightly. Tim followed. His hug was brief, but he kept a hand on my waist while pulling back. He smiled and looked me up and down.

"You look gorgeous in that," he said.

"Thanks," I said, reciprocating with a hand on his shoulder while a warm flush ran over me.

Their presence threw me off-balance. They were an attractive, penetrating pair, one of them wearing leather pants, the other leather shorts and harness. Kaspar had a tall, thin yet muscular body. His lips were full and wide, his icy-blue gaze was sharp. He had a blonde buzz cut and a gentle demeanour. Tim was shorter but bulkier, with more fat yet in shape nonetheless.

"We noticed you come in," said Kaspar.

"You were hard to miss," added Tim, intense with his stare and soft with his smile.

My face turned warm, and I began scratching my wrist.

"There you go," said Thomas, handing me my cocktail.

"Thanks, sweetie," Ana said, touching Thomas to show appreciation for his service.

My skin crawled when hearing the word again. I sipped on my cocktail while keeping my eyes on them.

"Jasmin, would you like to join us on the sofa?" said Tim.

"Uh," I said, turning my attention to Thomas. "Do you want to sit down, babe?"

"You three go ahead," said Ana. "There was something Thomas and I were discussing. We'll join you in a minute."

"No," I said with a level of force that surprised me. "I need to speak with Thomas about something."

"It's just a few minutes," said Ana with a dark tone, my skin turning cold from her stare. "Then he's all yours." Her face softened again, and she smiled.

I hesitated while looking at Thomas. He remained quiet, looking sheepishly into the distance. I waited for an eternity, but he still said nothing. *Fine, then.*

"Ok," I said, turning away.

With a warm hand Kaspar ushered me towards an empty sofa, where two beers were waiting on the table. Tim sat first at the end, then smiled again as I balanced my cocktail and took my place beside him. Kaspar completed the Jasmin sandwich.

I crossed my legs and sat with perfect posture. I looked around while sipping on my drink, feeling the heat of my companions' attention. The energy of the place had stepped up. The chatter was denser, the crowd had swelled. People migrated in and out, some holding hands.

"Ah!" came a scream from the bar. "Yes! Yes! Oh, shit!"

Apparently two people could not hold it long enough to make it inside. Bent over a bar stool with only the tassels of her buttplug visible was April. Her screams of pleasure became shrieks of ecstasy while a guy jackhammered her from behind with his shorts pulled down to his knees and everyone watching on.

"So, Jasmin," said Tim, grinning and shaking his head. "How do you like the party so far?"

I took a deep breath and flicked my eyelashes.

"I'll be honest. I have no idea what to make of all this."

"It's your first time?" said Kaspar.

"Yes. It's written on my face, isn't it?"

"A bit," said Tim with warmth in his eyes, shifting closer. "But you're doing fine."

I tensed up and looked at Thomas. He and Ana were leaning on the bar facing each other. Ana chuckled, and bent forward to tell him something while placing her hand on his chest. I tightened up even more.

"I remember my first time," said Kaspar. "When I got home, I had no idea who I was or what had happened."

"That's because I fucked you so well that night," said Tim, and all three of us broke out laughing while Tim's hand touched my back.

I stole another look at Thomas. He was staring directly at me before Ana reclaimed his attention.

"Look at her," said Kaspar, gazing across at Ana. "I don't know what you're doing with us. You should be over there getting your boy back."

I chuckled and smiled through the spike of concern. *I knew it.*

"Oh?" I said. "Is she going to steal him from me?"

"Not exactly," said Kaspar. "But she has this way about her. Every guy who spends time with her changes."

"In what way?" I said, my curiosity perking up.

"They come out of their shell more."

"She's a sorceress," cut in Tim.

I narrowed my eyes and smiled.

"She's not a sorceress," said Kaspar, shaking his head. "But honestly, she's something else. You have to be for a porn star slash sex therapist slash party hostess."

"She does all that?" I said.

"No, she quit the porn industry years ago. Jordan as well."

"Jordan did porn?" I blurted, fighting to keep my eyes in their sockets.

"Well, yeah," said Kaspar. "But not hardcore porn. Ana and Jordan aren't that. Not on camera, anyway. They did real sex porn. Choreographed, beautiful stuff. The young couple in love kind of thing. Those two made some stunning videos back then."

I took a second to suck in air again. *Of course Jordan was a porn star.* It had me picturing what 'real sex' with him would feel like.

"Ana gave up sex therapy only recently," continued Kaspar. "It had something to do with Jordan, I think. Even the parties stopped for a while."

I studied Ana again from my seat with far more care.

"Now Jordan and Ana are back like never before," said Kaspar, looking around bright-eyed with a wide smile.

"Don't worry," said Tim. "Thomas is in good hands."

"I'm sure she's making a man out of him right now," said Kaspar while observing the two of them with a wide smile.

"Why did she give up therapy?" I asked, my heartbeat picking up.

Kaspar and Tim exchanged a look, then Kaspar leaned into me.

"She can get a little bit too hands-on with her work, if you know what I mean," he whispered.

"She had sex with her patients?" I said with a scandalous expression, as though we were discussing a reality TV show.

"It's more complicated than that," said Kaspar. "She just got too obsessive. Blurred the client-therapist line."

"I think she did amazing work," Tim said. "Imagine Ana guiding your sex life. It's like having Serena Williams helping you improve your stroke."

"Come on," said Kaspar. "How many sex therapists do you know are actively recruiting for their sex parties?"

"I wouldn't be here otherwise," said Tim.

"Exactly," said Kaspar. "It's wrong."

"It's genius," Tim shot back.

As Kaspar and Tim debated sex therapy boundaries, I was compelled to check up on Ana and Thomas again. Ana's hands were on her cocktail, and the two of them looked to be casually chatting. I pushed away the sick feeling in my stomach and turned back to the boys, who were watching me intently again.

"They're just talking, dear," said Tim.

"I know," I said. "So what's Jordan's deal?" I tried to ask as coolly as possible.

"Who?" said Kaspar. "Berlin's most fuckable man? The guy's a living legend. Girls travel to Berlin from all over just for a chance to sleep with him. Without him, J&A would be nothing. What rock have you been under?"

"I don't know," I said, my face blushing. "Amsterdam?"

The boys chuckled in unison.

"You're adorable," said Tim, moving close enough for me to feel the heat of his body.

Kaspar followed Tim's cue and pushed against me also. I clamped up, feeling suddenly engulfed. Kaspar took my hand and began gently stroking my palm, and I felt myself relax into his energy. *Damn, he's good.* I pushed my legs together, but the tingles broke through nonetheless.

"Is this ok?" said Kaspar softly. "Tell us if you're not comfortable."

Oh, God. I had no idea what comfortable was anymore. My senses had been inundated. I saw Jordan devouring those three beautiful harems. I felt the ache of being a world away from Thomas, but also excitement. Tim and Kaspar were so confident, so beautiful, so attentive. They had made me the centre of their world, and it felt damn good. And had Kaspar said 'us?' Of course. They wanted a three-way. I sucked on my lip and pictured myself with the two of them. What would happen? A lot, judging by their expressions. I opened my legs again. My g-string was soaking wet now. My thighs were trembling.

"Jasmin?" said Tim with a whisper in his voice, stroking the inside of my leg as though sensing my excitement.

It felt like someone had turned up the heat in the room. Ana had her body against Thomas', and she stroked the back of his neck before whispering something in his ear. He looked at the floor, then made eye contact with her. Then he looked over at us, and his eyes widened. A hand pushed up between my legs. Thomas lifted off the bar and gave me an incredulous stare. I jumped forward and stood abruptly, picked up my glass and sculled my cocktail.

"Sorry," I said, my attention on Thomas and Ana. "I need to go."

I half placed, half dropped the glass on the table and marched over to Thomas and Ana.

"Excuse us," I said to Ana, grabbing Thomas' hands, my heart pounding.

I led us hurriedly inside, beyond the dance floor and into Jordan's den. It was empty. I took off my white kitten socks and tossed them away, trying to push back the embarrassment I felt for storming out of the bar like that.

"I can't handle this anymore," I said, shoving Thomas onto the mattress.

He said nothing, and I kissed him, almost eating at his lips like it was my first meal in days. At first I could barely feel him. He was overthinking. We kissed for a time. *Come on, Thomas.* I bit his lip to up the ante. He rolled me over and bit my lip in return. He nibbled at my neck, then moved his head down. When his tongue touched my nipple, it burst like an exploding star. I moaned, reached down and grabbed his semi-hard dick.

"Choke me," I said, envisioning Jordan's brutish hand.

"What?" said Thomas, hesitating.

"Choke me."

He put his hand around my neck with a weak grip.

"I don't want to hurt you," he said.
"It's ok. I want you to."
His grip tightened somewhat. He hesitated again.
"I can't."
"Babe, I'm so horny right now," I said.
He clutched my g-string, pulled it down, and left it at my ankles. I turned around and went on all fours, kicking my string off. I gasped and shook when he entered.
"Fuck me," I whispered.
He pushed hard into me, and I sucked in all the oxygen in the room.
"Spank me," I said. "Hard."
There was a hesitation, before I felt a slight impact on the outside of my butt cheek. The hand came down again, this time with less force. His thrusting inside me was like a resting heartbeat; it sustained our love-making but nothing more. His dick was barely stiff. I felt my arousal leaving.
"Pull my hair," I said.
I pushed my ass back against him, hungry to feel his power, but almost knocked him off balance. A shadow appeared to the right. Kaspar, Tim and two other girls had come into the room. They were looking down at us with bemused smiles. Thomas' thrusts died off before he pulled out. He looked at the new arrivals, and his face turned bright red.
"Are we disturbing?" said Kaspar, chuckling.
Thomas jumped off the bed and wrestled with his half-erect dick to put it back inside his shorts, then marched out. I looked up at the still smiling Kaspar, who pulsated his eyebrows.
"The four of us are going to play here. Want to join?"
I pulled up my g-string and chased after Thomas. The thumping beat from the dance floor hit me on the way through. I continued by the other rooms, the odd scream or ecstatic moan harassing me as I passed. In the bar, Thomas was standing and frowning while Ana held him in place with a hand on his chest.
"Don't leave," she said to him as I approached.

"Can I talk to you?" I said. "We just need a minute, Ana."

"Of course," said Ana with a touch of my back. "Sweetie, it'll be fine," were her parting words to Thomas as she walked away.

"Babe, I'm sorry," I said, guiding Thomas to the side.

"Why did you drag me along on this trip?" blurted Thomas. His face had turned crimson, and he was breathing heavily through his nose.

"I don't know," I said, tossing my hands into the air. "I thought..." Ana had opened a conversation with another girl but was watching us intently from a distance. "To have an adventure together, I guess."

"Why can't you be honest?" said Thomas, sharpening his eyes and shaking his head. "Just for once."

"What do you mean?"

"You knew I wasn't made for this. Look at these people. It's all a power trip to them."

"It's not like that. Maybe if you weren't so rigid you'd see it—"

"Rigid?" cut in Thomas with a hiss and a scowl on his face.

His stare cut into me and held me in place for what felt like an eternity. Then his expression turned cold. I felt the chill of him pass over me.

"I can't do this," he said flatly.

"Do what?" I said.

"If you want to be a whore, go ahead. Fuck ten guys tonight if you want. Have fun. I'm going home."

He walked off and took with him the floor beneath me. The chatter and the music faded away. I did not follow him. Could not. A giant hole opened in my chest and pulled me down while I remained paralysed. *Whore?* Had he just called me a... I turned to the side, and my eyes snapped onto Jordan's like magnets. He was standing upright in the doorway wearing a golden silk robe, his hair in a mess. His legs were firmly planted into the ground, his chin slightly raised, his self-satisfied grin on show. I remained caught between the competing pull of my heartache and Jordan's stare. Then it came like wildfire, barrelling out of my belly, spreading to my entire body. *Fuck them both!*

I fetched my bullet vibrator from the cloakroom and cat-walked inside, heading straight for Kaspar's group. Tim had his hands around his partner's peachy ass, moaning with pleasure from the power of her head movements. Kaspar and his girl were in missionary. I approached the bed, admiring their bodies in harmonious flow. Kaspar gradually slowed his thrusting. He turned his head towards me, then grinned.

His partner was the girl from the foyer. Her pink and blue bathing suit was in a crumpled heap on the floor beside her white kicks. Her boyfriend was gone. She looked up, a twinkle appearing in her eyes when she recognised me. *Second contact.* I dropped the vibrator onto the mattress and stepped towards them. Kaspar sat up, taking his condom off and placing it aside. I dropped to my knees on the mattress, and the girl came to me. I was struck by how flawless her rich, dark brown skin was, which pulled me in to kiss her. Her mouth was exquisite like mink. Our tongues melted together, and she sucked on my lower lip, delicate with her pressure in a way only a woman could be. Then Kaspar came forward on his knees, and she stood up and kissed him, moving down to his neck. I stayed where I was. Kaspar was shaved clean, his dick protruding like a skyscraper. I bent down and licked the tip hungrily once, then twice, while maintaining eye contact with him as he towered above me. I saw the devil in his eyes, which reflected her back to me. Her name was Jasmin. I took him in, testing how deep I wanted to go.

Having three people watching while I went down on Kaspar gave me a surreal head spin. My brain checked out, unable to make sense of the situation, which was escalating quickly. Before long I was on my back, my body swarmed by four faces. The mind-boggling sensation of four sets of lips on my skin took me somewhere I had never been. The other girl was hovering between my legs, breathing over my pussy, teasing me with her tongue, kissing me inwards and outwards over my thigh. Tim's hungry tongue circled and sucked my nipple, while a gentler, more sensual tongue caressed the other nipple. My hot and heavy panting was all I had to regulate myself, until the mouth of the girl with the afro met mine again, her soft hand cupping my cheek. Now the girl taunting my pussy got to business. At first she ran her tongue gently and slowly over my clit, giving it the respect it deserved. Kissing it, massaging it with her lips. Then she began to flip it from side to side with a perfect rhythm, sensing and moving with my arousal. God she was good. Tim kept at my nipple, while Kaspar had gone exploring. Kaspar kissed and licked my stomach. My hips. Then he went up and nibbled at my neck. The rush of it was too much. I could no longer lay there passive and receive. I was full. Pleasure was leaking out of my mouth, my ears, my eyes, my pussy.

I became unleashed, sat up and pushed Kaspar down onto the mattress. I snatched a condom from the table and ordered him to put it on. He chuckled. Then obeyed. I felt the heat of the others watching, and it was thrilling. I put on a show for them, grinding backwards and forwards over his cock, unashamedly lost in the intensity of the moment. I had never felt so free, so alive, so *me*.

I could barely register what came next. At one point I had a girl at my front, and another on my back, both of them kissing me and holding me tightly. The love, the security and the arousal of their combined embrace were everything. It empowered me to give back. For the first time, I went down on a woman, savouring the feel of her pussy, her lips, her scent. *Third and final contact*. Her pleasure was a wonder. Experiencing the feminine so intimately and potently had me giddy with joy. Being fucked with my bullet vibrator held against my clit was beyond words. Having Tim's dick inside me and Kaspar's inside my mouth at the same time, was the strangest, most overwhelming experience of all. I surrendered to the beautiful insanity taking place. This was beyond sex. It was a spectacle I had no chance of comprehending. I had been devoured in the most stunning way.

Finally, the five of us collapsed in a pool of sweat, our bodies pressed together in various positions as random hands caressed each other's bodies. In that moment of pure bliss and serenity, where everything around me glowed bright, I had to think of Thomas. I narrowed my eyes.

How's that for whore?

5
HER

THOMAS

I paced from side to side on the pathway like I had hot coals under my feet. What a return to Berlin! Led into a hornet's nest of horny assholes by my own girlfriend. I preferred the emergency ward. Why did she bring me here anyway? Was she punishing me?

Out from the door came a blonde I had seen being finger banged on a sofa. The look in her eye as she passed enchanted me briefly out of my demented vertigo. Her gaze was bright and beautiful, but done. She had been fucked to a place where she needed no more. The girl was gorgeous, but more hypnotic was her calmness. A serenity of someone who had experienced something I could never give.

"Hi there," she said with a sing-song voice and a wave.

She graced me with a smile as she looked back over her shoulder. It seemed like an after-party invitation. A second chance. Then I imagined that same satisfied look on Jasmin's face, her need for me satiated elsewhere. The thought of it set me alight, and gave me an unbearable impulse to get back in there. Nausea rose up with it and knocked my legs out from beneath when I thought of Jasmin being stuffed by someone else. Giving herself to *him*. *Jordan*. The way she looked at him fucking those girls. I had followed her to see why she left so suddenly, sensing a chance to play together. Then I saw her rocking on her toes, biting her lip at the sight of him, and I knew it was not simple voyeurism. She was entranced. She wanted in.

My shoulders dropped suddenly, and my chest ached when I remembered how I had run out of the party; with my tail between my legs and my dick hanging from my shorts. Those smug assholes laughing at me. What a shit show. I was even the one who suggested going to J&A. I had put aside my pride to fix us, and here was my reward. I punched the air.

"Fuck you!" I screamed.

The flame of fury went out as quickly as it lit, and I looked down at the ground. *Nice, Thomas. Embarrass yourself some more. Idiot.* I tried to pretend as if nothing had happened. The blonde scrunched up her nose at me and picked up her pace down the street. Second act of the shit show.

I found myself stepping back in the direction of the party. I had called Jasmin a whore. I had to apologise. I needed to fix this. Then I stopped again. A wave of heaviness came over me. I was eight years old again on the playground as the two captains, Kris and Martin, chose their teammates. The number of kids around me thinned out while the two teams took shape. My heart sank lower with each selection. I sensed the inevitable. Then my degradation was complete. The two teams were evenly formed, and I was the last one left. Nobody wanted me. The same had happened tonight. What would I do if I got back inside? I had already made an ass out of myself. What place did I have at a party like that? Those guys were leagues ahead of me. The groups were set, and Jasmin had found her team. She had wanted me to fuck her like a man, and I failed. Miserably. The people inside had a right to be there. I was a nobody.

I exhaled deeply. That was all true, but Jasmin had pushed those two guys away and taken *me* into the room. In the end, she wanted me and nobody else. Maybe I should— The flame of fury lit suddenly again, and I shook my head and marched away. Me? Apologise? Screw that. She was the one who snuck off, and she was the one who had brought us here, all because she was lusting for that meathead, Jordan. The way she watched him through the doorway, lingering, not giving a damn at all where I was. I could feel my doubt growing each second I stood there. The humiliation rising, my self-worth plummeting. No wonder I blew up the way I did. It was her fault.

I left the party behind for good. It was 2:53 am, and hardly anybody was out. I stood alone for a long time under the falling snow. I just wanted to go home and cover myself in a blanket and never come out again. A taxi passed eventually, and I hailed it and got in. The driver stared at me through the rearview and waited while my mind was elsewhere.

"Hallo?" he said, breaking the silence with a hint of the German impatience for indecisiveness.

I watched the snow outside. The white flakes falling in slow motion calmed me somewhat, and an idea hit me.

"Do you know Passion Parade?" I asked the man who looked as though he had not partied in three decades — if ever.

"Parade?"

"Hang on," I said, taking out my phone.

I found the address, and fifteen minutes later we pulled up to an empty concrete lot surrounded by decades-old warehouses.

The party was easy to spot. Flashing lights came out of the building at the end, where a handful of people were assembled at the front. I clutched the straps of my backpack and ploughed through the snow, then approached the bouncer.

"Name?" said the seven-foot monster with a black trenchcoat and shaved head.

"Jasmin Johnson," I replied.

The bouncer studied the list earnestly and then looked to my side.

"No Jasmin?" he said.
I shook my head. He signalled for me to enter.
"Have fun."

I marched through, intent on making this party my own. No Jasmin, no problem. The entrance to Passion Parade was somewhat similar to Ana and Jordan's party. It had a cloakroom and an open change area. Inside it seemed like just another Berlin club minus the clothes. Wearing my CK shorts, I observed lots of leather, lingerie and other skimpy outfits. There was a packed dance floor and bar. A door led outside to the garden, where a big white yurt was set up. I popped my head inside the ambiently lit space and found a dozen or so people cosied up and sprawled in different directions on mattresses. Nobody was fucking. Inside and out, I saw none of the pomp of Ana's party. No cocktail glasses, or guys with perfectly chiselled abs. A girl was up against a wall inside getting fingered by a guy. Otherwise, it was a tame affair. And I loved it.

Having felt the vibe of the place, I headed straight into the middle of the dance floor. The DJ set was peaking, and the anticipation was electric, like being on a slowly climbing rollercoaster. Ten minutes was more than enough for me to settle in. Everyone was facing the DJ, who led us harmoniously and meticulously to the top. I began floating along with the spirit of the crowd, settling deeper and deeper into my body. My worries dissipated in the surrounding ocean of energy. I inhaled deeply, and it was easy to give myself over. Then the rollercoaster dropped, and the crowd was unshackled, their joy shooting me straight to the ceiling and making me giddy. Now this was my kind of party.

Three guys dressed in matching leather harnesses and black sports shorts stood in a circle. Each of them broke their pill in half and took it. They then passed around a bottle of Club-Mate, the drink that kept Berliners partying longer. One of them caught me staring, and held his hand out. On his palm was the bright pink other half of his pill. He was a buff guy at least a foot shorter than me. He had a dark, stubbly beard, and his grin was child-like; bright and without a care. Something you only see on a playground.

His eyes told me that their team had three people. They needed one more.

I hesitated, brought back to my last trip to Berlin. Recalled the hours-long wait to see the doctor, as well as lying to her about what I had taken. The months of pain afterwards; a daily reminder of how lost I became here all those years ago. The concept of choice was washed away by a torrent of beer and drugs. I accepted anything offered to me. I had not taken another pill or snorted another line since. I wanted to refuse this smiling stranger's bright pink offering. To be responsible. But the moment took me with it, and I was ready to dive in again. I needed this. Whatever that meant. I accepted the pill, and the guy immediately handed me the bottle of Club-Mate. I took a swig, and the ritual was complete. He reached in and bear-hugged me, lifting me a few inches into the air. Then the four of us broke out laughing and dancing, and the music carried us away.

The beat was timeless. We stepped off the rollercoaster and onto a raft floating along with the river's current. We continued downstream to the music, our energies combining into four quarters of a whole. The melodies were like cold drops of water falling from above. The frequency of the sounds exposed any trace of tension in me. Having lost my physical and mental form, I left the past behind. Jasmin. Ana. Jordan. My humiliating entry into the kink scene. When the pill hit, I floated above while my body continued dancing without me. My senses came on like floodlights. The colours grew vibrant, the people became beautiful. Every one of them. I was born again, like seeing the world for the first time.

How I needed this. I remembered that it was not all hospital visits and chronic pain. It was also melting with the music, and love seeping in like a healing potion. The boys and I had not spoken a word yet, but none were needed. We felt our way to each other, with a glance, a touch, a nod, a chuckle. The pace of the music picked up, and I melted further into the flow. Love flooded me. The painful parts of me washed downstream and into the recesses of my being, while a heavy sadness remained. I emerged. The real me. I knew then I was not who Jasmin wanted me to be. A tsunami of emotion inundated me and showed me that my love for her was real, only it was obstructed. But by what? The crowd moved in synergy. Energy poured in and out of me like the sea. I looked at my hands. They were glowing. I could have cried from the joy. *Holy shit.* I was tripping. I fanned my face to try to cool myself.

A flowing white dress moved behind the boys, then disappeared. I tried to look for it, before the boys spotted my wandering eyes one at a time. They burst out laughing. The one who had given me the pill slapped me hard on the shoulder with a hearty smile and bear-hugged me again. I had love pouring out of my ears, out of the pores of my skin. I was sweating like a finalist at the World Sauna Championships. One of the boys noticed my discomfort, and he handed me a bottle of water. I slugged half of it, and bathed in the unconditional acceptance and care of my new friends. The flowing white dress appeared again. The girl wearing it lifted the garment, and revealed her bare, shapely buttock. I broke away from my spot and went in her direction, trying to avoid bumping into the dancing bodies, my coordination stunted by the drugs. She moved effortlessly through the crowd, and stopped on the edge of the dance floor. I saw the side of her face. Pouty lips, soft blue eyes with a burning intensity shining through them. Then she disappeared.

I returned to the boys, and we continued floating along together on our raft for four. The music peaked for the final time, and the crowd went wild, the rhythmic beat pounding every heart in the room open. My face, my heart, my stomach exploded with ecstasy. The moment remained intact for a time. Blissful. Perfect. Then the DJ's set gradually concluded, and we broke out in applause. Clapping hands remained high in the sky, yells of joy and gratitude sounded over the music. The DJ placed a hand on his heart and waved back to his adoring crowd, then disappeared from the podium.

The next DJ took over, and the boys signalled that they were going to the bar. I told them I would be there soon. Something was calling me. I went in the direction of the white dress, ending up at the entrance to the yurt. I found her in the corner sprawled like a cat, staring into space, indifferent to the environment around her. Everyone else was swimming in choppy, hectic seas. I knew this because the pill had awakened my ability to sense energy flow. Hers was what I was looking for. She was like a maiden in a forest, bathing in a pristine lake as I approached from behind. I imagined myself watching her in secret from the trees as she washed her breasts, with her flowing honey-blonde locks running down her pearly skin. While I was lost in my fantasy, I realised that I had settled down on the mattress beside her. Her indifference was magnetic. I could sense her inviting me purely with her energy. I stole a look at her. She had on a see-through floral white dress and nothing underneath. Her body was firm, her curves smooth. I felt an abrupt movement at the side and turned to the guy next to me. He smiled and asked me if I wanted to do a line with him. I looked once at the white powder on the phone screen in front of him and shook my head. I was fine the way I was. The guy turned his attention elsewhere, and I stole another glance of her.

This time she was looking at me. I emerged from my hiding spot in the trees and stepped into the lake. She had stopped bathing, but seemed accepting of my presence. I went deeper into the water, allowing my energy to drift in her direction. Her glow, her tender smile invited me in further. Before I knew it, we were face to face in the pure water. The outside noise faded. *What should I say?*

"I feel like we're standing naked in a lake among the trees," I said, as though that were the most natural thing in that situation.

She came alive with a chuckle, her seductive energy transforming into something more engaging.

"I like that," she said with a strong eastern accent.

Encouraged by her response, I moved closer.

"Who are you here with?" I asked,

"With you," she replied while holding my eyes.

"I can see that," I said with a smile.

"And you?" she asked.

"Same answer, I guess."

"Good," she said with a stoic nod. "Then we are here."

"Here's nice."

"Yes. Are you enjoying your time?"

I recalled the events of Ana's party.

"I am now. But I wasn't before."

"What happened?" she asked, turning towards me and supporting her head on her palm so that she gave me her full attention.

My instinct told me to be honest. She had welcomed me into her oasis. The least I could do was be straight with her.

"I was at an underground sex party with my girlfriend. It was my first time, and I wasn't ready for it."

"What does 'not ready' mean?"

"You should have seen the guys there. Big muscles, super confident. I felt like she was pushing me to be like them."

"That is not your nature."

She made the statement not only with her words, but her eyes. At that moment I felt that she was seeing me. *Truly* seeing me. Who was this girl?

"No, it's not," I said, my entire being naked to her sight.

"What is her name?"

"My girlfriend? Jasmin."

"If this Jasmin is looking for something else, let her. Good luck to her."

"Easy for you to say," I said.

"You are holding on. It is also easier for you if you let go."

I paused and searched myself. Yes, I was holding on since the breakup, I realised. After a few sleepless nights without Jasmin, I was in panic mode. I woke up suddenly on the fourth night, and the pain had become a horrible, howling explosion in my chest. I had never felt that alone. So I came crawling back to her. I was afraid of what would happen if I let go completely. The thought of losing her for good terrified me to the bones.

"Letting go can feel good," I said, immersed in my state of surrender.

"Yes," she replied. "I see you are letting go. Now you see yourself clearly. You are not those men."

"So what am I?"

"You are *this* man," she said, poking my arm.

I blinked hard and looked closer at her. Her words were surreal, resonating in my being.

"What's your name?" I asked.

"Now you are holding on again," she replied.

"Sorry," I said, staring at the floor.

"Do you want to fuck me?"

I flinched and looked up again.

"Hmm?"

"You heard me."

"No," I said. "I don't know. I should want to, right?"

"I am not concerned about what you should do. What does *this man* want to do? Does this man want to fuck me?"

My head spun while a plume of fear scorched me, rising from my belly to the top of my head. Panic threatened to overwhelm me. I inhaled deeply.

"Be steady," she said, softening her eyes and placing a calming hand on my leg.

I inhaled again and focussed on slowing my breathing. Her soft touch melted me back to a state of calm.

"Now, tell me," she said. "What do you want?"

You want Jasmin.

"I want to dance with you," I said.

"How long have you been waiting for this dance?" she asked.

"My entire life."

I got to my feet. I felt steady on my legs now, more sure of myself. I was no longer drifting with the current. I was the captain of my ship. I reached a hand out, and she took it, letting me support her weight until she too was standing. I led her out of the yurt and inside. We walked by my three brothers, who looked at us from their bar stools while grinning from ear to ear. Her curly locks and flowing white dress trailed us while I led her to the middle of the floor. We began to move in unison, as our energies danced together and our bodies followed. I bathed in her presence and smiled with pure joy. She reciprocated, and the beauty of her gift was more than I could bear. But I had to. I steadied myself, reached around her sultry hips and pulled her in. She rested her hands on my shoulders and looked deep into me. Finally, we kissed, and our union was complete.

With her body still in my grasp, the pill began wearing off. She sensed the withdrawal of my energy and led me aside.

"I know," she mouthed over the music with a nod.

I nodded back and took her into my embrace for the last time. The intensity left her eyes, and her smile bloomed like a flower — slowly, beautifully, gloriously. My brothers gave me two warm hugs and one bear hug on the way out. We still had not exchanged words. At the door I looked back to see her one last time, but she was gone. I got dressed and picked up my belongings, then nodded my thanks to the bouncer and came out into the snow. I felt like an angel glowing with light as I walked the streets of Berlin. Every inch of it was beautiful. Its grey buildings, its swarm of graffiti tags, even its overflowing bins and footpaths covered in vomit. I walked happily for a long time, absorbed in the afterglow. Eventually the sun rose, and I hailed a passing taxi.

Jasmin and I needed to have a conversation.

6

THE RULES

JASMIN

"Two guys *and* two girls!?" came Michaela's voice through the phone speaker. "Jasmin Freaking Johnson. Am I hearing this correctly?"

I squeezed my eyes shut and let those words sink in while seated cross-legged on the carpet. What had I done? Michaela's reaction told me exactly. I had cheated on Thomas with four people. That meant four times the guilt. A sudden explosion of nausea forced me to steady myself on the carpet.

"And at a J&A party!" continued Michaela. "Still can't believe you got an invite."

"I'm not sure what to make of it yet," I said, rubbing my wrist.

"It's fine, babe," said Michaela. "That's normal after your first time. There's a lot to process. I hope you don't regret it?"

I relaxed my neck and shoulders and thought back. If I had to be honest, I regretted only some of it. That it happened was not the problem. Four people also meant four times the fun. The aftershocks of pleasure were still rippling through my thighs. Rather it was the way it had happened. Why did Thomas need to be that way? We could have had a magical first group experience together. He had no idea what he missed. The beautiful, unfathomable insanity of it all. The stimulation overload. The terrifying yet exhilarating realisation that sexual pleasure was limitless. Wave after wave crashing onto you, eroding your resistance, carving into you the capacity for even greater pleasure.

"No, I don't regret it," I said instead, my smile growing from the echoes of pleasure now allowed to run free again. "It was so much fun."

"I knew it!" yelled Michaela. "I fucking knew it! You loved it!"

Michaela's enthusiasm was contagious, and caused me to burst out laughing.

"That's my girl!" she yelled. "Yes, yes, yes!"

"I really did," I said, smiling from cheek to cheek.

"Of course you did!" said Michaela. "What about Thomas?"

My smile disappeared. Too soon. I was not ready to go there.

"He couldn't handle it," I said and stopped at that.

"Really?" said Michaela, pausing for a long time. "And Jordan? Tell me he got in on it."

"No," I said. "He was busy with... other girls."

"Yeah, no surprises there," said Michaela. "That guy never changes. I swear he thinks he's all that."

True. And for good reason. He was a sexual adonis. But I had seen other sides of Jordan. The little boy behind the sharp facade got me curious, but it was the man who inspired the masses who had me paying attention. The community seemed to orbit him like a king, and he clearly cared about his realm. I had watched him closely as the party drew to a close. He got infinite love in the form of hugs, hellos and touches. People came close just to bathe in his grounded energy. One particular moment made me weak. A young guy was sitting by himself, having struggled to get into the party flow. The longer the night went on, the more people ignored him. It was Jordan who fetched him a beer, had a short conversation with him, and left him with his chin a little higher. Nobody else noticed. Too caught up in themselves. But I did. Still, I was no fool. I also saw the *other* side of Jordan. The thing that made him so mysterious and alluring to me. It was not only his commanding presence which cast a shadow. There was pain in him. A darkness expertly concealed behind his dominant presence and self-control. It would have been easy to gloss over if I had not gotten a glimpse of it while at Äden.

"He's definitely something," I said finally.

Michaela went quiet for a moment.

"Jaz," she said with a heavy tone.

Dammit.

"What?" I said defensively. "He's interesting."

"Did you know he owns La Secreta?"

I sat up and moved my head closer to the phone speaker.

"That Michelin star Spanish restaurant in Mitte?" I said.

"He gave the star back last year," said Michaela. "Said it restricted his menu. But it just made the place more famous. Not that he needed that."

I straightened my legs out and began running my fingers above my chest. The way to a man's heart was through his stomach. It was the same way to my panties.

"I've been dying to go there and try the food, but the line's always too long," I said. "How do you know so much about him, anyway?"

"It's Jordan," said Michaela, like it was something everyone said. "Also, his mother was a socialite in Spain. She got pregnant by a wealthy Dutch businessman and voila, Jordan popped out. Set him up for life. And he fucked his way to his own empire on top of all that."

"Wow," I said. "And you never thought to mention him to me?"

"Well, excuse me," said Michaela. "You were supposed to go to Passion Parade. I had no idea you were going to meet him on your first day and go straight to the big leagues."

I fell quiet as I pictured Jordan's ocean-grey eyes.

"Oh my God, you want to fuck him!" blurted Michaela.

"Look, I need to pack," I said, snatching the phone off the carpet. "I'll call you from the train."

"Cheeky monkey," said Michaela with a sigh. "Fine. But be ready for more questions about last night."

"I will," I said. "Speak soon."

I hung up, and was met by an earlier missed call from my mother. My fingers felt like rocks, keeping me from pressing the callback button. No way I was going to speak to her now. How in the hell would I answer her nosy questions about my time in Berlin?

"How's the weekend going, dear?" my mother would say.

"Just wonderful," I would reply. "I had an orgy last night with four people."

"How lovely! The more the merrier, I say," my mother replied in my head, which caused me to snort out loud.

While I collected my clothes to pack, Kaspar's words about his first sex party rang in my mind. I also had no idea who I was anymore. Any concepts I had about my sexuality were swept away by the tsunami of ecstasy I had experienced during the five-way. I smiled to myself, acknowledging that I had taken part in an orgy. It was as though a goddess had risen from the dust and taken me over. She was endlessly curious and insatiably hungry. She lived in the eye of the hurricane, and had invited Kaspar, Tim and the girls to visit. For an enchanted time, she had been me. Not anymore. She was long gone. Thomas entered my mind. His frown, his sad eyes, his spiteful words. The venom returned.

I heard the rattle of a room card at the door while packing my dress into the suitcase. Thomas stepped in and froze when he saw me. His suit was crinkled and his shirt untucked, his hair more dishevelled than usual. I found myself drawn to his eyes. Why did his pupils look like that? We faced off without a word, him in the doorway, me on the floor in my bra and shorts. The silence squeezed into me like a vice, growing tighter with each passing second. When my heart was close to bursting, I sighed and stood up.

"What are you doing?" he said.

"Packing. Where were you?"

"I went to Passion Parade."

"Oh," I said, now feeling better about what I had done. Still incredibly guilty, but a touch less.

"Why are you packing?" he said.

"I'm taking the train home today."

"No, you're not. We're staying."

My jaw tightened and my nostrils flared.

"First you call me a whore, now you're telling me what to do? Besides, we're meant to be checked out in an hour."

"Already sorted," he replied calmly. "I'll explain it all. Let's go for a walk. I want to talk to you."

I hesitated.

"About what?"

He stepped forward and dropped his bag to the floor. He gazed into me with his strange-looking pupils, and his expression softened.

"Did you do drugs?" I said, leaning my head to the side.

"I'm sorry about what I said. I didn't mean it."

I studied his face, which looked earnestly back at me.

"Do you know how degrading it is to call women that?" I said. "How hurtful it is? How damaging? Thomas, you hurt me."

"I know," he said, lowering his chin. "It was a moment of weakness. I should never have said it. Jaz, I'm sorry."

"You don't just get to say sorry, Thomas," I said. "That showed me something about you."

"You're right," he replied. "That's why you need to hear how I want to correct it."

I sighed and relaxed my hand, still unconvinced.

"Get dressed," he said with an uncanny confidence. "Let's get a coffee and we'll talk about it. The sun just came up. It's nice outside."

I reluctantly put on my jeans and a warm sweater, and we left Äden. There was a thin layer of snow on the ground and the sky was bright blue. We walked east at a snail's pace through the streets. Neither of us spoke. At one point I felt Thomas' hand reaching for mine. He clasped it tightly, and we continued in silence until we reached Prenzlauer Berg. We settled into a cafe, and Thomas ordered two espressos for us.

I watched him carefully while he stood at the front counter talking to the barista. He held himself differently, looked around less than usual, and his expression was softer. All effects of the drug? I wanted what he had taken.

Eventually, he returned with two cups and sat across from me on the table. His pupils looked like moons, or a set of black holes. I felt compelled to look into them, becoming gradually hypnotised by their depth. I decided not to say anything. We had both done something crazy. No big deal.

"Things got out of hand last night, didn't they?" I said.

Thomas nodded and grinned.

"You could say that."

"Are you ok?"

"I'm fine," he said. "I needed some time to blow off steam. Get some perspective."

"I understand."

"What did you do after I left?" he asked.

I started rubbing my wrist. *A lot.*

"Just had one more drink with Ana and those two guys then went home."

Thomas' eyes darted left then came back. He said nothing for a long time.

"Jaz, you haven't been happy recently," he said.

"What do you mean?"

"I mean with us. I didn't tell you at the time, but that's why I wanted to break it off."

"Because I wasn't happy?"

"Because I thought I couldn't make you happy."

"It's not your job to make me happy."

"No, but if I'm your boyfriend, the least I can do is get out of the way."

"You think you're in the way of my happiness?"

"I do. Something's eating at you. And it'll keep going until you hate me for it."

I sighed and felt myself soften.

"I don't hate you," I said. "And I won't. No matter what happens."

"Look," said Thomas, holding my eye contact. "I can't give you what you want. Last night proved that."

"It's fine, don't worry—"

"It's not fine."

There was that new confidence of his. I liked it. I wanted to know where it came from, but if I dug deeper, he would be justified in asking me questions about last night. I decided to roll with it.

"So what do you suggest?" I said.

"I saw the way that guy was looking at you," Thomas said.

"Who?"

"Jordan."

I shook my head and leaned back.

"Forget about this whole thing," I said. "It was a stupid idea."

"Ana noticed it as well."

I paused.

"Noticed what?"

"How you looked at Jordan."

Wow, had it been so obvious?

"What did she say?" I asked.

"She said you and I are like two children playing in a pond while there's a whole ocean out there."

"Sounds deep," I said, rolling my eyes.

"Babe," said Thomas suddenly, his gaze sharp and intense.

"What?"

"All this stress about your thirtieth. The long distance. You need this. You've wanted to sail out for a long time. It's the relationship that's been holding you back."

I sighed and pursed my lips, thinking back while gazing through the window. People walked by with slow, casual steps, enjoying the snowy wonderland outside, absorbing the sunshine with smiles and chuckles.

"Yes," I said quietly. "Time's just going by so fast."

"It is," said Thomas. "Which is why you have to do this. Except I can't do it with you."

"Hmm?" I said, doing a double-take.

"You know how I feel about open relationships. I can't do it. Not forever. So let's make a compromise. You and Jordan, just for this week."

"What the hell are you talking about?" I said.

Whatever he took last night, it was clearly messing with his head.

"You're free to do what you want, for one week," he said.

I shook my head in disbelief while flapping my eyelashes like the wings of a crazed bird.

"That's insane," I said.

"Ana thinks it would be a good idea as well."

"You're listening to Ana now? What about what I think?"

"You want this too."

"Do I?" I said, shifting in my chair and huffing.

"You know you do."

"What else did Ana say?"

"She suggested I try it too. She said she had someone in mind for me."

"And you want that?" I said, still outraged by this whole discussion but intrigued by the idea of Thomas fooling around with a stranger.

Thomas paused and looked at the floor. He shook his head.

"I know myself. I'm not made for it."

"So what do you want?"

He looked into my eyes with that softness that never failed to melt me.

"You. I want you. When the week's over, I'll be here."

I grew lightheaded. Me and Jordan, for a week? And Thomas waiting at the end of it?

"I can't believe what I'm hearing," I said.

"There have to be rules, of course."

"Rules?"

"You use condoms. No exceptions."

"Wait."

"No staying overnight."

"Babe."

"You get tested afterwards."

"Thomas!"

He lowered his coffee and looked up at me like I was the crazy one.

"Slow down," I said, holding my hand out. "You've thought about this."

"Yeah," he said with a shrug. "Ana helped. And like I said, I got some perspective."

"You can hear what you're saying, right?"

"Jaz, we tried it together. Look how it ended up. Your words tell me you don't want to break up, your actions say you want to do this."

"And you're ok with me fucking another guy for a whole week?"

"A week ago we broke up. If we can survive that, we can survive anything. You said it yourself, we can't keep going like this. Something has to change. You'll regret it forever if you don't see this through."

"But why can't we do it together?" I said.

"Because I'm not that guy, Jaz. Jordan is."

I straightened up again and folded my arms.

"What makes you think he'll want to do it, anyway?"

Thomas tilted his head.

"Is that a serious question?"

"No, I mean he can get any girl he wants."

Thomas held my gaze without saying anything. My eyes lit up and I leaned forward again.

"What did Ana say?"

"One week. You come home after each date, you use condoms, and you get tested."

"And you're really fine with all this?"

"Of course I'm not," said Thomas. "It's killing me just talking about it. But I'll be fine."

"Are you sure?"

"Yes," he said with a resolute nod.

So far the rules were reasonable. Except Thomas forgot one major thing. The detail that would decide the nature of his sleepless nights during and after my dates with Jordan.

"Do you want to know what happens?" I asked.

His face turned neutral, and I could see him searching himself for the answer.

"No," he finally said. "I don't want to know."

"Ok," I said. "That's probably better."

"No marks on your body," he added.

"No bruises either?" I asked.

"No," said Thomas with a bemused expression and shake of the head. "What else did you think I meant?"

"Nothing," I said, looking away.

"No marks whatsoever, because that counts as me knowing what happened."

"Right," I said.

Got me on a technicality. What the hell happened to him at Passion Parade? He was never like this. My curiosity finally got the best of me.

"Why are your eyes like that?" I said. "Did you take something?"

He shrugged and looked coolly back at me with his celestial pupils.

"I told you. My eyes opened last night. Must be what they look like now."

"If you say so," I said with a smirk.

"So we're decided?" he said.

"Sure," I said. "I can't believe we're doing this. But ok."

Thomas nodded and leaned back on his chair while looking me over with a thoughtful expression.

"What about our accommodation?" I said.

"I've called in my holidays and booked us in until the end of the week. I know you need to be in London by the weekend."

"And when the week is over?" I added after some time.

"We put it behind us and plan our future."

Our future, I thought. A few hours ago I was being penetrated by two guys I barely knew. But what was done was done. This was worth a last try. As disappointed as I was that Thomas had copped out, what choice did we have? It was the best option.

We finished our coffees and left, walking home hand in hand in the sun, imitating what our days might look like after the week was over.

MICHAELA

I measured the sofa with my eyes, moving my vision from side to side.

"It'll fit," said Hendrick.

"Do you like the colour?" I said.

"It's a bit bright."

"Mmm," I mumbled.

I sat down, testing the sofa's cushion for firmness and comfort. Hendrick joined me with a thud as he sat.

"It's too hard," he said.

"I like it hard," I said. "Don't!" I quickly added, anticipating his *That's what she said.*

We stood and moved on to the other sofas in the store.

"So that's good news, I guess," said Hendrick. "She's had her first orgy. Without Thomas."

"Yeah, I said. "It's something. Now she sees him for what he is."

"What do you think's going to happen next?" said Hendrick.

"I don't know," I admitted. My phone vibrated in my back pocket. "I just hope she makes wiser choices from here."

I checked my phone:

Not going home after all. Got a date with Jordan tomorrow:)

I stopped walking. Rubbed my temple, and let out a strong sigh.

"You ok?" said Hendrick, stopping also.

"Jordan Fucking Rambone?" I said. "Out of all the guys in the world, she goes from Thomas to *Jordan*?"

"You're kidding!" said Hendrick. "That guy's going to eat her alive."

"Darling," I said. "I'll be right back. I need to catch a train to Berlin to slap that woman over the head."

"It's fine," said Hendrick, rubbing my arm. "I think it's a good thing. She needs this."

I sighed again and wrapped my arm around Hendrick's shoulder. Planted a kiss on his neck. Appreciated the man by my side, who had landed on my lap only after many years of struggle, mistakes and heartbreak.

"You're right," I said, tucking my phone back into my pocket.

Jasmin wanted to get there the hard way. And if I knew Jordan Rambone, he was going to give it to her. Repeatedly. Until she came. I just hoped she came to her senses after that. I shrugged.

"How about an L-shaped sofa instead?"

7
MEETING DADDY

JORDAN

My girlfriend had a wicked sense of humour. Maybe it had been a bad idea forcing Ana to give up her sex therapist job. She obviously needed more than parties and manicures to keep her occupied. Now she was back with another of her games. One week with that minx from Äden. Even by Ana's standards, it was ridiculous. And that cuckold boyfriend of Jasmin's was on board? Hilarious. I prefered to defile a man's girl without his knowledge. What got me off more than the sex, was the idea of her going home afterwards to her oblivious boyfriend. Smelling the fresh roses he bought her, cuddling into him, and telling him with a sweet pout about her 'night out with the girls'. And that comment about my dick? I saw the way she looked on speechless during my four-way with the girls. Her eyes told me everything.

Ana was pushing hard for this. Usually she made the introduction and left it at that. If she liked something about the girl, she might join in. But that had not happened in a while. Jasmin 'would do you good' were her words. When I asked her why, she told me to trust her. Always playing the Oracle of Delphi, my Ana.

I picked up a banana from the kitchen. Ran the Jasmin proposal in my head, turning Ana's true motive over and over while peeling the skin, revealing... I lowered the banana and shook my head. *Of course.* The boyfriend. What was his name again? Tobias? Ana had sized him up in seconds when he walked past us at Äden. Reluctant mummy's boy. Golden child. Repressed sexuality. Always followed the rules. She had spoken about her clients the same way. Body language, facial expression, posture, energy, it all revealed a story according to Ana. How she read people always impressed me. Not that I ever told her that. And that was only the half of it. I was sure she did it for her own amusement. She knew Tobias would look at her, and she was ready. Ana is always ready. A lick of the lips, a cute smile and a curious question, and he was jelly in her hands. I should have known then and there, before Jasmin popped up and distracted me.

I tossed the banana into the bin. Picked up a fig instead and tore open the pink flesh. If I knew Ana, she was about to make this Tobias guy her new project. With me taking care of Jasmin, Ana would have free access to him. That was exactly why I got her away from sex therapy in the first place. To keep her from playing saviour to another pent-up kid.

Ana was Ana. She was going to stick her nose where it did not belong. Ramping up the parties was supposed to be the solution, not the source of new problems. How many would be enough? Guy after guy, a long line of sex therapy graduates screwing their way through the rooms of J&A. Stephan. Olaf. Giacomo. Tim. I was beginning to lose count by the time Dante came along. I had a bad feeling about him the first time I met him and his girlfriend at a J&A party. Something in his eyes. I had no idea what came from Dante and what came from Ana. I had a sense Ana was punishing the girlfriend through him for some fucked up reason. Once his girlfriend confided in me, and showed me the bruises and lash marks he had pressured her into accepting, it was time to get Ana out of therapy for good. At least at J&A I could keep an eye on her.

But nothing kept Ana down. Soon her eagle eyes were scanning La Secreta and Äden. Now she had locked onto Tobias and swooped down. The red flag was waving again. But I wanted nothing to do with her bullshit. Unlike her, I had no need to get involved in other people's lives to avoid my own problems. Once the sweat was dry and the afterglow had faded, I had zero interest in what — or who — they did once they left my place.

As always, however, I would need to keep an eye on Ana from a distance but avoid pressing her buttons. Never an easy task. For now, I was still sluggish from the party. So I grabbed my gear and hit the gym to get a pump going. I warmed up on the punching bag. Halfway through some bicep curls my phone rang. Kaspar. *Here we go.* He must have left something at the party again. Typical. For once I wished he could grow up, take his head out of the clouds.

"Yep," I greeted, placing the phone between my shoulder and ear.

"Jordan! How are you, man?"

"Good," I said. "How was the party? Have fun?"

"Oh yeah," said Kaspar. "Sublime. As always. Glad you and Ana are back at it."

"Good," I repeated. "What's up?"

"I wanted to ask you about one of the girls from last night."

Bingo. Young Kaspar had fallen in love after the first fuck.

"Which girl?" I said, rolling the dumbbell back and forth on the ground to help me deal with my boredom of this guy.

"Jasmin."

I let the dumbbell roll away and sat up. That was the last name I was expecting to hear. What did he want from her? Of course I was not going to express any interest or even admit to knowing her name. I had a reputation to keep. No piece of ass mattered to Jordan Rambone.

"Don't know her," I said, clearing my throat.

"She's the new girl. Ana introduced me to her. Funny story. Her boyfriend almost wet himself when we walked in on them. It was so funny. You had to se—"

"What about her?" I cut in.

I had no time for gossip. There was too much of it in the scene. Tim was the worst. Who had fucked who. Who was fresh meat. Who was spreading the clap. Plus I already knew the boyfriend was a loser.

"I was wondering if you could give me her number?" said Kaspar. "She rushed out after our group action. I didn't get a chance to swap details with her."

"Maybe she didn't want to swap details," I said.

"I know, I know. I normally wouldn't ask like this. Rules are rules. Can you at least get Ana to ask if it's ok? I mean, you had to be there, Jordan. This girl was an absolute sex pot."

My eyebrows lifted right up, almost touching the ceiling. He must have had too much GHB.

"What did you take last night?" I said. "I told you about the drugs."

"I didn't take anything!" yelled out Kaspar in a fit.

"Ok, easy," I said, moving the phone away from my ears.

"Trust me," said Kaspar. "She's top class. First we thought she was a prude. Cute, but an amateur. Ana asked us if we wanted to break her in, give her an introduction to the scene. We were like 'why not?' After that she was being difficult. She was nervous, I think. Then she had this fight with her boyfriend and he left. He must have said something to her, because she came back different. Left the rails. Even the girls were impressed. She must have been holding it in forever. I can't stop thinking about her, Jordan. It's driving me nuts. Look, I'm already embarrassed about this. Can you just talk to Ana?"

"Sure," I lied, having heard enough. "I'll let her know."

"Thanks, Jordan," said Kaspar. "I appreciate it."

"Talk soon," I said and hung up.

"Are you using this?" said some random guy in a tank top.

I tossed my phone onto the mat and reached forward to pick up the dumbbell from where it had rolled. Started doing reps while giving the guy a hard stare. He sighed, shook his head and walked away, muttering something I had zero interest in hearing.

I was only going through the motions. My mind was suddenly on Jasmin. Sex pot? I knew there was something about her. To be honest, I expected the fucking to be mediocre. Shy and inexperienced girls were no longer my type. It took too much effort to train them up. Not to mention how clingy they got. On my way home after Äden, I pictured how it might be with Jasmin. She would likely chew my ear off, yapping about her feelings and dreams. Be a lame fuck, then fall in love. Call me all the time. Play all sweet and lovely, hoping to one day make me her boyfriend. Send some passive-aggressive text at 3:00 am asking why I never reply to her. Appear 'by accident' outside my apartment. Nothing Kaspar said had changed my mind. This Jasmin was a liability. A waste of my time.

I finished my workout, keeping the dumbbell close the entire time even though I only used it for one set. Waited until the guy was gone before putting it away. Then I had a shower, put on my suit and caught a taxi to La Secreta to check up on things, as well as meet Ana to discuss the upcoming party.

A line was already building outside. I forced open the door and stepped in. Took a moment. Admired the liveliness of my realm, the seamless and effortless way my people were running it. You could die happy after eating at La Secreta. Not that it was a secret anymore. People waited for over an hour just to take a food selfie at one of our tables. My no-bullshit host, Ilva, commanded the front with ease. A rude tourist couple were putting up a fight trying to get in, but quickly gave up. They realised. Everyone did. This was a place of flavour, not pomp. I had hand-selected Ilva to enforce that credo with her Swedish nonchalance, her ability to put out any spot fire with her stoicism and grace.

"You need to get in there," she said as I passed her.

Apparently things were not entirely seamless and effortless. I marched towards the bar. Accepted a panicked greeting from one of the waiting staff.

"Jordan, thank God," he said. "It's mayhem today."

I stood observing the open kitchen that looked out over the thirty tables in the refurbished bordel. The heat was on in more than one way. The chefs were frantically immersed in their work, and only the head chef Imogen could afford to nod her greeting while wiping her forehead of sweat, a stack of pans and pots towered next to her.

"The washer's broken," she said without blinking. "We're still waiting for the repair person to show up."

I pulled my suit jacket off, rolled up my sleeves, and got to work. Something primal awakened in me when I was called to action. I was in my element in the trenches. No Ana, Kaspar or Jasmin. No big shot Jordan. Just me and the moment. Jordan Rambone was the king of the scene, but here I could take haven as a mortal — a servant who oiled the cogs of a greater good. Here Imogen was the fierce queen. If she was not filleting a squid or wagyu steak, she was busy with the team, supporting them in keeping the ship sailing straight.

The kitchen assistants were fierce, dedicated soldiers. The waitresses were seductive temptresses, upselling the white Rioja at every opportunity. Ilva the gatekeeper guaranteed an opulent vibe. They were the key to my hidden kingdom, and I paid three-fold to keep them. And the best thing about them — they gave zero fucks about who I was.

After I had cleared the muck from the dishwasher I turned it on. I heard the plates clanging inside again, before Imogen signalled towards the sink, which was full to the brim with dirty dishes.

"We're behind with the orders," she said.

I got into it without protest. I could taste the scent of the flavours in the air as I scrubbed the plates one at a time. I took in the white noise of the ambience. The clatter. The screams of the chefs. The gaggle of the diners. It was music to my soul.

Ana arrived just as I was done with the last cup. I washed my hands thoroughly, unrolled my sleeves and put my jacket back on. Asked Ilva to organise some coffees and set a table for Ana and me. When I prepared to leave the kitchen, the staff sent some parting insults my way. It was their love language, after all.

I stepped out with a sheepish smile but my head raised. Imogen gave me the wink that everything was in order while Ana watched on. My girlfriend never understood why I got involved with the day-to-day. And that was exactly how I wanted it. We sat down to our coffees.

"Have you thought about my Jasmin proposal?" she asked before I had even taken my first sip.

I leaned back on my chair and stretched my neck, rolled my shoulders to ease the tension of the workout. This Jasmin business was getting old.

"I'm good," I said. "Tell her boyfriend no thanks. I'm not doing his job for him."

"You don't like her?"

I thought about the moment I first saw the girl at Äden. Ana was in the bathroom, Jasmin was walking along the pool with light steps while I watched her from the water. It was like she was moving in slow motion. It caught my eye. Made me notice her. But like her? I liked black forest cake. I had no intention of fucking it or getting to know it.

"She's irritating," I said.

"You like the bratty girls," countered Ana. "They challenge you."

I shrugged.

"Not interested," I said.

If I had to pick one thing, she had a nice voice. Gentle, musical. A shame she probably whined all the time with it.

"I know what this is about," said Ana.

I sipped my coffee and waited.

"You're upset because of what she said," said Ana, lifting her pinky finger.

I sighed.

"Don't start," I said.

Ana shrugged and picked up her cup, took a sip with her pinky pointing up like an aristocrat, keeping her eyes on me.

I scoffed and shook my head. As if she could get to me like this. She put her coffee down and chuckled. I curled my fingers. *As if.* Why should I care what some hussie said? I sat up in my chair and looked out of the window. I could feel Ana's eyes on me. When I turned back, she still had that smug look.

"You know who Jasmin reminds me of?" I said. "Caroline."

Ana's expression iced over.

"Your ex?" she said.

I pulsated my eyebrows.

"Are you sure she doesn't remind you of your mother?" said Ana.

This time it was me who chuckled. *Nice.*

"No one compares to Arabella," I said, relaxing back into my chair. "Ok. Set it up. For tonight."

"Tonight?" said Ana. "We've got the meeting with Lars, remember? He just flew in from Barcelona."

I knew well about Ana's plans with the multimillionaire. Her collaboration with Lars near Berlin this Saturday was supposed to be the party of the year. An enormous opportunity for J&A to solidify its reputation and go Europe-wide, maybe further. Ana's dream though, not mine. Lately I had been feeling like a supporting act rather than her partner. It might as well have been called an L&A party. Besides, there was something more important at stake for me. Even though I was on edge this week, I was going to let the dick thing slide. But Ana had just tipped me over. It was petty, and I was playing into her game, but I had to defend my honour. You could only push a man so far. I was going to teach Jasmin a lesson for that comment of hers. Leave her high and dry, which would leave Ana with nothing. Two birds with one dick.

"I didn't forget about Lars," I said. "What time's the meeting?"

"8:00 pm."

"Great. Set it up with Jasmin for 8."

Ana's smug look was long gone now.

"I can organise it for 10:30," she said. "That would give us enough time—"

"8:00 pm. Or you can forget about the whole thing," I said.

"Darling," said Ana, measuring me up with her eyes. "What's this all about?"

I knew exactly. Ever since Lars came into the picture, my blood had been on a slow simmer. But Ana was not finding that out. It made me too vulnerable to her influence. Another button she could press. So I kept my cards close.

"Remind me why we're doing another event this weekend?" I said. "We've barely finished picking up the condoms from the last J&A party."

Ana sighed and gave me a condescending expression.

"We've had this conversation," she said. "It's time to expand while the wind's in our sail."

"Why do you keep doing this?" I said. "Like I keep telling you, it's a mistake to collaborate with Lars. The guy's a misogynistic pig. Do you want to be associated with that?"

"Oh, come, darling," countered Ana with a dismissive wave. "It's not like you have a perfect record with the ladies."

I shifted in my chair and stared out of the window.

"Besides, you were never the jealous type," continued Ana. "Why start now? Lars is harmless. He's got the global connections, nothing else. The people love you."

"Stop buttering me up," I said. "We're in the money already. Why do you need this power trip?"

"Oh, stop being so sensitive," said Ana with a contemptuous headshake.

My simmering blood spiked a couple of degrees. I stood.

"Tell Lars I said hello," I said, walking away and leaving Ana and a half-full cup of coffee behind.

A few steps later I stopped. She looked up doe-eyed from her coffee when she realised I had not yet left.

"I'm thinking about opening a new restaurant," I said. "With a new name."

Ana looked doubtful for a moment.

"What are you thinking?" she said.

"A menu from scratch, with some of those vegan dishes you've been experimenting with."

"Is that so?" she said with an earnest expression, tightening her lips.

I nodded.

"And what are you going to call it?" she asked.

My face softened. Her anticipation became mine.

"Ana's," I said.

It had been a long time since I saw that on her. A smile. Spontaneous. Genuine. *Alive*. It moved me into appreciation. Even in war and power, we could never stray too far from each other. Without our humanity, we were lost. Arabella taught me that. I had felt J&A dying in me recently. Things between Ana and me were growing routine. Lifeless. The threads which bound us together were fraying. This idea was my last stand, my way of resisting, of giving love a chance. And as long as I had some left, it was my duty as a man to pour it into my world.

JASMIN

I pressed the doorbell to Jordan's apartment building, rubbing my wrist while waiting. 'J. Rambone' was printed beside the button. *God*. He was born to be a pornstar. I wondered how Thomas was doing, and what he would think of me wearing my white datenight string for Jordan instead of him. I was in the middle of checking my phone for messages from him when the door squealed and clicked open. I hurriedly tossed the phone into my handbag and pushed my way inside.

My heels clacked on the tiles and echoed off the walls as I walked through the lobby. Jordan's apartment was in the rear house on the top floor. When I emerged into the yard outside, I looked up. A shadow moved in the top window then disappeared. I wiped a fleck off my blazer and straightened my crop top, pulling it down a few centimetres to reveal more cleavage. It had been one of the strangest feelings getting dressed for a sex date with another man in front of my boyfriend. For a moment I wanted to ask Thomas his opinion. That would have been awkward. And cruel. I was new to this whole thing, but I had the brains to stop myself. In the end I went for sharp and cute with a touch of sexy. Topped it off with some boycut jeans and a pair of closed at the toes pointed heels.

After climbing five floors worth of stairs I was out of breath, and found Jordan standing in the doorway. He had on black trousers with a black, tucked-in vest. His chunky arms hung to the side, and his eyes did what they always did when I was around; they feasted on the sight of me. I stopped in the doorway, immediately met by a field of tension. He held back his invitation for me to come in and imprisoned me in his sight. I held firm, my chest still heaving from the climb. We remained suspended in the game of chicken, both knowing the deal. The neighbour's door behind me opened and someone stepped out. I stayed locked in his game. The door behind me shut, and there was a pause before I heard steps descending. Jordan did not flinch, did not even acknowledge his neighbour's presence. They might as well have been in different solar systems.

Finally, a smirk came. He shook himself out of our mutual hypnosis and moved aside.

"Come in," he said.

I stepped into his lair and dropped my handbag to the floor. As I went to take my coat off, he stepped around from behind and took it from me. He picked up my bag and disappeared into his bedroom before emerging again empty-handed. Through the doorway I could see a gigantic bed with black sheets and a black metal bed frame.

"Some wine?" he said.

"Sure," I replied, following him into the living room.

The penthouse itself was exactly what I had expected. Spacious, modern, well-lit and central. The style of the place I had not seen coming. It was like a set of rooms had been transported from a Spanish villa and slotted into a Berlin apartment. The terracotta-washed walls, the white linen curtains and rose-gold lanterns, even the floor tiles looked Mediterranean. Not an inch of space was wasted. Someone had paid very close attention to the details.

I sat on the sofa and crossed my leg over the other, perching myself in a way that accentuated my femininity. The lanterns were dimmed low, and Jordan had lit up the entire room with candles. The popping sound of a cork came from the kitchen, followed by Jordan appearing with a bottle of wine and two glasses.

"This looks Spanish," I said, running a finger over a white porcelain vase on the side table with blue flowers painted on it. "And expensive."

"It's both," he replied and took his place next to me and placed the glasses on the coffee table. "It was a gift."

"From who?"

"Someone."

"Did this someone decorate your place?" I asked, inspecting the hand-made oak dining table from afar.

"They helped," he said. "But I called the shots. Do you like it?"

"It's beautiful," I said.

"Good."

"I also like white Rioja," I said, taking in the bottle label. "Are you a connoisseur?"

"Importer," he said.

"For La Secreta?"

He hesitated, knowing now that I knew. Then he nodded and began pouring his glass, turning the bottle without spilling a drop.

"I know what I like," he said. "The rest I don't care about."

"I noticed that. When you fix onto something, the rest of the world seems to disappear."

"Does that bother you?" he said, moving onto my glass.

Bother? It terrifies me.

"No," I lied. "But you should learn to lighten up a bit."

He looked up suddenly.

"Why?" he said, his eyes becoming spotlights which exposed my being and knocked the breath out of me.

Nevermind.

After some time I noticed he had slid my glass over. I picked it up, and he leaned back with his wine, slightly turned my way while showing no interest in a toast. Why was he being like this?

"You're quite the gentleman," I said. "Is this how you greet all of your lady friends?"

"No," he said, and waited.

So it was personal. I sensed a crucial moment in our story, which gave rise to the question I had put off answering: Who was I going to be? A sub that did whatever *he* wanted. Or a brat who made him earn it? In any case, it was about trusting him. Something about him told me not to. But my gut was telling me I was in exactly the right place. Still, this had nothing to do with dom or sub. It was about respect. We remained in our opposite positions with our glasses full and held steady.

"I'm not taking a sip or saying another word," I said, sharpening my stare so he understood. "Until you welcome me properly."

He nodded gently and held out his glass. We clinked them together and stayed in that space for a moment, holding each other in our eyes. He looked magnificent again suddenly. The boyish curves of his face shimmering on a frame of a man who could raise a mountain. I felt the knots in my body loosen, opening me to him.

I took my first sip, and let the wine swirl in my mouth. *Damn.* It hit every note. I almost lost focus, admiring the Rioja's regal taste. Much better than the riesling Thomas and I always ordered. Jordan's wine came from an exclusive world, which I wanted to be a part of.

The old me would have made small talk at that point, hoping to ease the tension, to bring things down to a somewhat safer level. But the new me kept her promises, and she swore she would never back down from what she wanted. I locked eyes with him again, took another sip, and stayed in that fierce, unforgiving space.

"I was surprised you wanted to meet me," I said.

"Don't be," he replied.

"Well, I am. Are you telling me what to do?"

There it was. Jasmin was going to be a brat. Jordan licked over his lower lip; the only sign that he was feeling the pressure. He was an enigma of dominant proportions. My tiny act of defiance caused a crack in the pressure cooker between my legs. The anticipation got the best of me. I placed my glass on the table and shifted towards him.

"Enjoy your wine first," he said bluntly.

I froze.

"We're not doing anything," he added, swirling his wine against the rim, looking at it like it was a lottery ticket. "Until I finish this glass."

I sighed and shifted back to my place.

"Not thirsty?" he said.

There was his game, but there was also levity in his voice. *Stay cool, Jasmin.* I could tell what he was playing, and I was going to play along. I picked up my glass, and we sipped quietly for an eternity as the candles flickered around us.

"What's your boyfriend up to tonight?" he finally said, breaking the silence.

"Same as us," I said smugly. "Probably having a glass of wine."

Jordan put his glass down on the coffee table.

"I guarantee you he won't be doing the same thing as us tonight," he said, leaning forward with that immense heat in his eyes.

"Oh no?" I said, moving back slightly, inhaling deeply.

Jordan gently shook his head and smirked.

"I figure we could chit chat," he said. "Or we can focus on what you came here for."

"Fucking," I said, which unleashed a spike of adrenaline that made me tremble.

"Fucking," he echoed, his husky voice forcing that adrenaline back between my legs.

He looked as calm as a spring day. I was hanging by a thread. I bit down on my lip while rubbing my finger along the top edge of my glass. He was utterly still, stalking me but refusing to pounce. *Take me, damn you.* I rotated my entire body towards him, leaned slowly forward, looking for clues as to why he was holding back. There was nothing. I found only an impassable wall inside those intense ocean-grey eyes. I had nowhere else to go. I placed my glass on the table and jumped in head first, hungry to immerse myself in the cold waters of his dark soul.

I felt his hand against my chest, holding me back. I was now on top of him, huffing, lusting, my whole body shaking.

"Relax," he said with a poise that snapped me back to reality.

I looked at him in a daze before blinking rapidly and lifting myself off his lap. I dragged myself away to the opposite end of the sofa. The sexual river inside had nowhere to go, and surged into a flood of embarrassment.

"I didn't know you were the type to relax in these situations," I said.

"You don't just roll up in here and get your way," he said. "There are rules."

He reached down and took his glass again, smelt the wine and slowly savoured the scent. I sighed, lifting my face. *Men and their fucking rules.*

"Ok. Tell me, Mr. Big Shot," I said.

"Daddy," he said, taking a sip. "You call me daddy."

I snorted suddenly, putting my hand to my face and laughing.

"Daddy?"

Jordan maintained absolute poise, which sucked the air out of my amusement.

"One of my friends calls her boyfriend 'daddy' in bed," I said. "She also loves it when he calls her his 'little whore'. I find it so weird. Are you going to call me that as well? Is that what we're playing?"

"We're not playing," said Jordan, his expression still deadly serious.

I adjusted my top and crossed my legs away from him.

"Thomas wasn't playing either when he called me that," I said.

"He called you a whore?"

"Yes," I said.

"What a gentleman."

"You're doing the same thing."

"Am I?" said Jordan. "Do you know who the goddess Kali is?"

"Well, this is total bullshit," I said, standing up.

Jordan sculled the rest of his wine and put the glass on the coffee table with a thud.

"Get on your knees," he said, the intensity in his eyes pouring suddenly out.

I froze as he sat back like a king on his throne. I felt the urge to leave, to count my losses. That was not an option. I came this far. I had invested so much already. Had put Thomas through hell. I hated to admit it, but Jordan had the upper hand. I could see it in his demeanour. His face. He did not need this, and it made me want him even more. I dropped to my knees.

"Come here," he said.

I crawled towards him, trembling with anticipation. I lifted my arms as he reached over, pulled my crop top up and tossed it aside. With an effortless flick of his fingers my bra came off, and I guided it off me before letting it fall to the floor. I unzipped him. Just as I was about to grasp his dick, his hands reached into the porcelain vase and pulled a thin black rope out.

"Hold your wrists together," he said.

Straight into it. I obeyed, and he worked the rope smoothly around my wrists, turning it twice around then twice over and finishing with a knot. His experience with rope play was obvious. Some seconds later, I had my eyes covered by a silk blindfold. He picked me up. With my arms tied together, he walked me into the bedroom like we were newly-weds and tossed me onto the mattress. My heels came off, then my jeans, while my pulse quickened. He left my datenight string on. I allowed him to tie my arms and legs to the bed frame. My entire body was heaving in anticipation.

Everything went quiet. I tried to sense him but found nothing. Were those footsteps inside? *Oh no.* I remembered the candles on the table. I had seen a photo on social media of this gorgeous young woman covered from neck to belly in candle wax. Was I going to let him do that to me? Would that leave me with burn marks? The weight of the situation then hit me with force, and I began to wish I had gone when I had the chance.

A long time passed with no sound.

"Jordan?" I said.

I listened hard but found only more silence.

"Daddy?" I yelled reluctantly.

A minute became two, two became ten as I lay there, helpless. I yelled his name loudly again, then at the top of my lungs, but no answer came. *Bastard.*

THOMAS

My video game ritual was bulletproof. Some heavy metal on the speaker, a first person shooter game on my phone, and a beer by my side. No matter what was going on in my life, I could get some aggression out while storming a virtual warzone, some joy from a good sip of a pale ale. I could dial up the volume and drown out my worries.

Tonight was different. Tonight my brain had a splinter in it the size of Jordan's dick.

All I could think about was Jasmin being Ramboned by that arrogant asshole. Him having his way with her, defiling her beautiful body, doing anything he pleased. Her letting him. That was what tore at me the most. The thought of her giving him the green light to do things to her that I never could.

I was on the outside again, while Jasmin and Jordan had formed their team. Letting her go was the right decision. But I was the one left with the consequences. The discomfort of what Jasmin might be doing ate at me like termites. *To know or not to know.* That was the torturous question. Knowing the details would light me on fire. Not knowing meant I was filling in the gaps myself, imagining countless scenarios that killed me with a thousand cuts.

Wait, I thought, lowering my phone. *No way.* I had a sense at Äden that Rambone looked familiar. Ana as well, now that I thought about it. I tossed my phone aside and tapped into my laptop, opening an old bookmark folder of my favourite porn videos. I had not looked in there for years. I flicked through a few, catching glimpses of horny step-sisters seducing their disinterested brothers, and librarians with thick-rimmed glasses getting pounded over their desks by their students. I thought for a moment, then an image of a beach appeared before me. I clicked on the video 'SUMMER SEXING INTO AN OCEAN OF BLISS.' I remembered being relieved at the lack of mindless anal and face fucking, and enjoying the old fashioned grinding of 'real sex.' The title screen flashed by, then there he was. Fierce and tanned, the embodiment of masculinity. His partner was voluptuous and stunning, her tits magnificent. *Ana.* The glamour herself. In the video Jordan threw her down onto the bed, driving into her, penetrating with power and ease. He would be doing that tonight to the woman I loved.

The moment I first saw Ana at Äden, I had also wondered how she would feel in bed. I paused the video and scanned the hotel room. Basic checks. I drew the blinds. Tore some toilet paper from the roll and laid it beside me. Made myself comfortable on the bed and hit the spacebar. Jordan resumed masterfully fucking Ana the way I had in my mind. I took his place in the video, and took out my dick. I started off gently and purposefully to get a feel, then accelerated my tugging as the pace of the fucking picked up. With the spike of intensity coming from the porno and from my hand, I could almost feel Ana's fit legs wrapped around me. She looked into the camera. Those sharp, commanding eyes almost talked to me. *This is as close as you'll get, loser,* they said. I jerked harder to force the thought away. Focussed on the shape of her ass instead. Those juicy tits. Her body flinched occasionally from Jord... *my* ferocious penetration. Her lush lips opened wide to accommodate her heavy breathing. My fucking grew feverish, animalistic, causing her pupils to scatter suddenly from the immensity of my cock driving into her.

She climaxed, and her ecstatic moan blared from my speaker while her legs began shaking. She almost took me with her, but with the finish rising in me, I fell into the deep hole of self-pity, where the fires of self-loathing awaited. I had been there a hundred times. The bright bliss of ejaculation would be followed by the coming of the night of despair. I let go suddenly, my cum stopping just at the tip and receding back into my balls, along with my shame. I snapped my laptop screen shut. *Enough.*

There was no need to rub my face in it. I pushed my pants back up. Soon after the sweat-covered Ana in the video had came, so did a text from her:

Hey sweetie:) Thought about my proposal? Trust me, she's amazing. Let me know xo

I stared at the message then closed it. Began scanning my contacts instead. I paused on 'Mia,' and saw her understanding eyes. Remembered the last time we were together a few weeks ago. Our walk from work to the bar. The yearning I felt for her. The way we kissed. The awkwardness that followed. The guilt. The pain of knowing I had to end things with Jasmin. Mia had told me not to contact her until Jasmin and I were done. *Guess I could call her now.* I could say Jasmin and I broke up and got back together, except she is fucking someone else. So, technically, all good?

The album playing on my speaker had ended, and I was now sitting in dead silence. There was no escaping myself. I could see everything clearly. All those times I had secretly swiped on a dating app, flirted with a random girl, then deleted my profile in a fit of guilt before getting back on some weeks later. My near affair with Mia. All the hours I spent with her without telling Jasmin. I had always explained those moments away. It was 'just venting.' I had never imagined being honest with Jasmin about it. Impossible. She would dump me in a second.

I finished my beer and popped open another one. Picked up my phone and opened my dating app. Began swiping on the girls of Berlin. Too hot. Too ugly. Too hot. Not my type. The bell of a message then caught my attention. The name on the screen was 'Giacomo Prevet Paade:'

Hey Thomas! Was great meeting you last night. Having a gathering at a friend's place. Music. Vibes. Other stuff. Wanna join?

I looked at the words in a daze. I had given those guys my number? I must have been *really* high. And what was 'other stuff' supposed to mean? I wondered if I should just stay home and wait for Jasmin. *Screw that.* She was having her fun, I should do the same. Plus the drugs were wearing off even more. The dark tide was rising, and I was looking at a difficult night. It was smarter to go out. To have a distraction. Avoid the comedown by staying high.

I tossed on a sharp white t-shirt and chinos and checked over my hair. Texted 'Giacomo' back asking for the address and left Äden immediately, wanting to be on the move even before I knew where I was going. A hundred metres down the road, the reply came. *Neukölln.* I should have guessed. I took the underground train. Twenty minutes later I got off at Hermannplatz, shoulder to shoulder with the uniquely strange Berliners.

I walked a couple of blocks to Giacomo's friend's apartment, where I found even more strange Berliners. The buff guy with the stubbly beard opened the door as I came up. I recognised the childish grin immediately. I hesitated, and he laughed heartily.

"It's Giacomo," he said.

"Right," I said, laughing as well. "I seriously had no idea."

"Man, you were so high!" he said with a thick Italian accent and a warm laugh. "Come in."

I tossed my shoes aside and entered the living room, which had been transformed into a drug den. Slow, moody electronic music was blaring from a speaker. One dim lamp was on in the corner. In the middle of the coffee table was a collection of bright-coloured pills and powder as well as the longest line of cocaine I had ever seen, spanning the entire width. *We meet again, my friend.* Giacomo bent down and pointed to one end of the winding white line.

"Berlin," he said, travelling along it with his finger. "To Tokyo!" he yelled with a chuckle when he reached the other end. "Help yourself," he added, holding up a metal straw.

I took the straw, dropped it on Tokyo and snorted all the way to Beijing. It hit me like a light switch. I had a bit more, and the light became a bolt of lightning.

"Easy," said Giacomo, slapping my shoulder.

I was back from my comedown and feeling good. Better than good. I found a seat on the sofa, leaning back and looking around with a wide grin on my face. It was Giacomo, me, and...

"Luca," said Giacomo, pointing to the lightly bearded, gentle-faced guy seated across from me, whom I recognised immediately.

"Oh, hey," I said, leaning over and shaking his hand. "Nice to see you again."

Luca gave me a dopey smile, his unfocussed and glazed-over eyes gifting me an unsettling chill.

"Did you work things out with your girlfriend?" said Giacomo.

I turned my head towards him.

"I told you about that?" I said, dumbfounded.

"For like half the fucking night," interrupted Luca, closing his eyes and grinning wide. "Man, I'm seeing colours."

Giacomo chuckled with a sparkle in his eyes and ignored Luca.

"Yes, you had a fight with her."

"Oh," I said. "We're in the process of opening the relationship."

"Cool," said Giacomo with a self-evident nod. "So she can party with us," he added, pulsating his eyebrows.

I tensed up. Did he mean an orgy? I pictured Giacomo and the other guys pile-driving Jasmin one at a time. But just as ever, my powdery friend pitched me a new, more extreme angle, twisting my confidence upwards. Suddenly I welcomed the image of Jasmin with the boys. I could even find my own plaything. The juices swirled between my legs. The adrenaline had me wanting to do *something*. Or someone.

"Sounds good," I said, breathing in deeply to calm my nerves and rolling my shoulders.

"There's a big J&A party this weekend in the countryside," said Giacomo. "I can get tickets for you and your girlfriend."

"You know J&A?" I asked.

"Everyone knows J&A," chimed in Luca, following up with a snigger.

Great. Even the most spaced out guy in the room was laughing at me. Jordan was a top-tier pornstar who was fucking my girlfriend and hosting famous parties, impressing even my new friends. But it somehow was not getting to me. The blow had me feeling just fine.

"Why weren't you guys at the J&A party last night?" I said.

"Sometimes you just want good music and dancing," said Giacomo, lighting up a cigarette.

"I get that," I said, reaching for and receiving the cigarette from him. "J&A was too serious. I felt better at Passion."

"You were dancing like crazy," said Luca, swinging his arms from side to side in slow motion and bobbing his head to an imaginary beat.

His eyes remained closed. He was half with us, half elsewhere. His face and hair were sweat-covered, and he was getting paler by the minute. The sight of him creeped me out. Luckily Giacomo was there to take the edge off with his silky personality, so I focussed my attention on him instead.

"Man, do you remember that girl with the white dress?" I said while exhaling some smoke, going back to the lake in the forest. "She was stunning."

"Maybe you'll see her again," said Giacomo with an all-knowing smile, taking the cigarette back.

I decided I liked the guy. He seemed content with life. It would help me to be more like that. For the moment, I needed another bump. I leaned over and snorted from Beijing to somewhere in Mongolia. As my senses peaked, my attention was drawn to the moaning noises coming from the bedroom.

"What's inside?" I said, wiping my nostrils clean.

"Let's go see," said Giacomo, snorting a bump after me.

Luca had his head bent over the backrest with his eyes closed. He was smiling and laughing at whatever he was seeing. I stood and approached the bedroom, only making it as far as the doorway. Giacomo put a hand on my shoulder from behind while I absorbed the orgy of seven men and women taking place on the two mattresses that had been pushed together.

"Recognise her?" he said.

I nodded. How could I forget those honey-blonde locks and pearly skin? I also recognised another of Giacomo's friends from Passion Parade. She was on top of him, riding him with her hands on his chest. She looked like another woman. It was not just that her flowing white dress was replaced by a black latex boob tube. It was the sharp determination in her face, the way her body was pulsating back and forth like a force of nature. She had left the lake behind and gone on the hunt. Caught her prey, and unleashed the full potency of her sexual energy on him. The sight of her in that position turned my heart to stone.

"Wanna join them?" said Giacomo.

I turned away and went back inside and sat on the sofa. Giacomo came next to me as I wiped my nose clean again.

"You know her?" I said, turning to him while feeling my chest somewhere in my stomach.

"We all know her," replied Giacomo.

My throat grew into a tight lump. How could she? *I thought you were different. Angelic. Decent.*

"What's wrong?" said Giacomo.

"I can't handle this," I said.

I grasped the metal straw and travelled into Siberia. It felt like a stampede of wildebeest climbing my back, my neck and over my head. My heart was going so fast I could barely make out the gap between the beats. I lost touch with my body from the belly down while the knot in my chest eased off. The swirling energy in my pants caused my legs to shake.

Giacomo took a tiny plastic bottle and popped the lid. Tapped some minuscule crystals onto the table and began crushing them with the tip of his health insurance card into a fine powder. Gathered it into a line.

"This will take the edge off," he said.

The fog of deja vu came over me. I had been here before. I ignored the feeling and snorted Giacomo's powder using his metal straw. Within seconds a wave of calm came over me, and my panic and confusion washed away. The impatience and adrenaline had the edge taken off them. I now wanted to join the action inside. Honey-locks getting pounded inside suddenly felt like an old friend who would give me anything. And I wanted all of her.

"Come," said Giacomo, signalling towards the room. "Let's go play."

JASMIN

The terror had set in quickly. What if my insult about his dick had made him furious enough to end my life? Was he making preparations to dispose of my body? I broke out all over in sweat while trembling violently, my teeth chattering. I remembered that Thomas had the address, and the shaking calmed somewhat. Jordan and Ana were well-known in Berlin. I was at Jordan's apartment with the knowledge of two other people. He had shown no signs of violent intent. I relaxed, and the sweating stopped. He was no killer. I began thinking clearly again, and it became obvious. He was making a point. Teaching me a lesson. Somehow that was worse than the murder option. Was he petty enough that a penis joke would offend him?

The rope was softer than it looked. It took me what felt like an hour to realise that Jordan had left some slack around my wrists. The knot he had used allowed me to reach it with my fingers if I rotated my arms a particular way. I picked at it over and again, making slow progress for what felt like another hour, before the rope began to fall apart. Eventually I got my arms free and took off my blindfold, then freed my legs. I got to my feet and walked to the door and switched on the light. My jeans were scattered on the floor. I collected them and went inside, finding the entire apartment shrouded in darkness. I exhaled like a bull. The bastard had left me there and gone out to have his fun. I switched on the rest of the lights and got dressed. Put on my heels and found my jacket and handbag in the bedroom.

Before I left, I wanted to give him a parting gift. I went to the kitchen and took out a closed bottle of milk. Opened it, and poured it all over his expensive-looking rug. Every drop. Slapped the bottom a few times to be sure. But I was not done yet. I picked up his special Spanish vase from the side table and hurled it against the wall. The sound of the porcelain breaking made me hornier than Jordan had all night. I turned off the lights before leaving his apartment — some civility had to be maintained. I walked home to Äden to help blow off some steam, arriving at our room half an hour later. Thomas was not there.

I brushed my teeth while reflecting on the evening. *Idiot*! I told myself, and tossed the toothbrush angrily into the mirror, leaving a long white line running across the glass. I had never felt so humiliated.

I texted Thomas that I was home then took a shower without washing my hair, and jumped into bed. He came through the door at 7:30 am. I was still awake, still ruminating about Jordan fucking Rambone.

"Hey," said Thomas when he noticed I was awake. "How was it?"

"I don't want to talk about it," I said.

He undressed and got into bed beside me without showering, smelling like body odour and cigarettes. I could feel he also had his back turned to me. That was the end of it. I did not care where he had been. Eventually, I fell asleep, just as a vague plan developed in my mind to make Jordan squirm. I was stubborn beyond measure, and Jordan Rambone was going to learn that the hard way.

8
WOMAN SCORNED

JORDAN

Arabella's vase. She shattered Arabella's fucking vase. I shook my head with hands on hips, staring bug-eyed at the slush of milk covering the carpet. I knew who to blame. It was 6:18 am, but I could not have cared less about waking her. I called Ana.

"Yes, dear," came her sleepy voice.

"She trashed my apartment!" I yelled.

There was a pause.

"Who?"

"Jasmin!"

Ana yawned.

"Why did she do that?"

"Because she's a—" I stopped. "This is your fault. You set this up. I told you there was something wrong with the girl."

"Darling, wait a minute. How did she trash your apartment? Weren't you there? Last I checked, you had the size advantage."

I huffed.

"She broke the vase," I said, ignoring the question.

"The one your mother got you?"

I snorted out, letting go of some of the anger with it.

"Jordan, what did you do to her?" said Ana.

My woman knew me too well. I hung up. Thought for a moment, then called the cleaner. A few hours later the carpet was sorted. The vase was a different story. There was no fixing that. My eyelids were heavy from a sleepless night at the Berghain scouting talent for J&A, but I was too worked up to go to bed. I went to the gym to pump out some of my frustration, then picked up a smoothie and a takeaway acai bowl and walked home. It was overcast with a cold breeze.

I could finally think straight. Fair was fair. An eye for an eye. I had gone too far. But what else could I have done? They pushed me. Jasmin knew that the vase was important. She broke it anyway. *Hell hath no fury.* Losing my mother's vase hurt, but I had to get over it. The justice of the jungle had been served.

I assumed I was never going to see the tramp again. I had begun to put it behind me when her text arrived:

Next time double check your knot ;) Busy tonight?

I stopped my walk. Sucked on my smoothie. This girl was batshit. She wanted to meet again? I had no idea whether to be impressed or put off. Luckily for Jasmin, my line between the two was non-existent. Batshit meant she fucked well. Young Kaspar had discovered that for himself. Now I was convinced. I wanted a taste. Breaking through was going to be a challenge, but when did Jordan Rambone back away from a battle? No more underestimating her. I hit reply:

Come over at 8:00 pm.

Her response came a minute later:

Your place is a mess, remember? Take me out like a gentleman.

I sighed. A date? That would set the wrong precedent. Maybe it was a bad idea. *No.* She broke Arabella's vase. That was not for nothing. I hit reply:

Fine. Meet at Heidegger's Katze.

One drink to loosen her up, let her air out her bullshit, then back to mine for the main event. I had made it home and was eating my acai bowl when she wrote:

Looks fancy. See you then.

The girl was getting cocky. I practically inhaled my food, then began planning how I was going to turn back the tide.

She turned up her arrogance to the max after I got comfortable at Heidegger's Katze. I had ordered and paid for a bottle of Fleury for us. Just as the barman popped the cork, my phone vibrated:

On second thought, I don't feel like a fancy place tonight. Meet me at Cockerspaniel.

I sighed and rubbed my face. Cockerspaniel was a swamp for hipsters. And here I was ordering the girl expensive champagne as a peace offering.

Cockerspaniel was five minutes away, so I decided to play along for now. I stopped before I got there and rolled my shoulders to get rid of the irritation. Bent my head down to stretch my neck and eased into my body. When the dynamic and dominant Jordan was back, I lifted my head and marched through the door with my fitted navy-blue shirt and neat ivory trousers.

The second I entered it was clear to all who the alpha was. I glided through the space, a man in his element, shoulders wide and nimble, chest open and chin raised to take in the environment. Every eyeball had yours truly in its vision. All the panties in the room had become damp. Each guy was forced to question his life choices. Nobody knew what to make of me.

The cackles of two girls came from a sofa to my side.

"That walk," said one of them to me. "Are you putting it on?"

I looked the girl up and down. Her words bounced off me like bullets to a tank. I scrunched my disgust at her, then forgot her. Went off to search the area, first skimming the seats, then walking back and forth and double-checking the corners. No Jasmin. She

must have been in the bathroom. I settled at the bar and ordered a Scotch, sixteen-years-old, neat. Sipped on it, and waited for Jasmin to be done. Five minutes passed. I scanned through my text messages. Five minutes became ten, then fifteen. Was she constipated in there? Wait, was she actually here? I shot her a text:
Coming or what?
She got the message, but never read it.
Another ten minutes passed with no sign of life. What was wrong with this girl? The irritation scratched at me, forcing me to pull in a deep breath to calm myself down. Had she gone to the wrong bar? No, she would have texted.
A half-decent brunette arrived and sat ten or so stools away from me. She began tapping on her phone while waiting for someone. She stole a look. I recognised her immediately from J&A, but had forgotten her name. On a few occasions she had sat close to me and lusted from a distance, but I had no interest. I ignored her and texted Jasmin again:
What's taking so long?
After a few minutes, I got restless and clocked a look at the brunette. One shy, sideways glance after another came from her. A play of the neck. She looked naive, but cute. Someone who wore their heart on their sleeve. The perfect sub. Would never bust my balls like Jasmin. Speaking of. Where the hell was she? Soon after, the brunette's friend showed up.
"Hey, Audrey. Sorry I'm late!" said her friend, looking flushed and out of breath.
Audrey. Right. Together they found a seat on the sofas, leaving me there alone, still waiting for Jasmin, that tardy little girl. I was ready to lose it. Was she that careless? I tried to take another sip of my Scotch, but found the glass empty. I slammed it on the bar and sighed irritably. The disrespect on this girl was beyond... I froze, thought hard, before it hit me, and my head fell. I smirked, shaking my head. That little... She got me. I kicked the bar suddenly, getting a stare from the bartender. Exhaled sharply, steadied myself. *Easy, Jordan.*

I measured the situation. Decided to adapt on the fly. I put Audrey in my sights and kept her there. She noticed, upping her hopeless effort to focus on her friend. She pushed her hair over her ears and stole another glance. I kept it going. Then came my opportunity. Her friend stood up to order drinks, and Audrey turned my way. I held her in my radar, pulling her in, and felt no resistance. I could see her blushing from where I was sitting.

She smiled again and shifted around in her chair, looking like her panties had chillies in them. It was still early, and the place was barely full. I signalled to the bathrooms with my head and stood. Went inside and waited in the hallway. Audrey appeared soon after, her eyes sparkling with desire, her sweet perfume wafting behind her. I got her up against the wall. Hovered over her like a wolf with his prey, pushing my body against hers. Her bright eyes invited me to ravage her as I pleased. Her pretty lips were parted, her soft cheeks flushed red. It had all been so easy, so effortless. Why was I wasting time with Jasmin? Audrey breathed in rhythm, anticipating me, hungry for me to take her. I held her in place with the strength of my energy, bathed in the power of my dominance.

I turned and left. Marched out of the place, burning with shame and anger at myself. *Fuck!* How did I let this happen!? I reached my apartment fifteen minutes later in a huff, got undressed and tossed my clothes to the floor. I had a shower, then decided to put on a movie to deflate, turning away from the shards of porcelain collected on my table as I walked by.

THOMAS

Beer number five was a mistake. Jordan's dick-sized splinter was starting to protrude through my skull, making it hard to function. I belched like a beached whale while steadying my bloated belly with my hand. The Späti inside was full of people buying bottles for their journey around the city on foot, heading to a house party or a club. I stood on the pathway with nowhere to go while people were forced to walk around me. The comedown had arrived. My chest turned to quicksand and sucked me in, leaving behind a hellish ache. A whole barrel of beer would not have been enough to plug the hole.

Jasmin was off on round number two with Rambone and still had not spoken a word about the first time. That was the agreement, but I sensed something wrong. She was struggling with it. Fighting some battle with herself but wanting no help from me. What good was I, anyway? I was hopelessly drunk. Today there was no party to save me. Giacomo and the boys were sleeping off their three-day binge.

I still had not responded to Ana, who had followed up with another message:

Waiting for you, big boy. Let me know xx

A warm flush ran over me. If Ana knew my state she would be feeling very differently. I had to put an end to it. I wrote back:

I can't. Sorry.

Her reply came swiftly:

The door's always open x
I swiftly pushed away the notification and wondered what Mia was doing. It took all I had to keep from messaging her. My strength was leaving me. I walked around some more to distract myself from doing something stupid. Eventually, I finished the beer and left the empty bottle on a bench. Sat on a concrete step at the old amphitheatre in Mauer Park and people watched. Droves of Berliners strolled through the cobbled pedestrian road in the middle, flanked on one side by a remnant of the Berlin wall on a hill. The grass was patchy like my beard when I grew it out, the ground dusty like the skeletons in my cupboard. The stones were filth-covered like my conscience. The Berlin wall was a freaking allegory for how stuck I felt.

So. This was what life without Jasmin would be like. I burped up some beer and took out my phone. Swiped on the girls of Berlin for some minutes, before I got a text from Jasmin:

Decided not to go out. I'm home if you want to do something.

A spike of guilt forced me to put my phone away. I left Mauer Park immediately and caught the tram to Äden. Back in our room I found Jasmin on the floor with her back to the bed and a glass of riesling in her hand while watching something on her laptop. She had a towel wrapped around her wet hair and another around her body. She looked fresh and rosy without makeup, her vulnerable beauty on display.

"Hey," she said, turning her attention to me.

I glanced at her screen. Makeup tutorial video.

"I prefer you without makeup, you know," I said.

"Want some?" she asked, raising her wine.

"Why not?" I said, fetching a glass from the cabinet and taking a seat beside her.

"You've already been drinking," she said.

"I had a couple," I replied. "You're home early. Everything ok?"

She poured me half a glass and shrugged.

"We said we wouldn't talk about it."

I took a sip and thought for a moment. Nope. Still did not want to know.

"Are you ok?" she said.

"We said we wouldn't talk about it," I said.

"That was the Jordan thing. It doesn't mean we should stop communicating. I thought being open would help us, not close us off from each other."

She was right. A fault line had opened since date one and was growing wider by the hour. I worried it would get too large to bridge. Having let Jasmin go to Jordan, I felt myself transforming. The fear of losing her dissipated, and out came my reckoning. Having let Jasmin go, I had nothing left to lose — except my burden. I wanted to spill everything now. Last night. Mia. The girls I had flirted with online. *Shit*. How could I have forgotten that secret date with that Swedish girl last year? I had pushed it out of my memory. That night we drunk ourselves stupid and made out in the back corner of the bar. I got overexcited, pushed too quick and scared her off. Went home in a daze, vomited for an hour then forgot the whole thing. There was something seriously wrong with me. In front of me was the perfect woman. For years I had been dishonest with Jasmin, and worst of all, with myself.

"I went to an orgy last night," I blurted.

Jasmin lowered her glass, appearing to process my words.

"Ok," she said with searching eyes. "Who invited you?"

"Some guys I met at Passion Parade."

"How was it?" she said with a cool, detached look.

I shrugged.

"I don't know. It's a total blur"

"I didn't see that coming."

"Me neither," I said. "It just happened. I think this whole kink thing is having an effect on me."

"Obviously," said Jasmin. "Did you like it?"

"Don't know. It was a bit awkward, but I didn't hate it."

My burden grew into a ten tonne gorilla. The guilt ate up the last of my strength. I had to say something now. But my throat was swollen shut. My hands trembled, and tears built up around my eyes. The enormity of my actions over the years rose to the surface. Here I was explaining the 'rules' to Jasmin, when I had been a lying pig the entire time. A sob broke out. The crying grew stronger, and I let go. Spilled everything. Mia. The online flirting. The Swedish girl from the bar.

"So what you said at the cafe," said Jasmin. "About breaking up because you couldn't make me happy. It was bullshit?"

"No. That was some of it, but there was more," I replied, wiping the snot off my nose. "It was the guilt about what I'd done."

Finally, the truth. Rather than be honest, I had found an easy way to keep the weight off my back — I tried to run away. I laid it all out to Jasmin. I wanted to be loved and celebrated by her. To be seen as her man, and not some liability which she tolerated. The pain of not having what I desperately needed drove me towards other women. It was an immature way to handle it. I knew I was chasing a pipe dream. But the chase was all I had to sustain me. It kept me from having to deal with my shortcomings.

The crying soon subsided while Jasmin sat silently by my side. I could have sworn I heard church bells in the distance.

"Are you angry with—" I began.

"Shh," she said, cupping my cheek with her hand.

She kissed me, massaging my lips without her tongue. After a moment, she reached down and unzipped me. I could barely believe my luck. When her hand touched my dick, I breathed deeply and my shoulders tensed forward. She sucked on my neck, and began stroking the shaft. My body gradually relaxed and gave in to her tender hand. She straightened herself and sped up the thrusting as my breathing grew shallower. Without slowing down, she forced out a volcanic eruption of cum all over the carpet. The aftershocks shook through me while I tensed up all over and convulsed, moaning out all of my guilt and shame. She took her hand away, and I collapsed against the side of the bed, breathing hard. She moved her body against mine and supported me in lying down onto the carpet. Soon the fatigue, the drugs, the alcohol, the heavy emotions and the bliss of being jerked off melted together, turning my eyelids into steel.

I opened my eyes again after dark with sandpaper for lips and a backache. I struggled to lift myself off the carpet, and checked the bed with hazy eyes. It was still made. The bathroom was empty. The heaviness of sleep was too much. I got up and collapsed onto the bed and closed my eyes before drifting back to sleep.

JASMIN

It was 11:30 pm. I stood on the sidewalk near the Charité hospital rubbing my wrist in circles, watching the clouds while waiting for Kaspar. The Berlin northern sky never went completely dark, always keeping a slight bright hue. Like a party that never ended. My relationship with Thomas had felt that way, the sun rising and setting on us and rising again but it never going dark. Now the strobe lights and music had gone off suddenly. In the resulting silence, the illusion had been broken. Here I was feeling guilty about what I did at the J&A party, and Thomas had been the one fooling around for years. *That cheating bastard.*

Then there was Jordan. That move he pulled with the rope had earned him far worse than I had given him. Behind his darkness was someone beautiful. I was sure of that. But he was protecting it in the cruellest of ways. Why were men like this? They had to make everything so difficult. Thomas and I could have had something wonderful. Instead he was fucking some girl called Mia behind my back, and flirting with anything he could online. I had to give him credit for owning up, but he *cheated on me*. That was unforgivable. I kicked myself for even thinking I could forget the Jordan thing and go home with Thomas. That ship had now sailed. I was staying in the deep end.

It left me with Kaspar, who had just finished his paramedic shift at the hospital. Hands in his pockets, he came around the corner. He had on a black jumper and a black rucksack on his back. His smile widened when he saw me.

"Hey," he said, reaching over and giving me a long hug, pressing his entire torso against me, matching his energy with mine.

When he pulled back we stared into each other without a word. His smile grew, and so did mine. He looked happy to see me. *Sweet.*

"So," I said, breaking the growing awkwardness. "What are we doing?"

"I know a bar nearby," he said. "Or we could just walk the streets with the flow. I love doing that in Berlin."

"Option two sounds wonderful," I said.

The streets were wide and spacious, and it was freeing to walk side-by-side at a snail's pace. Kaspar looked vastly different outside of the kink scene. His smile was raw, charming in a vulnerable way. The leather hunter guise was sexy on him, but this get-up felt nicer, more comfortable.

"So you finally messaged," said Kaspar. "I thought you'd gone home."

"It's been a complicated couple of days," I said.

"I bet," he replied. "It's nice to see you."

The hungry intensity in his eyes forced me to look away from him. How had I ended up on what felt like a first date?

"How was work?" I said.

"Tiring," said Kaspar. "I'm still hungover from J&A. We had an afterparty at Tim's. I didn't get to bed until the evening the next day."

I sighed. Did everyone in this city have to party all the time?

"That was my first party in three months," Kaspar added. "We were celebrating my thirtieth birthday."

"Oh," I said, relieved by the added information. "Happy birthday."

"Thanks," said Kaspar.

"I'm turning thirty this Saturday. I'm a bit scared, to be honest. What's it like on the other side?"

"The same," said Kaspar. "Just a couple of extra moles and some white hairs."

I snorted suddenly, and we chuckled together. Our 'date' only improved from there. We walked into the early hours, from Mitte to Prenzlauer Berg, to Friedrichshain, through to Kreuzberg, and circled back around the centre. It felt creepy being outside at that time, but our mutual bubble made it seem fine. Kaspar described his hometown in the south of Germany. I shared with him my West London upbringing. My dream of earning money travelling the world and writing about food. We exchanged stories of first kisses, first love, first heartbreak. How we imagined our thirties would be. All in all, it ended up being a wonderful first date. Except it was not a date. Or was it? I had no idea.

Our circle complete, we were back where we began. I could see in Kaspar's determined gaze that he wanted something which I could not give him. He reached over to kiss me, and I let him. To my surprise, it was one of the nicest kisses I had ever felt. Our lips were a match.

"Do you want to come back to mine?" he said.

His proposal was beyond tempting. It felt right to say yes.

"I can't," I said, shaking my head. Jordan's ocean-grey eyes were all I could see.

"Ok," said Kaspar, doing a good job at concealing his disappointment.

He ordered me a ride and waited with me until it came. We shared a final hug. His body felt wonderful, and I found myself resisting letting him go. I craved his touch. Probably because Thomas and I had barely laid a finger on each other since before the breakup. Kaspar released me nonetheless, and I walked for the backdoor.

"Your thirties are going to be amazing," he said. "Just see."

I stopped, and smiled to myself before turning his way with pleasant tingles.

"Thanks. I needed to hear that," I said.

He nodded.

"Goodnight."

"Goodnight," I said, and got inside the car, thinking about our 'date' the entire ride home.

THOMAS

Daylight was coming through the window when the sound of Jasmin's room card shook me awake. I sat up as she walked in and found an older, more mature looking woman in front of me. She had her hair done. Cut it to her shoulders, had it straightened and layered, and coloured it platinum blonde.

"Did you sleep well?" she asked.

"What time is it?" I asked.

"4:00 pm."

"Shit," I said, blinking the sleep from my eyes. I looked her over again. "You had your hair done?"

"You like it?"

"Umm," I said, rubbing my eye and standing up. "Yeah, I guess. It's different."

"I'm going out soon," she said.

"Where to?"

"You know where."

"You don't want to discuss what I said last night?"

"Let's leave it for later," she said, searching through her luggage and taking out her black cocktail dress.

"Ok," I said reluctantly.

A stranger was lurking in our room. Her demeanour, her movements. I seemed to be a stranger to her too. She went about her business as though I was not there. I then looked at myself in the mirror and understood. Staring at me was a gaunt, haggard little boy. Jasmin had put on her dress and completed her makeup, looking ravishing in comparison. I sat on the bed and watched on in a flaccid, dazed state. Eventually she was ready. She walked over to me and kissed me on the cheek.

"See you," she said and walked out, leaving me in the sorry pit I had dug for myself.

9
TAKES TWO TO MILONGA

JORDAN

Jasmin and I were an old married couple celebrating our fiftieth anniversary. Our sparkling youthfulness had solidified into an artistically-wrinkled, clay-like form. I was rowing us down a river in a sun-dappled gondola. Trees hugged the river on both sides. We were heading to my mother's place. Jasmin's idea. All was peaceful and quiet, besides the sound of insects crawling and buzzing. Cool drops of water fell from the trees onto us. There was a slight breeze. I heard the *clap clap* of an approaching animal and caught a stag standing proudly on a river bank opening. The handsome creature inspired me, with its antlers pointing to the sky like swords on a battlefield. I tried to row towards it to feel its majestic power, but the current was relentless. The river led us instead into a tunnel surrounded by vines and foliage. We entered, and Jasmin came forward and placed her hand on my shoulders while I rowed. We continued down the dark tunnel, descending underground, while the space around us gradually got smaller. And smaller. Until the gondola became jammed. Suddenly I was alone, trapped underground in a tiny coffin, the fear in me swelling rapidly.

I woke up gasping. My heart was knocking against my chest like it too was trapped in a coffin. *Only a dream.* I took a deep breath to settle myself. Rubbed my eyes to get the sleep out. Now I was dreaming about this girl? That fifteen-minute power nap felt like it had gone overtime. I rolled to the side and checked the time on my phone. 6:03 pm. A couple of hours, to be exact. I saw two missed calls and a message from Ana reminding me about dinner at hers before meeting Kaspar and the others for drinks. I rolled out of bed.

Dreams were moronic. This one was pointless for two reasons. First, I was never getting married, let alone making it to my golden anniversary. Second, my mother would be long dead by then. I shook my head and got to my feet. Threw on the shirt and trousers from last night. Went to the fridge and sculled some orange juice from the bottle. Left my apartment in a daze, still with the after effects of the dream — or more like nightmare.

I took a taxi to Ana's, who was waiting for me at the door when I came up. I leaned forward for the usual peck on the lips, and got a long, lustful kiss from her instead. Tongue. Passion. Urgency. She rested her hand on my chest, and her glowing eyes lingered on me. *What's going on here?* On the surface, it was a nice thing. But Ana's passion never came free. Our fifteen-year anniversary was tomorrow, but Ana was not a sentimental woman. Not even now had she suggested for us to move in together. No, something was bothering her.

"Come in," she said and left me in the hall to remove my shoes while she continued with the salad in the kitchen.

I grabbed a beer from her fridge, popped it open, and sat on the bar stool on the kitchen island in front of her. She seemed distracted, chopping cucumbers mindlessly while lost in thought. She remained gone for a long time, before she broke out of her hypnosis and looked up. She blinked twice and smiled, then noticed what I was holding.

"Beer?" she said with a judgemental look, briefly pausing from her work.

I shrugged. We both knew I never drank carbs. Tonight I was craving it, feeling it could take the edge off after that dream. Ana took a sip from her glass of white wine then continued cutting.

"I had a productive talk with Lars," she said. "He was disappointed you didn't show."

"What did you decide?" I said, taking a swig of beer.

"Nothing," said Ana. "He said he prefers to negotiate with a man. Chauvinistic bastard. Lives in the eighteenth century."

"So it was a waste of time?"

"No. I found out what he's got in mind."

I looked at her and waited with the bottle resting between my legs.

"His business partners are funding the party," she said. "They're from Galicia, connected to the Colombians. Lars is coming with them and a group of high rollers."

"So what do Lars and his drug buddies want?" I said.

"Playtoys," said Ana. "Young, starry-eyed lovers for entertainment."

"Oh?" I said cautiously, my mind turning briefly to Tobias.

"Mhm," she said. "I've already made a list."

I took a cucumber slice off the chopping board and ate it, and got a stern look from Ana. She sighed loudly, wanting to remind me of her stealing-off-the-chopping-board peeve. I knew. Did not care.

"How's Jasmin?" she said.

Here we go.

"A pain in my ass," I replied. "Not seeing her again."

Ana froze, and her face fell flat. She kept her eyes on the cucumber. For a time she said nothing. I inspected my nails. She chopped a slice off the tip before stopping again. Guillotined another with a loud snap. My legs pushed instinctively together, but I forced them apart and straightened up. Her breathing grew heavy. She drove the knife in again halfway through the cucumber, paused there, appeared to be thinking, then sliced off the rest. The volume of the clock ticking on the wall went up.

"You can't handle one little girl?" she said, looking at me.

"I already told her to get lost. She's not coming back."

I knew that look. Ana's stare gradually intensified. I sensed what was coming. I had a choice to make. I could bow down to her, or I could stand my ground. There would be consequences with the second option. As always, I had to choose my battles with Ana.

"You and I both know that if you called her now, she'd come running," said Ana.

"Absolutely," I said. "But I don't want to call her."

Ana sighed. Her expression was demented and grave, deathly even. She was on the precipice.

"Why not?" she said with a shrew voice.

"Because someone will get hurt," I replied, anticipating the breaking point. "I know what you've got planned with this... What's his face? Tobias?"

"Thomas!" she said cuttingly, her face washed over with disgust. "His name is Thomas. Can't you remember one name?"

"Thomas," I said as calmly as I could while the pressure in me grew.

Ana turned her face away. I could see her trying to keep it together, to avoid going to that place. Neither of us wanted that, but what was I supposed to do? Keep putting up with this charade?

"Look," I said. "Whatever you feel you need to do, go ahead. Just don't involve me. I'm out."

Ana's stare began to bore into me, and I could sense she was holding on by her manicured fingernails. I had delivered my message. It was time to backpedal. To pull her up to safety before she fell into that pit of chaos. But the trickster inside me would not have it. He had lit a fire in my belly and nurtured it to life. Was whispering sweet insults in my ear, telling me how weak I was for not standing up to her. I spoke again, knowing better.

"He's a hopeless cause anyway," I continued. "A loser. He'll piss his pants at the party, and you'll look like an idiot. Just give it up."

As soon as the last word left my mouth, I knew my instinct was correct. I felt it in the immediate change of mood. Ana was trying to recruit Thomas for J&A, and he had proven a disappointment. What did she expect? I sat up straight and looked at my woman. She grasped the edge of the bench with her free hand as though she wanted to tear it from its hinges. Her gaze was far off, and she was breathing heavily enough to hear. She suddenly looked all alone, free falling into the black with nothing and nobody to save her.

I would have felt sorry for her had her eyes not looked like that. Fierce. Hateful. They were shooting out acid from the pupils. *She's baaack.* The knife dropped with a bang on the bench and she came around to me, now looking perfectly composed. Too composed, her aura like a Siberian winter, her other-worldly expression forcing me to shudder and look away. She pressed her face to my shoulder and sniffed my shirt.

"Whose stink did you bring to my apartment, darling?" she asked, straightening up and staring hypnotically at me.

"I met Jasmin last night. Did you forget?" I lied.

"That's not Jasmin's perfume," she hissed. "I know her perfume. She wouldn't wear this."

For God's sake. Nothing got by this woman. I knew better than to wear the same clothes twice. It was one of our oldest rules; we never brought traces to each other's apartments. We stayed silently locked in opposition like two rams.

"Don't ever bring the stink of one of your conquests here again," said Ana forcefully. "Understood?"

I tensed my hand into a fist. *Jasmin.* That was exactly why I was putting an end to it. This would have never happened otherwise. I stood and pushed by Ana, knocking into her shoulder.

"Come back here!!" she screamed at the top of her lungs before tossing a handful of cucumber pieces at me, one hitting the back of my head, the others flying past.

I stopped and turned around. *Easy, Jordan. It's just another episode.* I knew the drill.

"Darling," I said calmly, picking up a slice off the floor. "I'm going inside to take a piss." I tossed the cucumber into my mouth, grinned while chewing it.

I winked at her and walked away. Locked the door when I got inside the bathroom, and exhaled slowly. I lifted the toilet seat and unbuckled my trousers. Enjoyed the sound of water hitting water while staring at the forbidden peeing man sign on the wall. If I never saw Jasmin again I would die happy. But I might change my mind if the toilet was her face instead. I shook my little man dry. I knew Jasmin would only bring misery to his and my life.

I stared at my reflection, becoming aware of just how much of an impact Ana's episodes were having on me. There was a weariness in my eyes that no amount of fucking could iron out. A stiffness to my lips that made smiling impossible. A darkness in my pupils where no sun could reach. I blew out my frustration and got back on the horse. As always, I had to be the one to guide us through the choppy waters.

After splashing some water on my face and rolling my shoulders a few times, an idea hit me. Something that would turn this night around. I went back inside and found Ana slouched on the stool staring at her feet, her mouth turned into a deep frown, the cucumber slices sitting untouched on the floor and bench. I calmly cleaned up the mess on the tiles, tossed all the vegetables together in a tupperware and put them in the fridge.

"Put on your dress," I said as I shut the fridge door. "We're going to a Milonga."

Ana's eyes twinkled and she shook her head, appearing to not understand what I had said.

"Tonight?" she said.

"Yep," I replied. "At the Apollo. Invite Lars. If he wants to negotiate, we'll negotiate."

"But I look terrible," said Ana.

"In twenty minutes you'll look smashing."

"And what about Kaspar and the others? We're meeting them later."

"We'll go to the bar straight after."

Ana thought for a moment, then nodded and went inside. I heard the muffle of her voice while she made the appropriate phone calls. I came into the bedroom and put on the spare suit I had at her place. Ana got busy putting on her makeup and I waited in the living room, tossing my 'filthy,' Audrey-infested shirt on the hallway table. I left the beer to get warm and poured a Scotch instead. Sipped on it while returning some texts.

Ana came out soon after in her burgundy velvet dress and red stilettos, tastefully made-up. Her hair was parted and tied into a ponytail. The manic Ana had disappeared. She was back to her stunning and confident self. Amazing what an outfit and a good plan could do to her mood — and mine. I lifted myself off the sofa and stood straight with my chin raised. Smiled and nodded approvingly. She walked up to me and placed her arms over my shoulders. Rested her forehead against mine.

"Tell me you're sorry," she said.

"For what?" I replied.

"Tell me."

"You're the one who put me in this position with that Jasmin crap."

She stepped back.

"You look absolutely stunning," I said with a hand on her hip.

"Let's go," she said, trying to pull away.

I reached around and snatched her back in, holding her torso tight against mine.

"Where are you going?" I whispered, breathing slowly over her neck while running my free hand up her thigh and over her ass, enjoying her firmness as well as the velvety feel of her dress.

She went quiet. I heard her breathing turn heavy, felt her energy seeping into me. It was all I needed. There was no time to get comfortable. I pushed her up against the wall, pulled her dress up and her thong down to the floor. Lifted her leg, propping it up with my elbow. Meanwhile, she undid my belt and pulled my trousers and boxers down. Took it out. I was good to go, and after sliding two fingers inside her, confirmed that she was too. I pushed up against her g-spot, inviting her in with a come-hither motion, which amped up her breathing even more. Then I pushed my hardness inside her, enjoying her sudden gasp, feeling her lungs fill with air against my body.

I had placed us carefully and purposefully in that exact position. Behind me against the opposite wall was the body mirror, where Ana could watch us fucking from over my shoulder. I ravished her with deliberately slow thrusts, penetrating her with my gaze, my energy, my focus. I had a singular goal — make my woman feel sexy. It worked. Too well. She forced me onto the sofa and kicked off her thong. Got on top, her dress wrinkled around her hips, and showed me how sexy she was. What a sight it was. I watched passively in awe as she went off her hinges. Then I sat up and embraced her, supporting her while she unleashed her sexual tsunami. I held firm like a mountain while wave after wave of her intensity crashed into me. There was a reason J&A had a *J* in it, and not some other chump's first letter.

We grinded chest-to-chest, two bodies merging into a singular flow, before it was time to bring us home. I stood and picked her up without pulling out. Took us back to our spot on the wall while she wrapped her legs around me. Thrust into her with an even greater fury as she groaned to my rhythm. Finally, I slowed, enjoying the sound of her breath, welcoming her energy further into me, before her pelvic floor took over. Her body levitated as she neared the edge, and she took me along with her like a wild river. Her moan poured out and reverberated around us while I began fucking her rapidly again with all my might. We came together, exploding like the second Big Bang. I grunted while I filled up her pussy. Then, just like that, it was over. We came down from the ceiling, both of our chests heaving against each other. When we had safely made it back to the floor, Ana lowered her legs, and I pulled out. She quickly covered her pussy with her hand to keep my cum inside her.

"Now I have to fix my makeup again," she said with a huff before going to the bathroom with her hand still between her legs.

I pushed my back up against the wall. Breathed into the sexual high running through me. It faded quickly, however, and left me with an empty feeling in my chest. A sense of sorrow. Of encroaching death. I poured an extra drop of Scotch and sculled it, then washed up while Ana was in her bedroom. Soon she was ready again. She picked up her handbag and marched straight out of the front door. I searched around, double-checking the hallway table.

"Where's my shirt?" I shouted.

I heard Ana's stilettos clacking down the stairs. I followed her, locking up behind me. We met outside. While we waited for the taxi to arrive, I looked back towards the path. Blinked twice to make sure of what I was seeing; my shirt on the ground in a scattered heap. The taxi arrived, and Ana marched forward. She opened the door and stared impatiently at me. I sighed and left the shirt behind, walking around to the other side and getting in. The taxi pulled away and I smiled, shaking my head. I glanced at Ana, and caught her smiling as well. We both chuckled, and she reached her hand out. I rested mine on hers. She was never going to change.

The taxi pulled up in front of the Apollo twenty-minutes later, and Ana walked ahead of me to talk to some girl she knew. With a hand in my pocket I stared off towards the river until she was done. She gave the bouncer a hug and continued through the door, and I could sense her excitement pulling her along. I had seen the bouncer at a few events, and we exchanged silent nods as I passed through.

The Apollo was packed when we came in, with a tanda in motion. The excitement hung thick, and Ana began working the room immediately, planting an air cheek-kiss on the first person she knew. I was still a bit touchy from the dream. I stood by and watched on. Admired my woman in her element. Felt tingles of appreciation, which I would never share with her. We were not twenty anymore. She looked over at me while talking to an older couple and smiled. I blew her a kiss and turned back to the river, which was visible through the floor-to-ceiling windows that lined the outside of the venue. The Jasmin dream crept into my mind and the claustrophobia returned. I shook my head and took a seat at the tables surrounding the dance floor. Watched the couples floating around in a sea of smiles. Studied and secretly laughed at the terrible fit of the men's suits. Admired the way the women's dresses accentuated their curves.

It was a decent spot. High ceiling, classy furniture, neat floorboards. Ana and I were among the youngest couples there, and I recognised a few faces. That was about it. For me it was all about the dance. Ana loved the community, and I could see it in her bright face as she migrated around. She took this milonguera business seriously.

Abba started blaring out of the speaker, ushering in the cortina break which replaced the smooth Argentine tango vibes. A few minutes later I felt a hand on my hip.

"Shall we, darling?" said Ana over the sound, having come up from behind. She appeared to have had her fill of socialising.

I got to my feet, adjusted my cuffs, and took her hand. 'Dancing Queen' faded away, and the next tanda came on. I listened briefly and approved of the selection, leading Ana into the flowing waters of passion. Pressed my chest and belly against hers. Her energy moved straight into me, and I took us out to sea. No matter what was happening in our relationship, it never got in the way of our flow during a milonga. Our steps were rapid, fluid and decisive. Fifteen years together, having immersed ourselves in every conceivable energetic act, we had something other couples could not even experience in their dreams. Ana's legs moved gracefully like a cheetah's, her ass swayed in a way that had the other men stealing glances any chance they got. I took her deeper into the flow, threw in a new transition I had dreamt up a few weeks back, and the surprise of it left her chuckling. I gave her a wink and a smirk. Her laugh was entrancing, her eyes sparkling. There was no resisting her in that state. *The darker the shadow, the brighter the light.* We were J&A for a reason.

There was no need to show off. Nothing to prove. Everyone in Berlin knew who we were. I felt the room and brought us down a gear to get us in line with the energy of the other thirty or so couples. We stayed there for a few songs. Neither of us wanted to interrupt the moment. It felt effortless, easy to enjoy, which was rarely the case in our relationship. Being J&A came with perks, but also headfuckery and stress. Which made this moment even sweeter. As the last song of the tanda came on, I took us back from the ocean and led us towards the shore.

There I could finally catch the wandering eyes of the other dancers in the reflection of the wall mirrors. Seeing who was getting bored. Who was interested in who. Most of the men's eyes were on Ana, while occasionally checking on me in case I saw them. I kept my attention on my woman, until I caught sight of a fine dish on the edge of the dance floor. In her sixties, white hair tied into a bun, a face for the ages and the glow of an immortal goddess. A flowing royal blue dress. The cortina came on to signal the break; some random pop song. I released Ana from my grip. The woman who had stolen my eye kissed her partner on the cheek to thank him for the dance. He clasped his hands together in gratitude and bowed, looking hesitant to leave. He eventually walked off, stealing a last look. He had discovered during that tanda what a sharp hawk like me could see in an instant. The woman remained alone at the edge of the dance floor with a content smile.

"Lars is here," said Ana.

"Go say hello," I said. "I'll be there soon."

"Who?" said Ana, sensing my attention elsewhere.

I signalled towards the majestic swan.

"Her?" said Ana, leaning her head.

"Her," I said, and walked off.

I approached the woman with absolute eye contact while the people parted for me. Stood in front of her, narrowed my gaze. Her smile faded like the sun during an approaching storm. Her eyes sharpened.

"Look who decides to show up," she said.

I reached my hand out.

"Be gentle," she said, taking it immediately.

"You too," I shot back, and led her to the floor.

We stood waiting for the cortina to end.

"I noticed you don't smile," she said.

"So you were watching me?" I replied.

"Sure. Handsome lad like yourself."

The tanda began. Some playful accordion invited us in, and I offered her my hand again. We started slowly, feeling into each other. My instinct was on the money. She was good. The experience showed in her movements, in her steadfastness. She kept up with my every step, lulled me into a feeling of strength, before testing my lead with a twist of the torso and a backward step that was out of sync. I let her go and we moved in unison while I stayed in her energy. We moved that way for a moment, before she spun herself and landed back into my arms, getting disapproving stares from the other dancers. I took her back with ease and pulled her in with a firm hand on her back.

"Not easily shaken, are you?" she said.

"Did you think you were dancing with a boy?"

"I knew."

"You have no idea," I said with a twinkle in my eyes.

"Darling, you couldn't handle me. I've had dozens of young men like you at my feet."

"Are we going to yap or dance?" I responded, picking up the pace.

She chuckled and went happily with me while I held a container for her infinite depth. By the second song we shifted into our private realm. We whirled and wheeled through the floor, and I varied the spacing of the steps. Rapid taps, long loping strides. Then I settled into a gentle rhythm, during which she closed her eyes, smiling angelically while surrendering entirely. She was different to the girls from the kink scene, even to Ana. Firmer, deeper, more grounded. We drifted along, watched on by Lars and Ana, who were standing on the side with glasses of wine in hand and exchanging the odd comment or laugh. During the third song, my dancing partner and I exchanged knowing, silent smiles. Enchanted moments needed nothing more. The tanda ended, and the regal lady chuckled, releasing all the tension of the dance while placing a hand on my chest.

"Thank you, darling," she said, continuing to laugh like a young girl. "That was divine."

I nodded and smiled, humbled by the way she had softened for me.

"I wonder if they have any sherry in this place," said the woman.

I gave her my arm, and she took it. We walked by Ana and Lars, and Ana shook her head, looking amused as we passed. I led the lady to the bar and ordered us both a sherry. When the drinks came, I paid. We toasted, and with a kiss on my cheek she walked back to her husband; a captain-of-industry-looking, silver-haired titan who raised his glass in my direction. I reciprocated, then went over and joined Ana and Lars, reaching over to shake Lars' hand.

"This dude doesn't give a damn how old they are," said Lars, slapping me hard on the shoulder and squeezing my hand like a vice. "Eighteen-year-olds, grandmothers. Whatever. He's going in!"

I squeezed back on Lars' hand and held it in place. I eventually overcame his grip, but let it go as soon as I felt him concede.

"Good to see you, Lars," I said.

"Still living at the gym?" said Lars, shaking the pain out of his hand.

"Gym has nothing to do with it," I replied.

Lars sniffed hard through his nose and cracked his neck to the side. His hair was shaved extra close, his hawkish eyes looked wired on cocaine. He had put on weight since I last saw him. Was well over a hundred kilos by now. Mammoth shoulders and arms. It made his chicken legs and belly look even more ridiculous. He was the most unlikeable guy I knew, but I respected one thing about him; his suits were always a perfect fit. He never let himself go in that department.

"Enjoying yourself?" I asked Lars.

He shrugged and made a rough face.

"Tango's not really my kind of party. But it's growing on me. This model I spent a night with in Ibiza, she showed me some tricks. You should have seen the ass on her, the way she moved. Mmm!" Lars bit into his knuckle. "It took all my power to stop from cumming then and there. We were at it until late in the morning. The tango wasn't bad either."

Lars finished his story with a wink.

Yes, we get it Lars.

"Maybe I can show you what she taught me," said Lars to Ana. He gave me a glance. "On the dance floor, I mean."

"Sure," said Ana hesitantly, ever the diplomat. "If you can handle it."

"I can handle it," said Lars quickly, sniffing hard through his nostrils.

"Ladies and gentlemen," came the DJ's voice over the speaker. "We have a special treat for you tonight. A one time only performance, to celebrate the sixtieth birthday of our wonderful organiser, Franceso."

The fat, balding Franceso waved from the side to the adoring crowd with a cigar in his mouth, his suit wrapped tight around his belly. The man was a proud pillar of the Milonga scene. Never missed an evening. His stories from Italy entertained me endlessly, but when it struck me that he was my mother's kind of man, that was it for me. I resorted to polite hellos from there.

"Coming all the way from Buenos Aires," continued the DJ. "Please give a warm applause for our maestros, Sylvie and Miguel!"

The three of us turned and found the area had been cleared. The crowd got to their feet and surrounded the dance floor. A band containing an accordionist, violinist and double bassist had taken their positions beside the DJ. In the middle stood a couple in their early twenties. The girl had her light brown hair tied into a bun, and was wearing a sparkling black dress. The guy looked swashbuckling on his feet, but needed a few years to fit into his black tux. They were in-shape. Bright-eyed. Their bodies electrified and ready to go. They reminded me of a couple I knew a long time ago.

The band started the proceedings with a funk beat and a swing tango musical style. An up-tempo song for a vibrant young couple. The DJ's words 'special treat' were on the mark. The crowd marvelled at the pace of the pair's dancing, and broke out in loud applause as the two of them separated and shared in what looked like a high-level tap dancing routine. They came together again, and he held her in a tight embrace. They mimicked each other with perfect synergy, their joy spreading like fairy dust, infecting each and every person in the room. Smiles and laughter covered their faces. I felt it too, especially in my throat and chest. The power of the feminine and masculine in unison. The young buck held his own, his energy vibrating a few inches beyond his limit, but the trust between him and his girl was solid. She willed him to keep it up, the overwhelm of the moment showing on both their faces. They had the audacity to go further yet, as young lovers always do. He showed no respect for the limits, and it was clear she loved him for it.

I glanced at Ana, and found her looking at me with the same inspired warmness. Was she reading my mind? Yep, we both knew the couple who had danced with the gods. It was fifteen years ago. I was on my last tether with the porn industry. It was my final filming session, and a budding young actress named Ana Nemati walked in.

"This one's different," said the director.

"Of course, she is," was my reply without me looking up from the magazine I was reading.

Then she came in. Confident, collected, feminine. Sexy as hell. The scene was by the beachside, on a bed covered in rose petals.

"This girl doesn't need instructions," the director said. "Go make some magic."

The beach location spurred uncomfortable memories for me. But like my father had experienced it with my mother the day they conceived me on the sand, I discovered a new beginning with Ana on the beachside. Our scene washed away the trauma of my first relationship, where I caught Caroline fucking my best friend Paulo on the sand in Barcelona. During our shoot, Ana and I reached a sexual transcendence for the ages. We finished the scene in one take, and got a powerful ovation from the film crew. Everyone in the room knew we had discovered something magical. Ana quit the industry soon after me. We had dreams. We wanted to fuck a new world into existence. To feel alive forever. Just like this prince and princess now being serenaded with applause after their magical performance.

The crowd was in rapture. My hands were clapping so hard it hurt.

"One last song," yelled the DJ. "Come on, everybody!"

Lars offered Ana his hand and she took it, giving me a panicked look as he led her onto the floor. I nodded to show her that I was watching. *It's just business, darling.* She could thank her stars it was only one song and not a tanda.

Lars and Ana moved into position, and the doubt seeped from her eyes. Lars took the first step, and Ana's body jerked when he made a sudden shift in a direction she was unprepared for. Ana adjusted on the fly, and they found a rhythm before he stepped on her feet and almost caused her to trip. I buried my head in my hands, chuckled and then looked away. *What a disaster.*

My attention got pulled to the side of the stage. I spotted the young lovers Sylvie and Miguel. The radiance in their eyes was gone. Miguel was radiating fury instead, grasping Sylive's shoulders and screaming at her. Sylvie looked shaken, yelling back at him and trying to escape his grip. She finally broke away and marched off before stopping at the edge of the dance floor. She looked out, and I could see her chest heaving. Miguel wiped his hand over his face and paced in circles. I could see him wanting to go after her but was hesitating. A middle-aged man approached Sylvie from the side, spoke a few gentle words to her and held his hand out. She ignored it and leapt into his arms instead, and he swept her off to dance. *So much for young love.*

A hand touched my shoulder, and I turned my head to find a smiling Kaspar standing beside me.

"They seem to be having a good time," he said, indicating towards Lars and Ana.

Kaspar and I watched them for a moment. They looked like the last two teenagers at prom who had nobody else to go with.

"Ana said to meet you guys here. Apparently we're joining everyone at Heidegger's Katze?"

"Yeah," I said. "Go fetch them and let's get out of here."

Playtime was over. I was done. I could see Ana was over it. Kaspar went off through the crowd as the night came to a close. I looked around for Sylvie, and found her beside the stage again. This time she and Miguel were passionately kissing. Miguel had swallowed poison, had one minute to live, and Sylvie was desperately wanting to join him in the afterlife by sucking in some of it as well. *Young love never dies.*

Lars, Ana and Kaspar came towards me, Ana talking to Kaspar, Lars walking ahead.

"This party's dead," he said as he approached. "Let's go get a drink."

I nodded and we walked out with Ana and Kaspar behind us. A black Mercedes was parked on the street at the front.

"You come with me," said Lars to me. "I told the other two to get a taxi."

I hesitated.

"It's fine, dear," said Ana with a reassuring hand on my shoulder. "We'll meet you there."

Lars and I got into the backseat of the Mercedes. The driver adjusted his cap and drove off.

"Hell of a woman, your Ana," said Lars.

I nodded, while the passing Berlin streets had my eyes. The wanna-be artists, the tourists, the dreamers who had escaped home for a taste of freedom; all roaming a post-Cold War concrete jungle, looking for the next pleasure high. What a world they lived in.

"Right," said Lars. "Now that we got you away from the wife and kid, let's talk business."

The guy was a moron believing I ran the show, but for Ana's sake, I decided to play along.

"Tell me," I said, giving Lars my attention.

"I'm sure Ana told you about my friends, and what they're looking for."

"She did."

"Your woman is a top operator. She's built this thing from the ground up. I hear about J&A all the way in Argentina. Ana this. Jordan that."

I shrugged.

"Lovely to hear, I guess," I said.

"Jordan, I'm here because you two are onto something big. J&A has a solid model. You bring in the ladies, Ana recruits the lads. You've built an empire with enormous potential. Only you don't realise it. Or at least *you* don't. I'm talking to you privately so you don't lose face with your woman, but you need to hear this."

Lars the businessman was in full flight.

"What is it, Lars?" I said with a sigh.

"You're a big boy, so I'll give it to you straight. You need to pull your weight. That no show the other night was unacceptable. Let's not kid ourselves; Ana is the head and heart of this operation. But Jordan Rambone is the enormous, throbbing cock. He's the man every guy imitates. He's the scalp the ladies want, so they can brag to their girlfriends the next morning."

I rested the side of my head on my knuckles while listening to Lars. The guy had a way with words, but he was still full of shit.

"Berlin's your stomping ground," continued Lars. "Your shadow covers the entire city. So I can't come here without having you on board. You see where I'm going with this?"

"Yeah, I do," I said. "You and your Galician buddies want to pedal coke in Berlin."

"The white stuff has nothing to do with it. We're already making great business here. It's snowing all year round in Berlin, not just in January."

"So... What?"

"Our crew runs parties in Spain. Private. High-end. These guys are rolling with millions, so they can get anything they want. They dream it, it happens. Supermodels, mothers with their daughters, young guys. Strange shit. Freaky shit. Other shit you don't want to know about. You name it, they've done it."

"We're almost there," said the driver through the speaker.

Lars pressed a button to transmit back.

"Do a circle," he said. "We need ten more minutes."

"Yes, sir," said the driver.

"My guys are bored," continued Lars. "They need something new. The kink scene is spreading everywhere. You and Ana are creating the most heat, and my guys want a piece. We want to take your model global. Carnival-themed sex parties in Rio. Beach orgies in Ibiza. Freaky hentai dress-ups in Tokyo. You'll earn a fortune. J&A's rep gets a monster bump, my guys get a good time, from London to Buenos Aires and back around to Barcelona."

"A good time?" I said, raising my eyebrows. "You know we have a code here, right? Openness, respect, consent. This thing didn't just happen by accident. You need to take care of it. Like a plant. Water it. Give it sun. Trim the branches once in a while."

"That's fine," Lars said, taking a moment to absorb what I had said. "My boys just want to pick some fruit from your tree or plant or whatever. If you don't share what you have, the fruit falls off and rots. Do you see where being selfish leads you? Farmers get their purse, the people get to eat. That's how the world works."

I had been around enough to know how this was going to end. But Ana wanted this.

"You stick to the rules," I said.

"Of course," said Lars, resting a hand on my wrist. "Ana told me all about the rules. We want a healthy, long-term arrangement. Win-win is the game."

"Anything else?" I said.

"I've heard rumours that you're unhappy about our collaboration. I can't have doubts in the air before our first event. No more complaining. I need you with us one-hundred-percent, otherwise this all goes under. A J&A party without you is like strudel without the apple, to use your metaphor."

"Don't worry about that," I said.

"Hear me out before you tell me not to worry. I made Ana keep quiet until I got a chance to talk to you. I wanted to tell this to you myself."

"You've got more demands?"

"I've got a vision."

Here I was again dealing with the consequences of someone's drug habit. This guy was coked up twenty-four-seven. Naturally he would start to think of himself as a visionnaire. I gave an impatient sigh.

"Your parties are too concealed," said Lars. "Too many rooms. Now, I'm not looking to mess with your formula. It works just fine. But you're missing something that can push you over the top."

"I don't want any sick stuff at our parties," I said, sensing where Lars was heading.

Lars sniffed deep and cracked his neck.

"You're being disrespectful," he said with a shift of tone. "I don't enjoy being disrespected."

"I'm just telling you *my* terms."

Lars gave a lopsided smile.

"What you're missing, Jordan," he said with newfound patience. "Is spectacle."

"You don't think a fuckfest with over a hundred people is spectacle enough?" I said.

"It's impressive. Not a spectacle," said Lars, shaking his head. "The party this Saturday is just the beginning. Villa Salace has a stunning location in the Brandenburg countryside. By a lake, surrounded by forest. Built by the Prussian Royalty. Inside you have over a hundred rooms. In the middle is the great hall. You instantly feel like a king when you walk in there. The perfect stage for our maiden party. On the first level is a balcony. My entourage will be seated there away from the rest."

"Sounds wonderful for you and your entourage," I said.

"All of that, my dear Jordan, is impressive," said Lars, ignoring my comment.

I closed my eyes for a long time. What was the point of arguing with all this?

"But like I said, we need spectacle," said Lars. "For the main event, we have what I've called the 'Maiden Consummation.'"

A sharp pulse ran through me. I did not like the sound of this.

"The theme for this party is 'young lovers'," continued Lars. "The girl I have in mind is special. A twenty-one-year-old from Galicia. Gorgeous. Skin like ripe fruit. Hair like a panther. The purest of the pure. The taking of her innocence marks the high point of the party. It'll be the most stunning act anyone has seen."

"Wait," I said, holding my palm out, blinking hard. "You want to parade sex with a virgin in front of hundreds of people? What kind of freak show are you running?"

"Jordan," said Lars, placing his hand on my arm, causing me to flinch and push it away.

Lars froze suddenly, staring hard at me before taking a deep, steadying breath.

"Obviously she's not a virgin," he said softly and carefully. "She works for me. But the people don't need to know that. Look, I respect what you've built here. But Ana pursued this partnership for a reason. You know the scene. You're the man. But I'm the *businessman*. I know how to take a decent operation and turn it to gold. You need to trust me. It's only a show."

"Decent?" I said, my shoulders tensing. "Show some fucking respect."

"Don't be so sensitive, Jordan," said Lars, rolling his eyes.

"And I don't care if it's just a show," I said. "I'm not interested in objectifying a young girl for your pleasure and gain. Let me explain something to you I don't think you understand. People come to our parties to explore their sexuality. It doesn't matter who they are. We offer them a positive space. Sometimes things go overboard, but there are consequences, and *everyone* gets respect. Not a freak show. This isn't what J&A is about."

"Come on, Jordan," said Lars with some force. "Get off your high horse and be the stallion everyone knows you to be. You're getting too caught up in self-righteousness. Look at the bigger picture. People aren't coming to the parties to be moral, they want to be *bad*. They don't want to explore their sexuality, they're looking for transcendence. They want to be wowed out of their fucking minds. Don't you see?"

My vision turned blurry, and my eardrums felt like they would explode. A visionnaire? This guy thought he was a Roman emperor. *Un-fucking-believable*. The car had long come to a stop in front of Heidegger's Katze. I opened the door and pointed a finger at Lars.

"You're a moron if you think I'll support this perverted plan you call a spectacle," I said and got out, slamming the door shut behind me.

I needed a drink. I pulled the front door to Heidegger's open, scanned the area and spotted Ana, Kaspar and one of his friends from the scene. Nice tits, sexy walk. Forgot her name. I signalled the waiter as I marched by the bar and found a seat on the sofas with the group. Ana gave me an expectant look. At the same time the waiter arrived.

"Scotch. Sixteen years. Neat," I said.

The waiter nodded and left. Lars stopped him on the way and whispered his order to him then found a seat next to Ana, stretching his arms over the backrest behind her and spreading his legs wide.

"Hello, boys and girls," Lars said to the group.

"Where the hell are Mimi and Jasmin?" said Kaspar's friend, looking in the direction of the bathrooms. "They've been gone forever."

My head turned suddenly.

I watched the bathroom door with absolute focus. The door swung open. Out came Mimi in tight pink jeans, followed by Jasmin, looking stunning in a black cocktail dress and her hair now platinum and short. I shook my head, forcing my smile down. *You never give up, do you?*

"Speak of the sexy devils," said Kaspar.

Ana was looking directly at me, beaming with glee, feeding her sick sense of humour with my confusion.

"Have fun in there?" said Kaspar to Mimi with a teenager's grin as they approached.

Mimi let out a laugh and turned towards Jasmin, who was looking directly at me, rubbing her wrist.

"Hey, Jordan," she said.

10
TO HEAVEN

JORDAN

That little hussy. Sitting all upright and proper with her little hands clasped together. Paying polite attention to Kaspar's pretentious travel stories. Giggling and cackling along with the girls. It made me sick to my balls. And that scheming girlfriend of mine sitting in between the four of them, looking as proud as a pig in shit. She had set up the whole thing behind my back. I should have seen it coming. Kaspar the determined prick went around me and got in touch with Ana, who gave him the number he was desperate for. Jasmin, horny to get a taste of the Great Rambone, made plans with Kaspar to get her foot in. Or maybe Ana had invited her. These manipulative games were getting on my nerves. Reminded me of the girls who showed up at La Secreta to get into a position to meet me. The lingering stares. The awkwardness of it all.

Jasmin was on a different level to those girls. Every time I tried to swat her away, her counterpunch came swiftly and twice as hard. I leaned back and put on a cool facade. It was tough, considering I was dealing with attacks on multiple fronts. Two scheming women in front of me, one arrogant pig beside me on the sofa. But I was Jordan Rambone. I thrived under pressure.

Eventually, Jasmin got up and went to the bathroom alone. I was ready. I straightened my cuffs, then stood and marched after her, catching her in the toilet lobby.

"Do you know how expensive that vase was?" I said on approach, forcing her to turn around. "Maybe I should make you pay for it."

"Asshole," she hissed. "You tied me up and left me there."

"Watch your mouth," I said. "Stop acting like a little brat."

"I'll act how I want," she said.

I inhaled deeply to steady myself while she tested me with her stare. My rising turn-on for her surprised me, before it switched back to fury. My face burnt up, and I scowled before turning away and marching back into the bar. I took a seat beside Lars, still fuming from the exchange.

"What's her deal?" said Lars while juggling his phone between his palms, focussing on Jasmin when she returned to her seat. "Is she as good as I've heard?"

I huffed a sigh.

"What have you heard? I said.

"That she's a sex pot," said Kaspar as he took a seat next to me, having walked over to join us.

My shoulders grew tight, but I held back the urge to roll out the tension, and stayed in my position.

"Kaspar here is smitten by her," said Lars. "Told me every detail."

I looked over at Jasmin the 'sex pot.' She was a contradiction with her perfect posture and sweet expression. The new hair suited her, though. Gave her an edge.

"I'm not smitten," said Kaspar. "Just impressed."

Ana's hands appeared from behind and crossed over my chest while she nuzzled my neck.

"Are you and Lars getting along?" she said.

"Perfectly," I said, tapping her hands twice as a signal to get off.

Jasmin looked directly at me from her chair, sucking her lower lip, gently patting her hair down. Mimi whispered something into her ear and cackled while also looking at me like I was a zoo animal. The two of them giggled together, seemingly at my expense. The tension in my jaw felt like concrete. *Anyone else want to take a stab?*

"Kaspar!" called Mimi from across. "What are you doing there? Let the adults talk their boring business."

"Come, Kaspar," said Ana. "Let's leave them to it."

Kaspar stood and rejoined the group with Ana.

"He makes an excellent lap dog," said Lars.

I exhaled impatiently.

"They're friends, Lars," I said. "Nobody's a lap dog."

"There's something about her," Lars said to himself, returning to Jasmin.

"You don't want to know," I said, crossing one leg over the other.

"What if I do?"

"Then knock yourself out," I said.

"What was her name again? Jasmin, right?"

I nodded before Lars leaned over with his hands clasped together. *This should be good.*

"Jasmin," he said, quickly catching her attention. "Come sit with us."

Kaspar's attention moved from the conversation with the ladies to Jasmin and Lars, and his face went from happy to constipated. He tried to focus back on the conversation, but stole another look as Jasmin sat across from Lars and me with her cocktail.

"That drink looks almost empty, how about another?" said Lars.

"Sure," said Jasmin with a soft smile.

Lars caught the attention of the waiter.

"What are you drinking?" said Lars to Jasmin as the waiter came.

"She'll have an old fashioned," I cut in, enjoying the sight of Jasmin's surprised reaction when she realised how closely I had watched her at the J&A party.

"My favourite," said Lars.

"I'll have a riesling, actually," said Jasmin, throwing me a steely look which had me back to being aroused.

Lars turned to the waiter.

"You heard her," he said.

The waiter nodded and left.

"Mr. Observant," Jasmin whispered to me.

I looked her over, from her peachy lips to the way her dress accentuated her hips. I took her in. Enjoyed her. Enveloped her in my attention. Then let her go. Leaned back, looking to stay in observer mode and enjoy the show.

"So, Jasmin," said Lars. "What got you mixed up with these charming deviants?"

Jasmin rubbed her wrist and glanced at me. I gave her nothing. If she wanted to play in the big leagues, she was by herself.

"Fate, I guess," she said, staring into my eyes with a vulnerable glow.

I cleared my throat.

"Fate?" said Lars. "That's it? You don't think we can make our own fate?"

"No," said Jasmin in a matter of fact tone. "We're powerless to it."

Lars broke out laughing and gave me a hard nudge.

"I like this girl," he said before turning back to Jasmin. "Did fate land you a piece of the Great Rambone yet?"

Jasmin was forced out of her tender position and went to scratch her wrist before stopping herself.

"Why do you ask that?" she said.

"Curiosity," said Lars, turning serious as the waiter placed Jasmin's riesling on the table. "I'm going to a dinner tomorrow evening with some powerful people," he said. "A thousand euros a head, some private fun afterwards at the Ritz-Carlton with the most stunning guys and girls you've ever met. Would you like to join me?"

Jasmin looked away with a serious expression, then at me.

"Are you going?" she said.

I shrugged.

"Why?" I said.

She shrugged back, and turned to Lars.

"Fate tells me no," she said and stood to return to the group, leaving the riesling that Lars had ordered her on the table.

I leaned back, allowing my smile to lift. She was a brutal sucker-puncher, I had to give her that.

"Now *that* was a spectacle," I said with a light chuckle.

Lars sniffed extra long and hard and twisted his neck.

"Whatever," he said, straightening up and slamming his palms on the table to gather himself. "Let's get this business discussion over with so I can get some sleep for tomorrow. She has no idea what she's missing out on."

"There's nothing more to discuss," I said. "My answer is no."

"Jordan, my friend," said Lars, his expression darkening. "Do you want to work together? If not, I can go a different route. One that you won't like."

"Do what you have to," I said, looking away.

Lars rested his chin on his fist and looked thoughtfully into the distance for a time. Checked his phone then tossed it on the table.

"So what's with this Thomas guy that Ana told me about?" he said to me suddenly with a business-like shift in tone. "She sold him as the ultimate toy boy. CK model material. She couldn't even get him on board. You two have lost your touch."

I ran my hand through my hair and rubbed the back of my neck.

"Don't get me wrong," continued Lars with a wicked twinkle in his eyes. "It's noble that you picked yourself up after that mishap with the sleeping pills. Really admirable. Lucky Ana came when she did. But don't you think it would be better just to pack it all in? J&A had a good run. You have your health. Focus on each other. Seems like the best option from where I'm sitting."

Time crept to a grinding halt. Lars' voice echoed off down a bottomless tunnel, leaving me with his exploding landmine as he slithered off to join the rest of the group. My legs started shaking. *Fucker.* Only deep breaths could keep me from landing a stiff hook into his face. I stayed where I was, choking in the waters of my inner darkness. I blinked twice, scrambling to get to the surface again. Anchored myself in Jasmin, who was the only one noticing my distress. Her focussed, knowing gaze was enough, and my body melted back into the moment. Lars stole Jasmin's attention, whispering something into her ear. Ana was busy chatting with the girls, barely paying attention to her surroundings.

The situation was getting away from me. I ordered a taxi on my phone then got to my feet and calmly walked over to the group, where Jasmin was now cosied up in conversation with Kaspar on the sofa.

"Jasmin," I said, looking into her and reaching out my hand. "It's time to go home."

She paused, turning to Kaspar with a twinkle of doubt.

"Wait," said Kaspar, blinking rapidly. "I thought you were out with us tonight?"

She froze, while Kaspar hung on her response, urging her with his eyes.

"I'm sorry," she said to him, placing her hand on mine and letting me pull her up.

"Enjoy the Ritz-Carlton tomorrow," I said to Lars with a slap on his shoulder, then invited Jasmin to walk ahead of me.

Ana stared at me wide-eyed with an empty smirk but said nothing as I gave her a peck on the cheek. I helped Jasmin with her coat then grabbed mine and tossed it over my shoulder. Held the front door open for her before we exited and got into the waiting taxi.

We said nothing on the ride to my place. I was holding too much in. Was still at risk of blowing my lid. Something touched my leg. I looked down and saw Jasmin's hand on my trousers. I grasped it and slowly lowered it back to the seat, then turned my attention out the window again until we reached my street.

Jasmin climbed the stairs behind me and we entered my apartment. I went directly into the living room with my shoes on and tossed my jacket onto the table. Jasmin came in a minute later barefoot without her jacket and handbag. She approached me with cat-like steps and stood face to face with me. I wanted to squeeze her as hard as I could, to brutalise her until she succumbed. *Go ahead*, her wide-open eyes told me. She looked like prey, enticing me with her pupils, which were enormous in the moonlight.

"What the hell is wrong with you?" I said. "Why are you doing this?"

"You know why," she said.

"I know you're an immature brat."

"Call me all the names you want," she shot back. "It won't make a difference. There's something between us. It was there the second we met. This goes deeper than me or you. If you're not man enough to go after it, I'll do it for us."

My pulse sped up at the sound of those words. *Not man enough.*

"Careful," I said. "Don't make me punish you."

"Go ahead. I've been numb for a decade."

My shoulders and neck tightened, but I was unsure if it was coming from my turn-on or my anger. This girl had *humiliated* me. I could not let that slide.

"At least I'm feeling something," she continued. "You're just hiding behind the tough guy act."

The pent-up frustration of the evening rushed out of me. I pushed my hand against her chest to keep her at bay. She took my wrist and moved my arm to the side, then stepped forward into my ring of fire. I grasped her throat with a solid grip. I wanted to… Just… Push her against the wall and fuck some sense into her. She straightened her arms out to the side and her shoulders lifted. I hovered my mouth in front of her's, feeling her shallow breathing on my lips, my face lurking over her like a wild beast.

The anger in my chest swallowed me whole. After some time it spat me out, and I saw the colour drain out of her. A bone-deep terror flooded me. There was no stopping this woman. I had nothing left to defend myself with. The fight left me, and I released my grip, now raw to her influence.

JASMIN

I rushed forward and kissed him, biting down on his mouth. He pulled his head away, which stretched his lower lip. I released it, my chest heaving up and down. He hesitated, before his eyes sharpened back to their usual intensity, and a boyish grin came to his face.

"Don't move," he said, standing up straight.

He pulled his shirt off with one motion, snapping multiple buttons and dropping the garment to the floor. I watched on, trembling with anticipation. With a hard pull of his belt, he snatched it off and held it to the side in a fist.

"Unzip me," he said.

I leapt up and busied myself with his buttons, then pulled everything down including his underwear, finally revealing my hard-earned prize. It was a wonderful specimen. Like a foreign artefact at a museum I had travelled half the world to see. Smooth all over with a slight upward curve, looking like a bent hammer, narrow at the base and thick at the end. The longest I had seen, although I had a small selection to compare. I only knew I was hungry to have it in my mouth.

He kicked off his shoes. Took off his socks and the rest of his trousers, then stood naked before me. The belt came around behind my neck and he ran it through the buckle to create a leash. He pulled me forward and down, and I welcomed his dick inside my mouth. I had learnt about the extent of my gag reflex from my experience with Kaspar. Jordan was a whole different level of challenge. The belt tightened around my neck, the shaft of his cock moved deeper down my throat. The desire to submit to his dominance was irresistible. The endorphin high urging me to let go was intoxicating. I wanted him to have his way with me. To feel his hammer cock throbbing against my tongue, fucking his excitement into me. To be his only source of pleasure.

Then I felt her. I had always felt her, trembling as she lay dormant for over a decade, biding her time, wondering which man would unlock the door and invite her out. I had held out hope that Thomas would find the key. It turned out I needed a hammer the whole time.

I snatched the belt out of Jordan's hands and stood. Pushed with all my might to get his massive frame onto the sofa. He allowed himself to collapse onto his back, then reached over to the coffee table and snatched the drawer open. Took out a dozen condoms and tossed them on the sofa while keeping one. I got on top of him, one leg at a time.

"Let me put it on," I huffed.

Jordan shook his head and slapped my hand away. He inspected the condom carefully, testing how it felt between his thumb and index finger. Took his sweet time while carefully inspecting the packaging. *Is this guy for real?* I lifted my dress off and tossed it away, desperate to have him inside me. Jordan was as focussed as a chess player, ripping the condom open with a smooth, deliberate flick. He checked which way it unrolled while I forced my wet g-string out of the way. He positioned the condom evenly on the tip of his dick and rolled it on delicately, his progress painfully slow while I watched on, livid.

"Hurry up," I said finally.

As soon as the condom was on, I pushed his hands aside and slid his dick inside me. The effect was immediate, and my body lit up like a Christmas tree. Jordan was also cranking into action. His breathing had sped up, and his energy shot between my legs and spread to my stomach and chest.

She was on her way, but I needed to rock the cage to force her out. I began moving back and forth over his rock-hard dick, my body coming more alive with each grind of my pussy. Eventually the charge took me over, and *her* fierce spirit came howling out of the cage. My body trembled with terror as I squeezed my eyes shut, feeling her roaming inside me. Her energy was a tsunami which came raging from my chest and burnt through every inch of me, leaving me nowhere to hide. I tried to shield myself from her incomprehensible fury, to survive intact, to keep Jasmin together long enough for her to leave. No chance of that. I was helpless. She was out now for good, and with my eyes closed I watched in awe, and let go.

I groaned with a deep, tortured voice and picked up the pace, twisting my head in all directions, my hair wild and untamed. With my tongue stuck out, I grinded Jordan's dick rapidly against my clit. Pulses shot out from between my legs and lifted beyond my skin, leaving me moaning like a possessed witch. Or was that her? The more I let go, the less that mattered. My movements picked up momentum, causing Jordan's dick to slip out. I scrambled to put it back in, as though it were sustaining me, as though having it out for too long meant certain death. He steadied me from the waist while allowing me full movement, and I came back into my body, now able to sense another foreign presence inside. Jordan's energy. We locked eyes, and he moaned, his eyes rolling upwards briefly before returning to me. His panting was in rhythm with my movements, his pleasure now under my control, his world consumed by my energy. The focussed yet vulnerable look on his face brought me to rapture. He had never looked so gorgeous, so soft, so pure. I thanked him with every cell in my body without knowing what for. Whatever he was doing, it was working.

We dissolved into a river, our grinding becoming an ineffable dance. He let her roam as she pleased while occasionally driving up into me, contributing his potency into our eruption of bliss.

My terror of her was well-founded. Her staggering intensity began to wear me out, and the power of my grinding began to fade. Jordan used the opportunity to lift me off the sofa with my legs still wrapped around him, holding me up with one arm while carrying me to the bedroom. He flung me onto the mattress, pulled off my g-string and immediately drove his head between my legs. I had no idea what he was doing, but he definitely did. With his firm fingers inside me and shark-like tongue swimming around the outside, a playful tickle formed in my lower belly and moved between my legs. My legs shook and tensed, relaxed, and then tensed again, over and over, forming a gorgeous melody of pleasure inside me. He was a talented musician, playing my pussy like a musical instrument, his passion transmitting pure bliss directly into me. I felt his tongue and his fingers between my legs, and his presence inside me, roaming around, enjoying the sights of my soul.

My entire body suddenly seized up as it approached. *Here we go.*

"Oh, God," I yelled in elation, feeling it spreading, growing inside me, expanding and expanding until it exploded out of my head. I left the room, feeling myself taken somewhere else entirely. "I'm coming! I'm coming!" came my voice as I was hurled down a tunnel filled with bright, colourful lights.

I convulsed all over, unable to control my screaming or my body. How could I? I was not even in the room anymore. He rubbed his fingers furiously back and forth against my spot without respite. My eyes opened wide and, for the first time in my life, I squirted. All over Jordan's mattress.

He removed his fingers, and I collapsed back on the bed. A warm glow covered me like a blanket, and I could feel my heartbeat pulsating through my body. My face and hands were numb. A fitting end to an amazing session of—

Shit! I thought as he twisted me around and got me on all fours. Did he want to clean up the mess first? Clearly not. He was just warming up. Could I handle anymore? *She* suddenly whizzed through me and assured me that yes, I could. I felt him inside me soon after, and he snatched a handful of my hair tight and pulled my neck back while pounding me furiously. I gasped and moaned when he sped up.

His fucking was unhinged. The immense intensity in his eyes which had quietly lured me in had manifested into a force of nature beyond imagination. My body rocked furiously back and forth, my hair and neck pulled right back. I dissolved into the ferocity of his assault like a bunny being devoured by a bear.

His hand came down on my butt with an unexpected snap that sent a spike through me and caused me to tremble and groan. He spanked me over and over, and my groans became wild screams of ecstasy. The sting was unbearable, and my skin felt more raw with each slap. *It's going to mark*, I thought, my mind turning to Thomas for a moment. But the momentum was irresistible. *Fuck it.* It was like remembering you left the oven on as an earthquake hit the city and the ground was rumbling and moving beneath you. I let Jordan continue, and moaned out as my ass and body burnt up from the infusion of pain and pleasure, each of which relied on the other and synergised into a mind-blowing concert. At some point he slowed the pace, and I could feel drops of sweat falling on my back. The respite was short lived, and the beast returned and took me with him again.

The endless waves eased into ripples before more waves arrived. He had shattered my reality. I came and came while the wall between bliss and orgasm tumbled down in the face of his relentless fucking. I had no idea how much more I could take, had no idea what it was to take, no idea what an idea was, no sense of anything. I just moaned and let it happen, feeling myself dissolve into the ether, where everything was still.

Eventually he pulled out and collapsed onto his hands, wiping the sweat from his face, his neck bent down like a warrior after battle, having given his all to the fight. Lying on my side, I admired his sweat-covered body and felt infinite gratitude. He had given everything. Well, almost. I still had something to take, and something to give. With intoxicating potency still coursing through me, I pushed him on his back, to which he was too weak to resist. With purposeful strokes I licked his nipples, enjoying the sound of his heavy breathing. My lips moved from one chest to the other, then to his stomach, pelvis, and finally his hammer-sized dick. *Hello, again.*

I caught sight of the black rope on the bedside table he had used on me. I gave a sly smile.

"My turn," I said, fetching the rope.

As I placed my hand on his wrist, he tensed up.

"Don't," he said, his eyes raw, his face unrecognisable in its softness.

"Trust me," I said as she left my body, leaving the two of us alone.

He exhaled, searching my eyes for a long time, then nodded resolutely and let his head fall back to the mattress. I tied his arms to the bed frame the same way I would do a shoelace, since I had no idea how to make a proper knot. When I was done, I was certain he could break free if he really wanted. I left it as it was. The fact that he let me tie him up at all was astounding enough.

I started gently, stroking the end of his dick with the tip of my tongue, experimenting with various strokes while gauging his reaction. He lifted his head and locked eyes with me, and I penetrated his spirit the way he did with me, only I had a mouthful of his dick, which I could feel growing and getting harder by the second. I pulled back the pace and continued teasing him for a few moments with my tongue, intoxicated by the need in his eyes. He acknowledged me with a weary grin, and the excitement of it turned me on so much that I was compelled to take him in all the way. With his hard-on pushed into my throat, he moaned and his body lifted into the air, his hips rocking back and forth with my motion. I used that as a signal to keep going, and I rocked up and down on it over and again. I pushed it in as far as I could take it, feeling it throbbing in my mouth. The longer I was at it, the wetter I got. His rising excitement became mine. I pulled out and looked over his saliva-lathered dick.

With some gentle tongue strokes to lull him in, it was time to end it. I sucked circles around the head, drunk on the power of owning his pleasure. At last came the moment that drove me wild. His moan grew louder until it became an eternal groan. His dick throbbed like a heartbeat, and I pushed down while his warm cum filled my mouth. I kept up a slow rhythm until I was sure I had it all. Then I stopped and ran my tongue through it, enjoying its consistency, spilling some in the process and swallowing the rest. I took him into my mouth again for a moment, teasing him while he twitched and chuckled heartily from the discomfort. I laughed also, touched by the sound of his sweet laughter. Who knew he had it in him?

I kissed the tip one last time and moved up, snuggling into his chest to share in the post-coital bliss. His heartbeat banged against my cheek, and his fast breathing gradually slowed to an easy rhythm. We remained that way in the afterglow. His energy was now nimble, and I rested deeper into it, enjoying his firmness and size in contrast with my tiny frame. I also basked in the fact that I had finally broken through. To him. To her. To heaven. The shift had been momentous, and it would take weeks, if not longer, to process what had just happened. For now, it was time to rest and enjoy.

"Are you going to untie me?"

"Huh?" I said, lifting my head and coming out of my hypnotic trance. "Oh," I smiled. "Yes."

I got his arms free and carefully folded the rope and placed it back on the bedside table, and returned to my place, this time with his arm wrapped around me.

"Better?" he said.

"Mhhm," I replied with a nod.

He stroked my arm gently, leaving a trail of delightful ripples behind. I cuddled deeper into him and let everything go. It was a moment to savour. We lay in absolute silence for who knew how long. Neither of us seemed to care.

Eventually the glow began to fade. I had to pee.

"I'll be right back," I said, and lifted myself off him then went into the bathroom.

I turned the light on and shut the door behind me. I stood in front of the mirror and looked over at the luminous woman in my reflection. She had transformed since I last saw her in the sauna window at Äden. Her pear-shaped breasts looked like ripe, hanging fruit, lucious and inviting in their maturity. Her small mouth was purpose-made to utter profound truths and give voice to the world's deepest secrets. I understood why people complimented her bright blue eyes and high cheekbones. They made her look regal. Her eyes were opulent, concentrated, all-knowing in their infinite wisdom, having seen it all from the beginning of time. I could barely comprehend her magnificence. I was just glad that she was with me. I turned to my side and twitched with surprise when I saw the red marks on my ass. Then I smirked and sat down carefully to pee, replaying the sexy scene with Jordan in my mind like a movie.

When I washed up and returned, he was in the same place I left him, and in the same peaceful state. He looked like a man without a worry in life, with his eyes closed and his hands behind his head. His legs were spread and he had a gentle smile on his face, which also brought a warm smile to mine. I wondered how often Ana saw this side of him.

He opened his eyes and looked me up and down with a twinkle in his gaze.

"You look amazing," he said with feeling.

I lay down and found my place again nuzzled against his chest. His arm came down to hold me again.

"I think I know who the goddess Kali is," I whispered.

"Magnificent, isn't she?" he said with a soft voice.

I shrugged.

"She's a bit of a whore if you ask me," I shot back before breaking out in uncontrollable giggles.

Jordan chuckled out loud and shook his head.

"Is she now?" he said with his rustic voice, which vibrated out of his belly and into my chest.

"So how are you feeling?" I said, relaxing again.

"Like I'm on a cloud."

"That's beautiful," I replied.

We said nothing for a while. Words felt optional with our energies aligned. I could sense his state. Every plume of gratitude, every quiver of doubt. I knew he wanted to tell me something, and I stayed silent while keeping the space open.

"Thanks," he said finally.

"What for?" I replied, turning my head up to look at him.

"Pushing so hard for this."

"What choice did I have?" I said.

"You really knew the whole time?"

"Yes. I felt it. Woman's intuition."

He ran his index finger gently along the nape of my neck, then continued down my shoulder. His eyes followed, watching over each place his touch explored, confirming it really existed. He was taking in my body. *Her body.* He paused above my sacrum, then touched over my vertebrae one by one. His eyes met mine again. There was someone else behind them. Not Jordan.

"I thought you loved your boyfriend," he said.

I sighed.

"I do," I said. "If only that was enough."

"What makes you think it's not?" said Jordan.

"We just have so many obstacles holding us back," I said. "For one, he watches too much porn to focus on me. It's messing with his head."

"As someone who had a career in porn, I can tell you he's a moron."

"No, he's a good guy. I just wish he could... mmm..." I hesitated, looking for the words.

"Get his act together?"

"Exactly," I said with a nod.

"Keep an eye on him," said Jordan. "He's in dangerous territory."

"That's fine," I said. "He can deal with it."

"Ruthless," said Jordan.

"When a woman's fed up, you're in trouble," I said.

"Amen to that," said Jordan, lightly spanking my ass. "That's going to mark."

I looked over my raw backside with concern.

"Is it bad?" I said.

"Yep," said Jordan. "It'll look worse tomorrow. Or better. Depending on how you look at it."

"Thanks for that," I said, shaking my head.

"So now we've fucked Thomas out of your system," said Jordan. "Is there anything in particular on your fucket list?"

I seized up. Felt the dark cave inside me where I kept all my forbidden desires locked up. Then I relaxed. Why was I so worried? This was Jordan I was talking to.

"My ultimate fantasy," I began, biting my lip and smiling sheepishly.

I told him how I saw it, the show that I only visited when I was playing with myself. The one I was convinced I could never have. The one that simultaneously filled me with dread, excitement and burning shame.

Jordan listened carefully, then nodded with an impressed smile.

"Insane, right?" I said.

"Nope," he said with a head shake.

"You don't think?" I said, giddy at the thought of bringing my idea to life, my whole body contracting as I squeezed my legs together.

He shook his head again.

"What about you?" I added. "I guess that's a stupid question. You've probably done everything you ever wanted. I mean, you have Ana."

Jordan snickered and gave a twisted, amused smile. A twinkle appeared in his eyes as he seemed to be scanning something in his mind.

"There's more to life than that," he said.

"I thought you loved her?"

"I do. But time takes its toll on love."

"What changed? Did something happen, or did you just lose the magic over time?"

"I lost something," he said.

He fell silent and looked down at the wet patch I had left on the blanket. His pupils retreated, opening the gate to his being. I felt his glow fade, and the room seemed darker now. With my body still connected to his, I sensed a heavy, downward pull in his energy.

"And I didn't think I'd ever find it again," he added.

"What's that?" I said, looking at him intently.

"Someone who could see me. Who could help me to feel again. You."

High-voltage electricity shot into my heart.

"I thought it was too late," he continued. "I thought that part of me was broken."

His words left me in a daze.

"I... I don't know what to say," I replied with a shaky voice.

"You've said it all already."

I cuddled further into him. Thomas drifted through my mind but I let him continue on by, content to let Future Jasmin deal with him. For now I had everything I needed, and with that I fell asleep to the vibrations of Jordan's breathing.

11
LOVE LOST

JASMIN

I woke to a flurry of messages and missed calls from Thomas stacked on my phone screen. Jordan was still asleep, and I turned to the side to read through the barrage, chewing on my nails:

4:01 am: Jaz, where are you?

4:47 am: I need to know you're safe. Text me even if you're not coming home.

6:30 am: Jaz, WHAT THE FUCK!?

7:01 am: I know I've been an idiot and that I lied to you. Please just let me know you're ok. I love you.

I was about to leap up and get dressed to rush home when another text came through:

7:03 am: Fuck it stay with him!!! I don't care!

My pulse slowed back to its usual rate. My skin cooled, and the sweating stopped. *Suit yourself.* I placed my phone back onto the bedside table and turned over to face Jordan. I watched him sleeping, paying close attention to the shade of his tan, the direction of his eyebrow hairs, the twitching of his face. *So handsome.*

His ocean-grey eyes then opened, and he gazed wearily at me. He impacted me instantly, not with his usual sharp intensity, but rather a gentle vulnerability.

"Hey, beautiful," he said with a sleepy smile.

I shifted forward and cuddled into him.

"You should head home," he said. "Thomas is expecting you."

"I will," I said. "Let's get some food first."

"Ok," said Jordan. "I know a spot."

"You do?" I replied, lifting my head. "Where?"

"It's a secret."

Our taxi pulled up to La Secreta; a charming red brick building with a black door. I got out of the vehicle in my dress and heels from the previous night, while Jordan had put on a neat pair of cream chinos and a perfectly-fitted navy-blue sweater. He held the door open for me to step in.

As soon as we got inside the restaurant, his shields came back up. The strut had returned. The youthful softness had disappeared, and the narrow-eyed stud was back on point. A deadly-composed, Scandinavian-looking woman in a black suit jacket and skirt came to meet him. She impressed me immediately. There was a bright elegance about her, and her posture and body-language told me she called the shots here. I wondered for a moment if Jordan had slept with her. He placed a hand on her shoulder and spoke something into her ear, and she nodded towards a corner table with a lavish, curved velvet sofa. The way they seemed to be all business told me no.

"What?" said Jordan as we reached the table, noticing the way I was now looking at him.

"Old Jordan's back," I said, overcome by a dull heaviness.

He lifted his chin, and his boyish grin returned.

"Don't worry, I'm not far away," he said with a wink.

That was enough to reassure me. He came over from behind and took my coat, and the heaviness lifted with it.

"Always the gentleman," I said.

Just as he was about to respond, the elegant boss lady from the front came up to us. She was even more intimidating up close. Some women just had it.

"A set of boxes came in for you with the food delivery," she said to Jordan. "Imogen put them in the fridge."

"Thanks, Ilva," he said, then turned to me as she left. "Give me five minutes, ok?"

"Sure," I replied. "I'll be here."

"You better be," he said.

Jordan placed my coat on the rack beside us and strutted off, leaving me alone with the lingering tingles of a spectacular evening. I felt fine initially, and took time to enjoy my surroundings, until the unsettling trembles crept in. I understood instantly why people gravitated towards Jordan. He made you feel steady and supported through his presence. To have the power of such a man focussed purely on me was intoxicating. To lose it felt like the building I was in might collapse at any time.

There was no sign of that as I looked around the place. The restaurant was starting to fill up for lunch. Waiters and waitresses marched by on light feet, carrying oversized porcelain plates with beautifully-stacked, vibrantly-coloured ingredients. The tavern feel of the place had me feeling at home, yet the regal table settings and furniture reminded me I was in the realm of the affluent. The walls were a dark emerald-green, lined with lamps over each table. Between the lights hung surreal art works in gold frames, along with red, yellow and green bouquets of flowers. Each of them protruded out and brought the space to life. The attention to detail was unmistakable. Jordan's world made me feel like a higher version of myself. As though I could be above my problems. But without him at the centre with me, the drug I was riding high on began to quickly wear away.

I checked my phone, dreading the awaiting half dozen angry messages from Thomas. I found only one. From Kaspar:

Hey Jasmin. Haven't heard from you. What you did last night wasn't cool. Text me back.

So much for being above my problems. I tucked my phone into my bag as though that would also rid me of my guilt. First I had Thomas at home fuming, waiting for me to arrive so he could let me have it. Now I had Kaspar expecting an explanation as to why I turned him down and went home with Jordan. *Whatever.* Thomas was a dishonest, cowardly cheat. Kaspar just wanted to get laid. I owed them nothing.

"You ok?"

I turned my head and found Jordan's curious eyes on me.

"Huh?" I said, shaking my head. "Yes, I'm fine."

"You looked like you were drifting in outer space."

Actually, I was swimming. In a sea of dicks.

"It's nothing," I said, waving it off.

"Come join us," said Jordan. "I want you to meet the family."

"Sure," I said, perking up.

I stood and began following Jordan towards the kitchen.

"I didn't tell you I was a foodie, did I?" I said.

"Food And All That Jaz," he shot back quickly. "One-hundred-thousand followers. I know about it."

I stopped briefly before resuming walking.

"You've done your homework," I said. "I figured you hadn't bothered."

"It's impressive," said Jordan. "I can almost taste the flavours in your photos."

I had received plenty of compliments on my food blog. For some reason, Jordan's went straight to my heart with the power of all of them combined.

"You don't have any social media accounts, do you?" I said. "For yourself or La Secreta."

"Don't need them," said Jordan, passing the bar and turning into the open kitchen.

We were awaited by a small group of waiters standing in anticipation, chatting among themselves. Five dozen or so oysters were sitting in boxes in front of them, while two chefs were left on cooking duties.

All eyes came on us. Well, me actually, with their looks having *who's the girl?* written all over them.

"Everyone, this is Jasmin," said Jordan, picking up a shucking knife and starting with the first oyster.

"Hi," I said with a wave, receiving a lacklustre greeting in return.

"It's early for oysters, I know," said Jordan. "But at La Secreta, we're oyster obsessed, so time is irrelevant." He turned to one of the chefs. "Paul. Can you slice up the lemons please?"

Dry as they were, I could see why Jordan called them 'family.' They were an honourable looking bunch, their faces worn out and layered with sweat, like those soldiers in the war documentaries my father always watched. I could feel the bond between them from where I stood, and something told me Jordan did not have that outside of La Secreta. One by one, he shucked the oysters and handed them out to his 'brothers and sisters,' while Paul doled out the lemon slices. Jordan waited until everyone had been served before taking his oyster. He lifted it and nodded.

"Credit where it's due," he said. "Outstanding work."

The oysters were fresh, immaculate and gone in minutes. They were also French, judging by how flat they were.

"Hi, Jasmin," said the head chef, coming up beside me, her tall white hat covering her smeared brown hair. Her face was angular and thin, her eyes brightly intense. She stared at me like I was an alien.

"Hello," I said cautiously.

"I'm just trying to work this out," said the head chef. "I know Jordan and Ana have an open relationship. But in five years of owning this place, he has never once bought another girl in here."

I stared dumbfounded back at her. Was she for real?

"I'll remember that," I said, allowing the weight of it to sink in.

She caught Jordan staring at us and immediately stepped away from me.

"Right," she said with a harsh shift in tone, turning her attention to the workers. "Back to it."

The kitchen surged back to its usual mayhem. Stove fires lit up, and smoke and aromas filled the air. Urgent yelling and insider communication shot through the room as the head chef coordinated her team, micro-managing and questioning their every move.

"Hungry?" said Jordan.

"Absolutely," I replied.

We sat side-by-side at our table in the corner, and our meals came soon after.

"To start we have poached eggs with fresh asparagus, basil pesto and salmon roe," said the head chef, personally delivering the plates to us and gifting me a smile as she left.

"This is amazing" I said, mesmerised by the immaculate dish in front of me. "Every meal really has a life of its own. You can feel the love oozing out of the plate."

Jordan's melting smile was the first indication that I had lost myself, having let my passion rush out without thinking. *That must have sounded so pretentious.* I tensed up, anticipating his reaction, expecting him to break out laughing. Instead, his eyes sparkled in their appreciation.

The world was in order again with Jordan like this. He really had it in him to be a family man. I could see his love for his employees, the sense of responsibility he held for them. Much like a father. J&A was a spectacular production, but witnessing Jordan in this environment told me he wanted more. Last night showed me he *could* be more. It had turned my curiosity into something far deeper. I felt it coursing through me now, a melting softness that opened me to a wider spectrum of possibilities. Happiness, fulfilment, and yes, family. I had not felt that way since... *Of course. The Dutchman.* Much like with Jordan, I had initially lusted for the Dutchman. It seemed purely sexual. And just like that moment in the cafe, something else came through now. A softness, a sense of surrender to the 'right' man. Whatever that meant. I felt suddenly exposed, terrified of what was inside me. I was not in love. But I knew the presence of it when it came. I could feel the first ripples of it now. And just like with the Dutchman, I resisted it. Urged it to leave my body. I had broken the rules and spent the night with Jordan. Had let him sex me deeper than any other man before him. And yet, I only now got the feeling that I was cheating. Fucking was fucking. This was touching me in the place I had only reserved for Thomas.

"Not taking a shot for your blog?" said Jordan.

"No," I said, now welcoming the feeling. "This moment is just for us."

Jordan nodded, again with that sparkle of appreciation in his eyes.

"Besides," I added. "You don't need any more exposure, do you?"

"No," said Jordan. "That's enough for one day."

While we had our three-course breakfast, a waiter came by and asked if we wanted coffee. The euphoria from last night was still there, so I ordered decaf while Jordan got an espresso. He spent the time with his eyes on me, and I enjoyed the way he was enjoying me, as though I were the only woman in the place. He sure knew how to make someone feel sexy and seen. Thomas would either be chewing my ear off or playing with his phone.

A mother pushed her stroller by our table, followed by her toddler son waddling behind her with a toy car in his hand. He stopped beside me and looked up with his big brown eyes.

"Hello, handsome!" I said, warmed by his presence.

The boy reached out and offered me his toy, which I gladly accepted, even after I realised it was covered in saliva. His mother stopped and smiled politely at me before picking him up. I returned his toy to her and waved him goodbye with a bright smile, which he reciprocated with a gorgeous smile of his own.

"So cute," I said, turning back to Jordan, who was abnormally quiet with his eyes on the boy.

I looked him up and down, confused by the sudden shift.

"You should probably get back," he said, turning to me.

"Are you ok?" I asked.

He leaned over and placed his hand on mine. He nodded and smiled.

"Listen, I had a good time last night," he said. "A really good time," he added, insisting with his focussed eye contact and the charm of his smile.

"Me too," I said, placing my free hand over his. "I won't forget it."

"Me neither," he said, kissing my hand. "Now go."

The pain in his stare was evident, the skin bunching and twitching around his eyes, his jaw tensed. Something had triggered him, and he was putting on a brave front. He was demanding space without wanting to hurt my feelings. I wanted him to have it, because that was what the feeling coursing through me demanded.

"Ok," I said gently, getting up and fetching my coat.

I said nothing about seeing him again. I had a feeling our story was not over, and that was enough. We locked eyes, sharing a final exchange of energy. He winked at me, and I smiled back before I left and walked out into the cold.

Even as it drizzled on me, I continued to smile. Someone once said to me that you should carry your own weather with you. I had no idea what they were talking about until now. Not even an angrily awaiting Thomas could kill my groove. I walked the entire way back to the hotel, feeling *her* circulating through me. A nine year blockage had been released, and it felt damn good.

I stopped by the bakery to pick up a peace offering for Thomas before getting to Äden. When I stepped through the door to our room, the Thomas effect hung thick in the air, and it immediately choked the joy out of me. Thomas was lying on the carpet staring at the ceiling. He did not acknowledge me. I dropped my handbag to the floor and tossed my coat onto the bed, my throat growing lumpy. I kicked off my heels, and sat beside him on the floor. He still did not look at me or say anything. His scrunched up face and pout said everything.

"Got you something," I said, placing a chocolate brownie beside him and opening the wrapper.

He gave it one look then turned his attention back to the ceiling. I waited with my eyes on the floor, held back from looking at him by the tension. After some time, the boredom got to me. Or maybe it was the unease. I poked a finger at the brownie, testing its firmness, then licked off the residue. Busied myself inspecting the state of the room, which looked like a hurricane had hit it. The bed was unmade, with one of the blankets hanging over onto the floor. Random clothes were tossed on every piece of furniture. There were scraps of paper and random bottles and bits and pieces on the desk. It was unlike us to let things slide this much. But here we were.

"Have fun last night?" said Thomas, breaking the silence.

My shoulders tightened, and I looked at him for the first time.

"Listen, I know I broke the rules," I said.

"Yeah, you broke the fucking rules," he said with force, turning to me.

"Rules aren't going to save us," I said, emboldened again by her. "We need to act outside the box."

"Unlike Jordan, who acted inside your box, right?"

His crass words crawled inside me, forcing me to twitch and shift my position to shake the feeling off.

"God, Thomas," I said, lifting my face. "Please see the bigger picture."

"I think I'm the only one seeing the bigger picture. The rules were there to protect us. Did you think about that when you fell asleep last night?"

"Of course, I did," I said unconvincingly.

Thomas studied my eyes intently, the intensity of his anger glowing bright for a long time. Suddenly, the light went out, and his eyes opened wide.

"Oh, man," he said, covering his face with his hand.

"What?" I said, struggling to take a breath.

"You fucking fell for him."

"No, I didn't," I said, sitting up defiantly, trying to force off the inevitable truth. "Thomas, I love you."

There was barely any heart in my words. They felt empty, and I sensed they did for Thomas as well. A force of habit, an echo from a time when the phrase meant something.

"Bullshit," he replied. "You did this to get back at me for what I did. Now it's cost us everything."

"What?" I said, knowing exactly what he meant.

"I was honest with you, and you punished me for it. You punished *us*."

My shoulders dropped while I slowly shook my head. My heart shrunk to half its size.

"That's not what I was doing," I said softly. "I want us both to tell the truth. We've been deceiving ourselves and each other."

"Ok," said Thomas. "Let's do that. I told you the truth. Your turn. What happened last night?"

I flinched.

"We said we wouldn't talk abou—"

"I don't care anymore," he cut in. "Tell me everything. I want to know every detail. How many positions he fucked you in. How long he fucked you for. What his dick tasted like."

I looked away before squeezing my eyes shut, formulating an answer to a reasonable question that Thomas had somehow made disgusting. The confusion lingered for a time, before slowly morphing into loathing, which lifted until it had nowhere else to go.

Nine years. I had put up with his bullshit for nine years. He had sucked me dry with his negativity and insecurity. Worst of all, he had put it on me. He told me I was never loving enough, supportive enough, committed enough. I was the one holding us back — according to him. I had to constantly reassure him, and he just sat around like a spoiled child. I gave up everything for him. I held myself back in every conceivable way so he could be happy. Yet he never was. *Behind every great man is a great woman.* I believed his weakness was my fault. That I needed to sacrifice even more for us to work. After all that, his solution was to cheat and lie. *This isn't working?* Well, screw that! I was working just fine.

"Look, are you going to fuck me properly or not?" I said.

"What?" he said, sitting up.

"You heard me," I said. "I'm horny. Are you going to fuck me?"

I put my hand over his neck and kissed him lustfully to show him I meant business.

"No," he muffled, pulling his head back.

"Yes," I shot back, kissing him again and grasping his dick.

He pulled my hand away. I reached over with the other and massaged his balls. After a long hesitation, his body kicked into gear. He sucked on my lip and dragged me in by the waist. Reached up and choked me for a split second before releasing his grip. His hand moved down my hips instead and he began to pull my dress up. We were both panting like animals on heat, both ready to take it to another level, to raise the roof—

Thomas' entire body froze stiff. I continued to kiss him for a moment before picking up on his withdrawal. I pulled my head back. He was looking at the side of my ass. I followed his gaze, and flinched when I saw the purple, blue and red fusion of bruises. Jordan had called it. It looked worse today. *Much worse*. Like I had been terribly beaten. *Whoops*. I had no idea it was going to look *that* bad. How had I missed it when I got dressed this morning? I must have been too distracted by Jordan.

"Jasmin, what the fuck?" said Thomas with a horrified expression.

I pulled my dress down and moved away from him.

"What?" I said defiantly.

"What did he do to you?"

"Nothing I didn't want."

"You asked for this?"

I wrapped my arms around my knees and looked at the floor.

"What the hell's gotten into you?"

"You see, this is why we're having problems," I said. "You question everything."

"Of course I'm questioning this," yelled Thomas. "He abused you!"

The word triggered me beyond madness. I was in survival mode, fighting to reclaim a love I had forfeited last night. Without it, I felt like a wild animal facing imminent death. Without love to guide me, the unfiltered truth came hurtling.

"No, he didn't!" I yelled, turning my fury outwards. "He *fucked* me! Over and over and over until I couldn't cum anymore." Thomas' eyes saw death, but there was no stopping me. "And I sucked his dick! And it tasted wonderful, to answer your shitty question. And guess what!? He didn't cum after two minutes! It was the most amazing night of sex I've ever had. And you know why? Because he doesn't question himself. He doesn't make excuses. He doesn't cover up his tracks. He's a real man. He knows what he wants and he goes for it!"

We had shot over the cliff and far into the abyss. I knew it. Thomas knew it.

"Get out!!!" he shouted, shuddering me into a freeze.

Silence hit the room, along with the sound of Thomas' heart shattering into a thousand pieces. My stomach hardened suddenly, and I grew nauseous. I snatched up my coat, handbag and shoes. Stormed out barefoot, leaving the door open behind me. Thomas' violent sobs reverberated out of the room as I stepped into the elevator. I desperately pressed the close button a dozen times before the door finally shut. I made it to the ground floor, shaking all over, relieved to not be hearing him anymore.

I immediately left the lobby and walked towards the pool, entering the changing rooms and stripping off. I stuffed my clothes and belongings into a locker, fetched a towel and went into the lounge. Fell onto a sun lounger. Finally, I could let out a breath of relief and gather my thoughts, feeling the tension in my body melt away. The first thing I did was laugh. It scared me how little I cared. How exhilarated I was to be in unfamiliar territory, doing as I wished without Thomas holding me down. My life was a mess, but I was free of his grip. *She* was with me now. Guiding me. Reassuring me. Empowering me.

My relationship issues felt insignificant in a place like Äden. I let everything go into its flow and gave myself over again to be guided. As I let my body melt into the chair, the impact was immediate. She directed my attention to the sauna. I stood up and let her energy take me to the door. I looked in through the glass, and witnessed a dozen people sitting on their towels, many of them with their heads bowed from the heat.

A man with glistening bronzed skin and thick, silver chest hair stood in the middle preparing for the 'Aufguss' ceremony. He had the charm of an expensive whiskey, enticing in his age. His steady eyes and poise lulled me into his sizzling realm. He removed a white towel wrapped around his waist, leaving him completely naked. Like a magician initiating his trick, he flicked the towel open and began waving it effortlessly in circles. Each rotation blitzed the room with a gust of superheated air which I could almost feel singeing into me from outside. From front to back, over his head and around his waist, he carried out what seemed like part ritual, part dance. The participants lowered their heads further, some of them forced to moan from the overpowering heat. I leaned forward and rubbed my wrist. One woman spread her arms out and bent her head back, further opening herself to the intensity. When the ritual ended, the Aufguss man returned the towel to its position as his toga.

I knew the next step. The people grasped their scrubs and began working their legs, arms and shoulders, with others having their backs exfoliated by a partner. Meanwhile, the man opened a bottle of scented essence and carefully poured a tiny handful of drops into the bucket of water. Once fully exfoliated, the others patiently watched him at work. He picked up the bucket and poured water on the stones with yet more care. Volcanic smoke rose. When he was satisfied, the man took a whisk made of tree branches covered in fresh leaves and began dipping it into the bucket of water. My skin prickled at the sight of him standing there. There was something erotic about the way he held himself in preparation while taking turns making eye contact with each person. A woman on her back nodded, and the Aufguss man proceeded to gently beat her skin with the whisk while she closed her eyes and absorbed the sensations. *Slap. Slap.* I felt a burning envy towards every stroke making contact with her skin. The Aufguss man went from person to person, stopping only to reheat the room using more essence-infused water. I felt urged to go inside and also receive my Aufguss sacrament. To blitz Thomas out of my system for good.

As though having sensed my thoughts, the bronze-skinned magician's attention suddenly turned to me. His eyes sharpened, and a smirk appeared, enticing in its warmth. He motioned with his head for me to come inside, breaking the golden rule of Aufguss — no entry allowed during the ceremony. I bit my lip, and could not help smiling. The charming fox invited me in with another tilt of his head. He could see how much I needed it. I envisaged the punishing sting of the tree branch on my body while everyone watched. The intoxicating heat. The exhilaration of surrender. The urge to flee the situation forced me to make a decision. So I went inside.

I layed out my towel and took a seat sideways with my legs up as the bronzed man continued whipping the others. After some minutes, I had warmed up and exfoliated myself with the help of an older woman who did my back, and whose curious gaze landed on my bruises. Our eyes met, and I gave her a coy smile. Meanwhile, the bronzed man lowered the whisk again into the bucket of water, rolled it around then took it out. He came before me, and I gave him the nod. The whisk came down on my back, and I bit my lip while the goosebumps of pleasure rippled all over. *Thomas, be gone.* He lashed my entire back and followed with my legs. The effect was both soothing and invigorating. *Thomas, be gone.* When he was done, the Aufguss man nodded and ended the sacrament, receiving warm thank yous from the people inside.

Every face was now flushed red and layered with sweat. The room began to clear out soon after. I took deep, calming breaths to help me with the heat, and pondered what my next move would be.

I had no idea, but she did. A stubbly-faced, shaved-headed guy was the last person inside. He stood up and sauntered by, noticing the bruises on the side of my ass before leaving the sauna. He had a cute, lopsided face and enormous hands and body like a construction worker. Looking back once, he slid through the gap into the darkroom like a spirit entering the afterlife. Within a minute I had left the sauna, tossed my towel on a sun lounger, and was standing in front of the darkroom entrance. This time I did not hesitate. I left all thoughts of Thomas at the entrance and went in, taking a moment to acclimatise my eyes to the dark. I went forward and followed the hallway deep inside. Now I was back at the same spot I stood last time. I immediately went further, turning the corner and peeking inside the barely visible first room.

"Who's there?" came a man's husky voice.

"Jasmin," I said.

"Come in, Jasmin," said the man. "I'm Ismael."

"And I'm Dion," came another man's silvery voice, causing me to flinch.

I walked forward, unable to see a thing, until I collided into a rock-like body I figured belonged to Ismael.

"Hello there, little one," he said playfully.

"Hey," I said, my voice higher than normal, my palms growing sweaty.

"We've got condoms," said Dion, his sturdy body pushing up against mine from behind. "Tell us if there's anything you don't like. Use your voice."

"I will," I said, reaching behind me and pulling Dion in close.

Ismael grasped my hair gently from behind and pulled me in. I felt his breath on my nose, and enjoyed the warmth of him pressed up against my body. He kissed me, his stubble tickling my mouth. I put my hands over his shoulders and enjoyed his wide frame. Dion's hand reached around and he rubbed his fingers between my legs. My breath grew heavy and fast as three more hands roamed over me, stroking my neck and back, clutching my ass and breasts. Finally, Dion drove his finger inside, and I gave in to my ecstasy as

Ismael found his way to my nipple and sucked on it. I moaned out loud, my pulse racing. I welcomed these foreign explorers with all of my senses. I breathed in their damp scent. Felt their passion with every cell of my skin. Listened to the symphony of their excited breathing. Tasted their intentions as they took turns kissing me while also kissing each other. Only my eyes were deprived, which heightened my other senses. The two lovers were commanding in their energy, but I was sure I could handle it. Dion removed his finger, and Ismael lifted my leg up from the knee. After a crinkle of a condom wrapper and a delay, he pushed his dick into me. I lifted my head to the black ceiling and groaned, flooded with jubilation from Ismael's confident fucking. Eventually he slowed to a soft rhythm, allowing me to take in every millimetre of his dick's girth. Meanwhile, I heard a squirting sound. Soon after, I gasped and twitched when Dion placed his fingers over my anus, rubbing a cold gooey substance around it. He waited for my protest, which I was not giving him. So he gently and gradually drove his finger inside. I smiled when it dawned on me, and I braced myself for what was coming.

JORDAN

The weather was grey and rotten in Berlin. Still, a two hour walk felt like the perfect way to get home rather than catch a taxi. I popped my umbrella open and left La Secreta, watched by Ilva through the front glass. I gave her a wink, and got a typical Ilva response back — nothing.

The neighbourhoods of Berlin each had a character of their own. Yet after decades of gentrification, the city was maturing away from its counterculture roots. Wilmersdorf had a middle-class, suburban feel. Perfect for Sunday walks and long dinners outside on the sidewalk. It took me over an hour to leave La Secreta's world behind and cross Schöneberg into Gleisdreieck Park. The typically bustling wide-open space located on a former wasteland was empty. The joggers, walkers, frisbee players and Berliners having picnics had taken shelter inside. Only a handful of people were walking through on this drizzly day as a bright yellow BVG train crossed over from above. I should have headed north to get home to Prenzlauer Berg and Mitte. Mitte had grown from housing squatters and artists to a chic and trendy cesspool of cool. The shabby and careless, typically-Berlin way of dressing was now carefully and neatly selected. I was not yet ready to head home, however. I continued east instead, preferring to stay on the move. Plus I was feeling nostalgic.

Kreuzberg was the last bastion of the 'real' Berlin, but it too was showing signs of losing its soul. I came to that part of Berlin years ago to escape the glitz of my mother's world. Dinner parties and yacht rides with crusty old men pretending to be my father were not for me. Here in the grime and edge of Berlin, the weight of Arabella's expectations fell off my shoulders. I could be who I wanted, rather than what *she* wanted. But the glitz followed me, and J&A was born. The Jordan Rambone everyone now knew came soon after. Since escaping my mother, I came to be what a whole city wanted instead.

Berlin had lost its Cold War identity after the wall fell. What followed was nothing short of magical. A fractured city without a status quo, where out of every crack came a rainbow of creativity and individuality. I had become Berlin, a legend in perpetual making. My walls fell when I came, and I embraced a new, authentic way of life. Now my destiny had become entwined with the city. I was *Mr. Berlin*. That authenticity had dried out like a river during a drought. Where had it all gone wrong?

My phone vibrated, and I checked the screen:
I'm thinking of you. Let me come over.

Another text from a fuck buddy. Lisa, this time. I tucked the phone back into my pocket. Typically I would have entertained the idea. Today the thought of a random fuck made me nauseous. A lot was different on this day. After a morning at La Secreta I would have gone to the gym, or checked in with Ana about the next party. Of all days, I should have been getting my head right for our crystal anniversary tonight. Fifteen years from the day we met at the studio and sparked a revolution. Instead, I wandered the streets of the city that had breathed new life into me all those years ago. My mother's wealth meant nothing after I got here. My old buddies and I, dressed only in worn black t-shirts and old tracksuit pants, let the current of the city take us. From an electronic club, to a woman's bed, and back to another club the next day, it was a blissful flow I never wanted to end. Yet it did. And my destination was empty and purposeless. I was dead inside. Until last night.

Now I was contemplating tearing down my walls again. To let go of the old, turn over the soil for something new to grow. With Jasmin. The girl who days ago I had wanted nothing to do with. I snickered and shook my head as I wandered through Kottbusser Tor with drizzle falling on my umbrella. I liked the edge that Kreuzberg had. The heaviness I felt when I came here. The undercurrent of unease, as though something unexpected and unpleasant could happen at any moment. Kreuzberg did not pretend; it was unabashedly filthy and imperfect. To me that was life. Real problems with real consequences. Not the dreamworld I had been lulled into since the inception of J&A.

I had enough women to fuck until my last breath. An inheritance big enough to buy a house for each and every one of those women.

"Hey, Jordan," came the voice of two passing girls I vaguely recognised.

I also had a reputation that made me king of the streets. Being Jordan Rambone came with responsibility. It meant having to constantly be somewhere or do something. Today, I just wanted to be.

With myself and my city. To be back in the flow. I felt content. I had everything I needed; a feeling I had not experienced in years. Jasmin had pulled me out of my numbness, and now I was awake. I was feeling again. It felt damn good. Hope had returned to me. Was that what it felt like? I had forgotten. There was also a dull weight inside, telling me I wanted nothing to do with Lars' party. Something massive had permanently shifted.

After a group of young bucks tried to pull me up and convince me to let them come on Saturday, I left the centre of Kreuzberg and wandered the quieter streets instead. Made my way uphill towards Friedrichshain, in the direction of my apartment. Top floor in the centre of Berlin. Where a king should live. Today I wanted to be anonymous. There was something pure and reassuring about the idea of nobody knowing who you were. The thought of flying out of Europe tonight with Jasmin popped up as I crossed Oberbaum Bridge. I had to laugh. I was losing my fucking mind.

The familiar shadow then descended, telling me to be careful. Caroline had injected me with the same hope. Look how that ended. She had my senses glowing bright. Vibrant colours paired with an intense aliveness. A heart gushing with love. A sense that I had the power to tumble mountains — as long as *she* was by my side. That kind of thing never ended well in my world. Being Jordan Rambone also showed me the harshness of the world. The price we paid for love. The inevitable pain and disappointment. The heartbreak that came from believing we could fool reality. It was a law of physics. The illusion lingered for a while, before the bubble burst and reality came howling in. Then it got ugly.

At least with Ana there was no illusion. I might not have felt *seen* by her, but she goddamn knew me. My history. My demons. My limits. And she accepted it all. I had inherited more than just a bundle of money from my father. My mother told me I had that same look in my eyes when the heaviness came. It had cost my father his life, and almost took mine. With Ana and I broken up that autumn years ago, I slipped. The pain quickly took me over. I cut off contact from my friends and made the darkness my only companion.

Soon I reached the point of no return. Hope abandoned me in that horrible place, and slipping away from the world felt like the most natural thing. The pull was irresistible. When I tried to end it, Ana was there to pull me back from the abyss. That was what made her my queen. It was cold by her side, but at least it was real. Love was for idiots who needed something to believe in after the tooth fairy.

I remembered that lesson this morning over lunch. The nurturing look on Jasmin's face when she was playing with that little kid had shot my nerves. I had no intention of falling for the same trap. But fuck was I tempted. It felt amazing to be *seen*. That moment at Äden where Jasmin looked into me was a spark in the darkness that had become my life. Now the fire had been lit. I interacted with countless people each day, both on and off the mattress, but nobody really knew me. Not even Ana cared to look behind the curtain. She was lost in the glitz of J&A. She might have saved me, but her band-aid solution was no longer working. The constant parties and sex were wearing me thin. Anymore of this and I would end up back in that place of despair. Something about this Jasmin thing felt so natural, like leaving everything behind could be the easiest thing in the world. Like the natural order of the universe would be restored if I let her into my life. Yet drugs left you feeling the same way. That was why I never touched the stuff anymore.

I arrived at my apartment with aching calves and feet and dropped my soaked umbrella by the door. Tossed my shoes aside and stepped inside my dead-quiet apartment. I put my phone and wallet on the coffee table, still not knowing what to do with myself. Not wanting to do anything. Trying to push Jasmin out of my imagination. Then my phone rang. Ana. I froze. The ringing persisted for a long time and eventually cut out. The phone sat still for a second before she immediately called again. I stared at her name for almost a minute before I finally answered.

"Yeah," I said.

"Hi, darling," she said with a flat voice.

"What's going on?"

"You tell me. How was last night?"

"You were there," I said. "Didn't Lars fill you in?"

"That's not what I meant," she said sharply.

I rolled my head around to get the tension out of my neck.

"That's my business," I said.

Ana fell silent. Transparency was our number one rule. We both knew that.

"You can tell me tonight," she said. "What time are you coming over?"

I rubbed my hand over my face and began pacing the kitchen.

"We also need to go through the plans for Saturday," Ana added.

I exhaled slowly and stared out of the window. A magnificent blue and white swallow flew by my window and continued up into the grey, wet sky. Regardless of what I decided to do with Jasmin, I knew now what I did *not* want. The truth hit me like a revelation, and I had to free it into the world. Real or not, the cold climate that Ana was taking us into was going to destroy my soul. There was just one question I had to ask.

"Did you sign off on this maiden thing with the Galician girl?" I said.

There was a long pause, before an impatient sigh came through the speaker. It told me everything.

"I'm out," I said, feeling the sudden tension that comes when you cross the point of no return.

There was a long, tense pause.

"You're what?" said Ana.

"I don't want to go on Saturday. Do it without me."

"Excuse me?" she snapped.

The screech of the doorbell sounded at the front.

"Hold on a second," I said, lowering the phone.

I went to put Ana on mute, then realised that she had already hung up. No surprises there. The doorbell sounded again, and then again as I approached the front door. Who the hell was that? And what was so urgent? I picked up the phone speaker.

"Hello?" I growled.

"It's me," came a soft voice.

I hesitated.

"Jasmin?"

"Can I come up?"

I hesitated again. *Fuck.*

I buzzed her in. A minute later she came up the stairs with her handbag, still wearing the same dress from last night. She looked like she had been swimming. Her hair was a mess, and her face was flushed red.

"You ok?" I said.

"I had a fight with Thomas," she said. "We're finished."

"Aha," I said.

This can't be good.

"It's my final night in Berlin," she said. "Do you remember what I told you? My ultimate fantasy?"

"Yeah," I said, taking my hand off the door and standing straight.

"I want to do it. Tonight."

Was this a play? Her boyfriend agreed to open things up, then flipped when the consequences hit. I had seen it plenty of times. The idea seemed fine until your partner left for that first date. Then you started sweating. It took a special breed of man to live this life. Fresh off losing her boy, Jasmin had freaked out, and now needed a rebound. But how to reel me in? *Sex.* Of course. A woman's ultimate weapon. The best way to slither into a man's affections. I could sniff it from the door. *Don't fall for it, Jordan.*

I was cornered. Seeing red. I tried to formulate the words to convince Jasmin to go home. I thought about the anniversary. Not spending it with my woman would open me up to a world of hurt. Sure, we lived apart, would never get married, and never exchanged cards on special occasions. But to skip it altogether? I had dropped out of Lars' party this weekend, but was I willing to go even further and put my relationship on the line? J&A? *Decide, Jordan.*

Standing moon-eyed in my doorway, Jasmin had the sunlight from outside shining over her wholesome face and through the strands of her tangled hair. That little vixen. She felt so undeniably right, even with the way she looked. *Fuck it*. Time to make a leap. I grinned, and moved out of the doorway.

"Come in," I said. "Let's get you cleaned up."

12
LICENCE TO FUCK

THOMAS

The sun was setting when I stepped off the tram and stood on the sidewalk with a monstrous pain in my chest. I checked my maps app to study where I was going, then looked around to catch my bearings. Berlin used to be one of my favourite cities. Now I hated everything about it. Every currywurst stand. Each anarchist graffiti tag. Every grey fucking wall. The place had ruined my life twice, and now it had corrupted my girlfriend.

Ex-girlfriend, actually. I had the urge to smash my fist into a wall. I was a fool, running to Berlin like that, just because Jasmin said so. I sighed and wandered reluctantly to my destination, towards that other manipulative hag who got me in this mess.

The entrance to the apartment block buzzed open and I climbed the steps to the second level. The door opened and revealed Ana, dressed in a tight black silk robe. My whole body immediately reacted to her. She had the sash tight around her waist, accentuating her hourglass figure. The lapel was open, and revealed the side of her breasts, which she made no effort to hide. Maybe she was not all bad.

"Hello, darling," she said with a lovely smile, making room for me to enter.

"Hey," I said wearily.

She came forward and hugged me, pressing her torso and breasts against my body, injecting me with some life.

"Come in," she said.

She walked away into the living room while her hips swayed from side to side, compelling me to watch her as I was taking my shoes off.

"Tea?" she asked as she entered the kitchen.

"I'll have a beer if you've got one," I said.

"Sure," she said.

I threw my weight down on her cushion-filled sofa, in front of which was a Scandinavian-looking television cabinet with incense burning on top. The only lighting was a collection of candles spread out across the living room.

"Actually, I'm going to pour a glass of red," said Ana, popping her head through the doorway. "How about drinking one with me?"

"No, I'll take a beer," I said with authority.

Ana took a moment to process the severity in my voice. Then she smiled and came back with a glass of red wine and my beer. She sat next to me, close enough for me to feel her heat.

"Cheers," she said.

Cheers? I had to laugh, barely believing where I was. It was Ana's proposal at Äden that had launched this comedy of horror, leaving me sitting loveless and girlfriendless on her sofa. Now I was supposed to toast with her? *Here's to fucking up my life.*

"Sorry," I said after a long delay. "Cheers."

We touched our drinks together.

"Don't be sorry," she said. "You've had a difficult week."

She held my eye contact for barely a few seconds before I was blushing and looking away. Damn she was hot. The way her thick lips gently pushed up on the edge of the glass as she drank, how that robe sat on her luscious body, the profile of her tits under the material. The intimate ambiance only magnified the effect. Her skin was also glowing. Her energy intoxicated me and made me want to fall into her arms. *No*, I thought, sitting up. She led me here. This was her fault. I would prefer to have her bent over the sofa with a sock in her mouth. Hammering her while she barely got out a muffled yelp. *Man.* This week was messing with my head. As a smirk touched the side of Ana's mouth, I could have sworn she read my thoughts. But instead of backing off, she leaned in a little further.

"So, if I got it right, Jasmin's fallen for Jordan?" said Ana.

"Fallen?" I said. "She's lost her mind."

Ana looked me over and smiled all-knowingly.

"Girls fall for Jordan all the time," she said. "It's only lust. Jasmin is going through a phase, and you need to let her have it. Jordan gets bored easily, and when he does, she's going to come back to you. But until then, there's nothing you can do. You can't do what he does."

I sighed and felt my shoulders drop.

"Not yet, anyway," Ana added with a hand on my knee.

"I told you," I said. "I can't."

"Jasmin couldn't either until she took the leap with Kaspar and Tim."

"With who?" I said, my head pulling back.

"At the party," said Ana. "After you left?"

My heart toppled into my stomach and exploded into a million pieces that ripped my guts open. Ana observed my reaction carefully, then shook her head.

"Thomas, sweetie," she said. "I'm sorry."

"What did she do?" I croaked.

Ana looked me over and shook her head dismissively.

"Tell me," I said.

"She had group sex with Kaspar, Tim and two other girls."

The image of Jasmin with two other guys swallowed me whole, thrusting me into the emptiest, furthest reaches of my loneliness. A place of limitless despair.

"Oh, man," I said, burying my head in my lap.

"Sweetie," said Ana. "Jasmin came here searching for something. You have to let her find it."

My eyes welled up. Ana placed one hand on my back and rubbed my shoulder with the other. The depth of my despair went further still, horrifying me beyond what I could accept. Only Ana's warm touch kept me anchored. But that was the problem, I realised. I moved her hand away. Soon after, the feeling washed away, and the tears stopped. An eerie sense of calm came over me. I lifted my head and straightened my shoulders. I was such a hypocrite. I had taken part in an orgy as well. How was that any different from what Jasmin did? A spontaneous chuckle escaped me.

"Pitiful, aren't I?" I said.

Ana shrugged.

"We've all been there. Love hurts."

"Yeah," I admitted. "So what now?"

"Thomas," said Ana. "When I first saw you at Äden, I sensed enormous potential." Ana's compliment had an immediate impact, and I became more receptive to her words. "I had a vision about the man you could be. But I saw the way you and Jasmin were talking to each other. It was obvious to everyone that she was holding you back."

I sighed and rubbed my eyes.

"That's difficult to hear," I said. "But you're right."

"It's time for you to swim out of that pond. Tell me, Thomas. What's your ultimate fantasy?"

I shook my head with a huff.

"I hate these kinds of games," I said.

"Jasmin is gone," said Ana unfazed. "You're a free man. What do you want?"

I pondered for a moment and shrugged.

"I don't know. I guess… To have sex with lots of hot women?"

Ana paused and looked into me before speaking again.

"Good," she said. "Let's start with one. If you do well, I'll give you five hot women at once at the next party."

"What do you mean?" I asked, sitting forward.

"We have a special guest coming from Galicia for this Saturday's party. The most beautiful girl you've ever seen. I've got plenty of guys in J&A willing to do it, but I want you to make a woman out of her."

My head pulled back.

"You want me to do what?" I said.

"It's going to be the show of the year," said Ana without losing her composure. "I believe that you have the potential to be the next Jordan. A softer, more refined version. The days of toxic masculinity are over. You are the new generation, Thomas. Women want men like you. Sexual and attuned, but open-minded. This show will capture their imagination and make you a superstar. You, Thomas, can be Berlin's most desirable man."

The idea tickled me in the place where dreams emerged. It seemed too good to be true. But if anybody could deliver on such a promise, it would be Ana. She had the connections. The reputation.

"And this girl from Galicia. All I have to do is fuck her in front of everyone?"

"Don't be so crude," said Ana.

"Sorry," I said.

"Give them a show to remember. Loving, youthful, lustful. It will be the most exquisite thing anyone has seen. And you will be the man who gave it to them."

I rubbed the back of my neck. Me? The centre of attention? The new Jordan? It sounded insane.

"You're messing with me, right?" I said.

"You need to stop messing with yourself," said Ana.

Holy shit. The woman was dead serious. I tried to imagine myself in a bed with a gorgeous model. She would laugh me out of the room.

"What makes you think I can do it?" I said. "Look at me."

"It's not potential that's your problem," said Ana. "Only confidence. I know the person who can help you find it."

"Who?" I said.

Ana smiled mischievously and picked up her phone from the coffee table while I watched on confused. She dialled a number, which I saw from the photo and the name was April, the fiery, auburn-haired girl from the party.

"Hey, love," said Ana after putting the phone to her ear. "Listen, Thomas is at my place. He's been telling me all evening about how he wants to teach you a lesson. Talking a big game. Do you think he could get his chance tonight?"

"Wait, what?" I said, tensing up and leaning forward.

Ana listened to the response, nodding repeatedly while her smile gradually widened.

"Aha," she said, smiling openly, "I'll let him know. See you in an hour."

She put the phone down and turned to me.

"What did she say?" I asked, my voice faltering.

Ana chuckled.

"She said she's had a stressful week, so you had better fuck her well. Otherwise, you can go fuck yourself. Her words."

I got a sinking feeling, sensing myself dragged even further into Ana's dystopian nightmare. It pulled me out of my seat, the rage lifting me into the air.

"I don't get you guys," I said, unable to breathe beyond my throat. "I'm here for two minutes, and you're already onto your next plan. This is fucked up on another level. I come in here, after a breakup caused by *your* idea, while your boyfriend, or whatever the fuck he is, is screwing my girl. And whose name is *Rambone!* Who the fuck is called Rambone?!" I was hyperventilating now, my hands trembling. The urge to punch something took me over again. "And now you invite your friend over, saying I want to 'teach her a lesson.' You're all depraved! All of you! Fuck you! And fuck J&A!"

I slammed my fist down on the cushion, and looked away with my chest heaving up and down. Ana remained perfectly still. Eventually, my rage subsided, revealing the acidic fear I had in me the entire time.

"Are you done?" said Ana.

"I'm gonna make an ass of myself," I added hopelessly.

"Thomas. Sweetie," said Ana calmly and matter-of-factly. "You know what your problem is?"

"What?" I said with a frown.

"You hate women."

"I don't hate women!" I shrieked. "You all hate yourselves!"

"All men hate women," said Ana. "They just don't admit it."

"Don't give me that feminist crap," I said.

"Think about it, my dear. Men hate women because they're powerless to them. Hate is the only feeling of control they have left. Just about every man, including you, was once mummy's little boy. You were totally dependent on her. She had you literally eating out of her tits. She had all the control, and you hated that. Unconsciously, of course. You grew older and you escaped. Then the first female with a sexy body walks by, and you're weak at the knees the same way you are now," said Ana, indicating towards my shaking legs. "Powerless."

I opened my mouth to tell her to shut up. That she was full of it. Then I closed it. My knees stopped shaking, and I suddenly felt a couple inches taller than usual.

"Wait," I said, briefly emboldened before hesitating yet again.

I thought for a moment, now able to see what she meant.

"It's also why Jasmin is acting like this," continued Ana. "You've been trying to take back the power by making her feel guilty, and she's not taking it anymore. You've been using her love against her."

A sickness crept into my stomach. I was forced to look at the floor. The woman in the tight silk robe had me. I only felt strong with Jasmin because I knew she loved me. I took her for granted.

"I never really thought of it that way," I said.

"It's fine, sweetie," said Ana. "It's not the end of the world. It can be a good thing."

"How can hating women be good?"

Ana smiled and sighed.

"It's never good to hate women," she said. "But it's important to acknowledge that it's there. That way you can channel it into something good. Use it to show her the time of her life, instead of making her life miserable."

"Who? Jasmin?"

"No. The woman you're about to have sex with."

"April?"

Ana nodded.

"I... I don't know, Ana," I said. "I need to see what happens with Jasmin fir—"

"Jasmin is out right now having the time of *her* life. With Jordan. Not you. You're not even on her mind right now. She's getting what she wants."

"Thanks," I said. "I feel much better now."

"Look," said Ana, a crack appearing in her mask of patience, the anguish in her face surprising me for a second. "Jordan and I have our anniversary today, and he hasn't even called. I'm just as affected by this as you are."

I remembered my beer and drank half of it in one turn.

"Thomas, darling," said Ana, regaining her composure as I lowered the bottle. "What do you want? Do you want to have a wonderful experience with a gorgeous woman?"

I pondered for a moment. When I let the idea of Jasmin go, ten Aprils appeared in her place. Their bras were gushing, their legs stretched up to the sky. Their asses were a kick in the guts the second you laid eyes on them. I wanted that. Every man did. I had fantasised about it thousands of times. A beautiful woman terrified me, but there was no denying that I wanted to be with one.

"Yeah," I admitted. "I want lots of them."

"Then stop letting fear hold you back," she said.

"I've seen April," I said. "She's going to eat me alive."

"Not if you hold your ground. Let your anger guide you. But don't forget. Respect. There's a line you can't cross, and you need to find it. Not that you need to worry. April's got a high pain threshold."

My eyebrows lifted.

"Pain?" I said. "That's not who I am."

Ana sighed impatiently.

"I've had so many clients like you," she said. "They miss the point completely. She doesn't want some random guy. She wants a king. One who dominates his realm. Someone she can submit to. She wants to believe in you. But she won't surrender unless you believe in yourself first. First you tame the dragon, then you take the throne."

I almost laughed out loud. King? Dragon? What was this woman talking about?

"If you say so," I said.

"I do," said Ana. "Now go have a shower and clean yourself up. She'll be here soon. Fresh towels are in the cupboard."

"Ok," I said reluctantly before standing up and dragging myself inside.

"And don't worry," yelled Ana. "She's a sweetheart. I promise."

I turned back one more time at the doorway and nodded before disappearing inside. Once I was naked in the bathroom, the gravity of the situation hit me, and my palms began to sweat. I wiped them off on the towel and stared at my boyish reflection in the mirror, looking for any traces of a king. If he was in there, he needed to hurry up. The dragon would be here any minute, and my sword was as limp as a rubber band.

JASMIN

What the hell was his problem? I crossed my arms and curled my toes. Jordan had been speaking with Tim for over fifteen minutes, leaving me alone with my stupid cocktail. We had barely arrived at the Aschinger shibari bar before Jordan ran into him on the way back from the bathroom and practically forgot I existed. They made no attempt to join me, or even acknowledge that I was there. There was no way I was going over to them. I could hear everything they were saying from where I sat, anyway.

"Everyone's excited," said Tim. "You and Ana are moving up. Hosting it at Villa Salace is going to be amazing!"

Jordan nodded and looked away. The eyes of most of the girls in the place were on him. Not mine. I was watching the two guys at the other side of the bar. *Cute.* They could have been in a boy band. Perfectly groomed. Fit bodies. Glowing skin. Immaculate shoes. I kept Jordan in my peripheral though. Tonight he was mine.

"Apparently Frederick the Great used to take his mistresses to Villa Salace," said Tim. "Or misters. Depending on which historian you ask."

Tim tapped Jordan's arm to help drive home his joke. Jordan raised his eyebrows and forced a smile.

"I bet you're excited for this," continued Tim. "It's going to be a fuckfest on Saturday."

Saturday. My birthday.

Jordan shrugged.

"I won't be there," he said.

I turned suddenly and looked at him. Surely he never skipped a party.

"You..." Tim stuttered, giving Jordan a baffled look. "This is the biggest party of the year. Lars fucking Lecker is bankrolling it. What the hell?"

Jordan shrugged and looked briefly in my direction.

"It's personal," he said.

Tim blinked a number of times and shook his head.

"I can't believe this," he said. "How the hell is there going to be a J&A party without you?"

"You'll be fine," said Jordan, slapping his shoulder. "You're the man of the house now. Make me proud. Come on. Let's grab another drink."

The boys walked off together, and I was left with Jordan's bombshell. Jordan skipping a party? It left me questioning what his life could be like outside of the kink scene. I had seen another side of him at La Secreta. Sentimental. Authentic. Humble. Those were qualities that had me daring to believe. But in what? A future together? Impossible. Jordan was Jordan.

Anyway, I was flying home tomorrow. Plus it was hard to visualise a happily ever after in a place like Aschinger, which looked like a dungeon. The ceilings were low, the walls bare brick and concrete. Only red and warm orange lighting was used. Black and white shibari pictures hung from the walls, with women and men tied down in various styles. Others were hanging from the ceiling while someone held onto them and looked out with a deviant stare and tongue out.

I trembled when I caught sight of the harness beyond the hallway hanging from the ceiling. The bundle of rope on the nearby table taunted me. I grasped my cocktail with both hands while being torn apart by conflicting impulses. My body was now screaming to be tied up from head to toe, to be immobilised to the point of utter helplessness. The thought of what would happen after had me wanting to escape outside into the near-freezing fresh air. The walls closed in on me and constricted my throat, but leaving was not an option. Thomas was out there, and I was inside my desired cage. Only Jordan's fingers and dick could free me. But he was busy talking to fucking Tim.

The place had filled out in the last hour. A group had congregated with their drinks around a stage at the end of the bar. On it were a couple, making deep eye contact and oozing with chemistry. It was a show of some kind. I went over and joined the audience. The trust and affection in the woman's eyes were absolute. Her sparkling silver one-piece was magnetic. His dark jeans and black leather vest lurked behind her. His arms reached around and grasped her throat, then ran sensually and gradually down her waist while she trembled from the anticipation. He took her roughly by the arms and forced her to her knees. Knelt behind her and moved his face sensually through her hair, embracing her lovingly around her chest. They remained that way for a time. He held her in his arms while their chemistry held the crowd's attention.

His hand reached behind and grasped the end of a massive bundle of purple rope. With his face pressed close against her, he worked the rope around and began furiously tying it into knots. Her arms were bound tight behind her back at right angles, her neck was bent while she kneeled in absolute submission to her captor, her hair covering her entire face. He continued his work while she slipped deeper into surrender, her body becoming more and more limp. Suddenly he sprang up and tied the rope to a harness, lifting her up until she was on her tiptoes. Now that she was suspended standing up, he began to work on her legs and feet. Soon enough she was floating, now also suspended by her knee on one leg and foot on the other. She looked like a human origami; a gorgeous floating statue. The ecstasy grew too much for her, and she moaned. The crowd broke out in applause while he spun his prize in circles, presenting her to the adoring audience.

I did not clap. Their gorgeous interplay had me under a spell, which I only came out of when I finished my drink, having taken a neurotic, unconscious series of sips. I started twirling the glass impatiently in circles. I forced myself to look at Jordan. As though sensing the heat of my stare, he looked over at me while listening to Tim's story. A twinkle appeared in his eye, then he turned back to Tim. *Bastard.*

I thought Jordan was done playing games. We had moved beyond that. Had come to a silent agreement to be respectful. *Wait a second.* In one context respect was a moving target. Another agreement we had decided on. The game would begin without warning. I had told Jordan I did not want the whole thing to be scripted. It had to be spontaneous and unrehearsed. I had told him what I wanted, what remained open was *how* it happened. I could see now that he was initiating the game by ignoring me. Leaving me out in the cold — to see how I reacted.

He wanted to play, did he? I cat walked towards the bar and spanked his ass as I passed, before claiming a stool next to the lads from the boy band. Getting their attention was easy. I was looking sexy as hell in the low-cut, sapphire dress Jordan had bought for me during the day. The boys would lose their minds if they saw what I had underneath it — hand-picked by Jordan for my ultimate fantasy.

The bartender came to me, and I ordered an old fashioned. While waiting, I sent the textbook signals to the two boys. Turned their way. Played with my hair. Pretended I was looking beyond them into the distance. Then I locked eyes with the hotter one for a second too long, then looked at the floor. My drink came. As I reached into my bag, a hand reached over to the bartender with a credit card.

"On me," said the hot guy.

"That's a good start," I said. "Maybe later I can be on you as well."

His head pulled back in surprise. He stared at me with an air of caution, forced to suddenly measure me up again. Meanwhile, Jordan's shadow appeared menacingly from the side.

"Boys, come here for a minute," he ordered, calling over the guy's friend as well.

If they were in a boy band, Jordan was their manager. They responded immediately, walking ahead of him towards the front door.

I watched Jordan at work. He towered over the boys, his dominance obvious from their hunched heads and deer-in-the-headlight eyes. They listened carefully to his words, and nodded enthusiastically while looking over at me. When they seemed to understand, he slapped one of them on the shoulder and came back my way.

"You're a little brat, aren't you?" he said, dressing me down with his stare, making me infinitely hornier in the process. "Did I say you could talk to anyone?"

Game on.

"I'm sorry," I said with a sweet voice. "I was lonely over there by myself. You didn't play with me, daddy."

Jordan snatched my arm by the wrist and forced me to follow him, through an unmarked door and to the top of a narrow set of stairs.

"Walk ahead of me," he ordered.

"Yes, daddy," I said.

This time I snorted with laughter when I had to think of my actual daddy, whose highlight for the day was watching his football team on television. The crossover with him and Jordan had never felt more ridiculous.

"Ah!" I screamed, jumping and contorting from pain when Jordan pinched my ass.

"No fucking around," he said with a fierce stare. "I mean it."

His intervention pulled me back to reality. I descended into hell one step at a time, feeling the heat of him behind me. The red lighting in the bare-concrete basement was dimmer than upstairs. There were two chairs in the middle. Beside them was a stage with a black leather mattress and a harness hanging above. At the side of the room was a long, tinted window which ran across the entire width of the open space, presumably for people to watch.

"Don't move," he said, pointing his index finger at me and giving me a powerful stare that froze me in place.

His acting like that was incredibly hot and terrifying at the same time. I started to wonder if he was serious or still playing? Maybe I had pushed him too far?

He disappeared through the door, leaving me alone in my invisible prison. The trembling moved from my hands to my legs, and began to affect my breathing. The claustrophobia came back like a wildfire and made me lightheaded. I waited. Jordan took his sweet time, and my throat became tight. He was taking forever. So I sat down.

His shadow appeared first and caused a hot pain in my chest, before he walked through and relief flooded me. There was now a black leather bag in his hand. He unzipped it and emptied out its contents onto a cloth on the floor. I saw a magic wand vibrator. A flat wooden spoon. A black leather flogger covered in tassels. A large white feather. My mouth fell open, and my belly had hornets in it.

"Didn't I tell you not to move?" he said.

"My legs got tired," I replied, putting on a pout.

"Stand up," he ordered.

I did as I was told. Who could argue with such power?

"Shoulders back. Stand straight."

I adjusted my posture.

"Straight," he said. "Do you want to get punished?"

"I am standing straight," I moaned.

His expression grew even more unimpressed. He picked up the other chair and dropped it in front of me. Dressed me down with his stare while removing his jacket, and carefully placed it over the backrest. Neatly rolled up his shirt sleeves, one by one, taking his time, letting me stew in the tension of anticipation.

"Sit down in front of me," he said.

I challenged him with a direct stare.

"No," I said slowly, a cunning smirk edging from the sides of my mouth.

"Oh, you want to play with me, do you? Come here, you little brat."

I kept my defiant eyes on him while I paced away with cat-like steps.

"Hey," he said forcefully after I was a number of metres away, to which I circled with a twirl before standing my ground.

"Come and get me if you want me," I said.

He sprang forward suddenly and grabbed my wrist. Led me back to his chair and sat, forcing me down stomach first over his lap. *Step one.* He lifted my dress to reveal my bare ass, and raised his hand into the air. Just as I was recalling what our safe word was supposed to be, his hand came down on me with a powerful snap.

13

WHAT APRIL WANTS

THOMAS

I was a dead man. A lucky one, who had breathed his last breath and made it to heaven. I sat up on the bed in my boxers, bathed in candlelight, watching in awe while two horny angels made out in front of me. April was down to her white lingerie, the v-string barely covering her ass, the bra barely containing her tits. She reached up and pulled Ana's silk robe lapel to the side, revealing a glorious tit. The chocolate kiss at the tip was begging to be tasted. April beat me to it, bending down and hungrily sucking on Ana's nipple. Meanwhile, Ana bit down on her lip and moaned with her deep, regal voice.

She looked directly at me, panting with her thick pink lips parted. Her x-ray eyes saw into me and transmitted her pleasure directly inside. April came back up, and her lips got acquainted with Ana's. The girls' bodies became like two snakes dancing, their lips like oceans colliding. The light in the room brightened, and I sent a silent thank you to the man upstairs, convinced that I would never experience anything this magnificent again in my life.

The girls pulled away and stared deep into each other's eyes, exchanging illuminated smiles of appreciation. April then turned her attention to me, and I flinched. She got on all fours and crawled towards me. Unclipped her bra and removed it, freeing her breasts in their glory.

"Cute shorts," she said with a chuckle, pulling at my ducky boxers. "But they have to go." She snatched them down, wrestled them off my feet, and tossed them aside. Then she moved straight down and began hungrily sucking me off. Meanwhile, Ana came around from the side and kissed my lips. Their combined energy was a tsunami, before which I grew petrified, and my legs began trembling.

"Oh my God," said April, lifting her head up. "Look! His legs are shaking."

Ana smiled and straightened up, covering her breasts again with her silk robe.

"Have fun you two," she said and left the room, closing the door behind her.

I exhaled and blinked down hard, relieved and disappointed that Ana had left. I was seconds away from an embarrassing and premature end to the evening.

"I see the way you look at her," said April, stroking my dick with her warm hand.

I moaned, feeling the rumble within as it threatened to erupt.

"Wait," I said, pushing her hand away.

I caught it just in time, my whole body lifting off the mattress while I created space for the energy to go anywhere but through the tip of my dick.

"You good?" said April.

"Yeah," I said softly, leaning my head against the bedhead and exhaling. "Too good."

"Should I leave?" said April, looking towards the door.

"What? No," I said, flinching and sitting forward suddenly.

With a mere twist of her head away from me, she delivered a direct shock to my system. In that fraction of a second, I pictured my lonely walk home, and felt the warm flush of shame that would infect me for days afterwards. The regret that would come in the following decades, when I would look back at my life, knowing I had blown my chance at bliss.

She cackled at my reaction, shaking her head and burning me with her stare.

"Ok, ok," she said. "Don't worry. Mummy's not going anywhere."

"Right," I said, my face turning warm when I realised her trick. "Nice."

"So predictable," she said.

"We're not going anywhere," I said, and rested my hand on her thigh.

Her face softened. Her untamed red hair was even wilder tonight. One moment her pupils were brown, then they became green in the light. The longer I stayed in her energy, the harder my heart beat. A long, deep breath did nothing. My legs trembled again. This woman was imposing. The way her tongue had moved over Ana's nipple made her look like a Komodo dragon I saw in a documentary. Exceptional hunter. Extremely toxic bite. Basically my first impression of April. She seemed innocent enough now. Angelic, even. She had lowered her guard. Her cheeks glowed like half moons. Her lips were strawberries inviting me to nibble on them. I leaned forward, entranced by—

"Do you like to get pegged?" she said.

I blinked twice as the words registered, before a stab in my heart abruptly popped our bubble of shared connection. The picture of the angel before me was in shreds. I focussed carefully. The Komodo dragon had returned.

"What?" I said, straightening up, feeling uneasy.

"Has a woman ever taken you from behind with a dildo?"

"No. What kind of a question is that?"

"What do you fantasise about then?"

"Not that," I said. "Jesus."

"I caught you staring at my ass at the J&A party on Sunday."

"Who wasn't?" I said as coolly as I could.

"You looked like a man who wanted his meal."

The heat of her scrutiny caused me to look at the floor.

"Now I see a little boy," she added.

I glared at her. *Boy?*

"Yeah. You know what I don't see? *A man*. A big, strong man with an even bigger, stronger dick."

"Whatever," I said, turning my whole body away from her, unable to bear her probing eyes anymore.

"No wonder your girlfriend is out fucking Jordan."

A pit of fire and lava opened up in my chest, oozing out from my inner darkness and filling my body.

"I'm starting to fantasise about slapping someone in the fucking face," I said, now staring directly at her.

"Good," said April.

With a hand on my chest she guided my torso back against the bedhead.

"Control yourself this time if you want to be a proper dom," she said before getting to work.

I had never had my dick sucked like that in my life. April grew hungry for it. Ravenous. She took ownership of it, making it her own play thing. Up and down, side to side, she whipped me into soft, smooth cream. Meanwhile, I laid back and enjoyed the sight of her wide, round orange ass, even reaching my hand down to grab it for a moment. She licked the tip of my dick as though checking it for taste, then drove the whole thing down her throat suddenly until her nose was pushed up against my pelvis. I lifted up off the mattress, flooded by the intensity. Sensing my excitement pouring over again, she lifted her head and gasped. She slowed down her strokes and resorted to licking the shaft gently up and down. My eyes met hers, and she winked at me before kissing the tip.

"You good?" she said, sitting up on her knees.

I exhaled slowly and checked again for my body. It was still there.

"Yeah," I said with almost a whisper.

"Your girlfriend wasn't woman enough for you. It's the woman who makes the man. And she did a lousy job. How long have you been together?"

"Nine years," I said, rubbing my hand through my hair and stretching my legs out, letting my dick fall soft again.

"Lousy," April repeated, looking me up and down.

"Think you could do a better job?" I said.

"Depends."

"On?"

"Tell me, *Thomas*," she said in a girlish tone, taking her v-string off and tossing it aside. She pushed her chest out and spread her legs. "What do you see?"

I held her eyes for a moment, then turned my attention to her body, which reacted immediately to me. Her chest lifted higher with each breath, her legs opened wider like a flower blooming in spring.

"Do you see me?" she said.

Did I see her? What kind of a question was that?

"I see you," I said, just to push her stupid question aside.

"No," she said with darkness in her tone. "Thomas. Sweetie. Do you *see* me?"

The way she posed the question shot an unpleasant quiver through me. The room grew bright again like before, as though someone had turned up the lighting. It was like the come up from the pill the other night, only now I was sober. High on nothing, except April.

I paid close attention to her body with my new awakened sight. Another feeling seeped into me. It felt icky. Heavy. It made me want to turn away from her. But I looked. Her tits were not as perfect as before, hanging a bit too low for my liking. I had taken for granted that she had the perfect ass. Now the angle she was sitting at revealed her cellulite. She sat down on the mattress and straightened her legs, and all I could see were her stomach rolls. She was quite chubby, when I thought about it.

"And?" she said.

"You look nice," I said.

"Tell me the truth."

Damn.

"Your body type is different to what I'm used to."

She got on all fours and faced her ass towards me.

"Of course," she said. "I bet the only person you've fucked in the last decade is that skinny little bitch."

Another bite from the Komodo dragon. Her poison seeped deeper into me.

"I bet the only person you *haven't* fucked in the last decade is me," I snapped.

"Do you like my pussy?" she said, unfazed.

I lowered my head and inspected the two lips between her legs. Reached my hand over and touched her, rubbed my fingers over her labia and inserted two of them inside. She moaned her acceptance of my intrusion.

"Yes," I said, enjoying the wetness and warmth of her. "It's like ripe fruit."

"Is it?" she said, inhaling as her body contracted. "So you want to eat it?"

I took my fingers out and stroked her freshly groomed pubic hair.

"Nice landing strip," I said.

"Thank you," she said.

I came around to the front and stuck out my two wet fingers for her to lick clean. She complied. I reached my head over and kissed her. She immediately made her presence known inside my mouth. Her lips were fuller and warmer than Jasmin's, her tongue slicker and busier. No surprise for a Komodo dragon.

Without warning she shifted away and lay on the bed with her back to me. Her skin looked like velvet, her natural curves were bursting with life.

"Hold me," she said.

I shrugged and took my position behind her, reaching my arm around her shoulder and spooning her. We remained there in silence while I wondered what the hell she was up to.

"How do I feel?" she said.

I sighed. *Fuck my life.*

"Normal," I said.

"Breathe," she said, and began gyrating against my crotch.

My body responded to her, and with that I sensed her aliveness. Her passion. Her potency. She was no Komodo dragon. She was a *serpent.*

"I can feel you," I said.

"I can feel your big dick," she shot back.

"How does it feel?" I said, remembering to breathe.

"Like a tree trunk."

I attached my lips onto her neck and sucked on it while our movements grew. I had to follow her or I would lose her. I turned her face back with my hand and took her tongue inside my mouth, driving my turn-on into her and feeling it pass from her body back into mine. The power of the energetic loop seemed to have no end.

"What are you afraid of?" said April, settling into a sensual, steady flow.

How the hell did she know what I was feeling?

"Mmm," she moaned. "I've never felt anyone like you. So tender. So deep."

Is she being sarcastic?

"You're powerful," she said. "But you're afraid to let go. What are you scared of?"

"I don't know," I whispered.

"Turn around," she said. "My turn."

I did as she said, and felt her hand reach around from the back and grab onto my so-called tree trunk. She had definitely made it as hard as one. She jerked me off while another finger rubbed up against my anus. I flinched, but let her do it. Like playing two instruments, she jerked me off with a steady rhythm while running her finger in circles over my ass, gradually pushing it in.

Her finger came away suddenly, and her body moved away from me momentarily. The warmth of her body then returned, and I felt something cold and sharp touch my butt cheek. Not her finger.

"What's tha—"

BAM!

An electric shock passed through me, and the pain forced me to suddenly jump, roll over and hop to my feet.

"What the fuck!" I yelled, looking down and seeing some kind of cattle prod in April's hand, the two metal teeth sticking out like snake teeth. "What's that?"

April cackled in hysterics. Before I could react, she leapt up and shocked my leg, laughing again as I yelled and jumped up into the air.

Her eyes looked wild. She had morphed into a Komodo dragon, a serpent and a witch; all rolled into one. With a mad shriek she came at me again. My instinct was to protect my face, and I got a sharp electric stab on my forearm and screamed out again.

"Fucking bitch!" I yelled, slapping her over the head.

The witch shrieked and zapped me again, driving me into the depths of my own hell. The urge to strike back grew irresistible. Not an option. A voice in my head told me to get out. I marched to the door and pulled the handle. Locked. *Shit*. I could hear Ana on the other side. Laughing. She knew about this!? Yet another zap struck me in the ass, and I convulsed so hard it hurt.

"Enough!" I screamed and turned as April was preparing to strike me again.

I managed to grab her wrist in time, and looked on at the cattle prod teeth's futile attempts to electrify its target — me. My pulse became electrified instead, the adrenaline had sharpened my focus. With one smooth motion, I snatched the cattle prod from April's hand then pushed the witch over onto the bed. Before she had landed, I was already on top of her. I pulled the trigger and held the cattle prod to her hip and kept it there. The ta-ta-ta of the electricity jackhammered her, and she screamed at the top of her lungs like a witch burning at the stake.

"You like that!?" I screamed.

Her yelling was not what I thought. Her body grew limp and she gave in to the punishment. Her screams were fused with another sound. Groans of pleasure. She was enjoying this?

I pushed the cattle prod harder into her waist, and the groaning disappeared, leaving only hysterical screaming.

"Stop!" she yelled. "Stop!"

"Fuck you!" I yelled.

The door burst open and Ana marched in. I took my finger off the trigger and pulled my hand back, which was shaking with fury. I shook my head and stood, horrified with myself. I had lost it. Never had I experienced anything like that before. This mad woman had turned me into a madman.

"Ana, you know bloody well my safe word isn't 'stop!'" yelled April from the floor, giggling to herself. "Woo!" she yelled.

I gave Ana a questioning look. *What. The. Fuck?* She smiled and shrugged.

"You were supposed to come in only when I said 'New York, New York,'" said April.

Ana shook her head and gave me an amused look before leaving. *She's all yours,* said her face. The door locked from the outside.

"I'm not done with you," I said, feeling the beast still circulating inside me.

"Give me your best," said April with fire in her eyes, panting in fearful expectation while covered in sweat.

I knelt down and slapped her ass with all I had. She giggled.

"Is that it?" she said.

I grasped her nipples with both hands and squeezed with all my might.

"Ah!" she shrieked. "New York! New York! New York!"

The door burst open again, and I let go. April's surrender was enough to quell the monster. He left me, and receded back into the darkness within.

"Do I need to stop this?" said Ana.

No longer filled with rage, I looked down and noticed my raging hard on. April was looking at it also with sweet hunger in her eyes and licking her lower lip.

"Is that mine?" she said.

I fell to my knees. April scampered over to the bedside table and snatched one of the condoms off and crawled back. I took it from her and ripped it open without breaking eye contact. Using my thumb I tested which way it rolled out, and then covered the rock between my legs. I fell down on April and pushed my tree trunk into her moist, peachy pussy. Her cheeks were now blushed red, and her eyes transmitted total surrender to me. Her face was a sunrise. Absolutely gorgeous. I smiled in awe and relief, and she mirrored me. We were connected in body and energy. I pushed deeper inside her, and she gasped. I fucked my prize with firm, commanding strokes, and melted into her. I could feel Ana's presence for a time, before the door shut and she was gone. I continued to pump my offering into April, and she proceeded to invite it deeper and deeper inside. And off we went on an energetic ride, from the floor, to the bed, to the dresser, against the door, and back to the floor, where April rode me. Until then I had experienced no other forms of her, only the surrendered April had revealed herself.

Now, on the floor, after what felt like an hour of mind-bending sex, she unleashed the witch again. Her eyes were filled with hysteria, and her face swung in all directions as she feverishly grinded against my dick while I steadied her by her hips. She stopped suddenly, reached down and began rubbing her clit. Her pussy seized my cock tight. I felt her arriving, like a strong wind through the crack of a window, before it blew open. She came, her body lifting, her voice lifting, sending me to the edge. Her weight collapsed back onto me, and she collected herself, panting heavily. Then her gyrating started again and took on its own momentum. I had no way to resist her as she fucked her prize out of me. I came, convulsing repeatedly while I filled the condom. She collapsed down onto me, our sweat combining as she nuzzled into my chest and I wrapped my arm around her, the two of us gasping.

The sweat on our bodies eventually dried, the high ceded, leaving me in a state of peace and satisfaction. I listened to April breathing while taking in the shining moment. I never would have imagined when first seeing her that I would end up here. I needed to piss, but I stayed in position. Accepted my responsibility. I was the foundation on which April was peacefully resting, and me moving would end that. The instinct to sabotage and destroy had left me, and preservation and creation suddenly seemed like the most natural things in the world. I wanted to be a pillar, someone others could rely on. And it started by the simple act of not moving, allowing April to rest. Within the resulting silence I could hear Ana walking around inside. April chuckled sweetly.

"I knew you had it in you," she said with a bedroom voice.

I smiled with gratitude for what I had just experienced. It would certainly be a night I would always remember — with zero regrets. I ran my fingers over her back, circling around her ass and grabbing it tight. Perception was a strange thing. Never steady. Now her ass looked glorious in the dim lighting; cellulite and all.

"I like your body," I said. "I guess I needed to test drive it first."

"Does it handle well?" asked April with a muffled voice, her head buried in my chest.

"Mhm," I replied. "Like a Porsche."

Cuddling with April was like having a glass of wine by the fireplace. Her body felt warm, alive, and comforting at the same time. After hours of mayhem, cattle prods and fiery passion, I felt relieved at the quietness that had fallen over the room. My eyelids grew heavy, before a loud, reckless rattle from the kitchen jolted me.

"What's Ana up to in there?" I said.

"I don't think she can sleep," said April with a sleepy voice. "She's got a lot on her mind."

"What's that?" I said.

"Jordan skipped out on their anniversary," said April. "And he told her he's skipping the party this Saturday. You can imagine she's a little stressed."

"What happened?" I asked, already knowing the answer.
"Your girlfriend happened," said April.
So there it was.
"She's not my girlfriend anymore," I said.
"Sounds like Jordan will be happy to hear that."
My bladder started aching, and I could no longer hold it in.
"I'll be back," I said, gently guiding April off of me.
"Sexy butt," came April's voice as I walked out of the room.

I entered the hallway and found all the lights off. The front door slammed suddenly shut. Where was Ana going at two in the morning? A day ago I would have frantically called Jasmin to find out what was going on. Tonight, I would do nothing. I felt calm and satisfied, and I wanted to stay in that space. Jasmin was no longer my concern. Instead, I was going to the bathroom to drain the snake, then I was going to hop back into bed with April and get some much needed sleep. I had to rest if I was to put on a show on Saturday with this 'purest, most beautiful girl' I had ever seen.

14

TO HELL

ANA

Fate had let me down once again. I should have seen her coming. That little Trojan horse bitch had infiltrated my man's heart and stolen his love. And I was the one who had invited her in. It was time to snatch back control.

"Don't let them leave," I said into the phone, rushing down the stairs.

"Not to worry," replied Tim. "They're not going anywhere. Or at least Jasmin isn't. She's 'tied up' at the moment."

I hung up and exited my building, stepping into the early morning street light with heavy eyelids. The taxi was waiting by the road, and I had forgotten about the driver's presence until we were well on our way. His voice briefly pulled my attention.

"How are you this evening?" he said.

Drinking and shibari, *on our anniversary*. Jordan was sending a message. I rejected the primal feelings of jealousy slicing through me. I had orchestrated their union, while falling for the simplest trap; believing that an unassuming little girl was incapable of bringing our house down. But how could I have seen this coming? Infatuation always came suddenly and unexpectedly. Now Jasmin was threatening our entire existence. Jordan's mental balance. Our relationship. And worst of all — J&A.

"We're here," said the driver.

My eyelids flickered, and I saw the red 'Aschinger' neon sign outside, before looking at the driver through the rearview. His mouth parted and pupils expanded when he saw me. I snapped the door open, slamming it behind me. I heard only the clack of my stilettos before a grey trench coat appeared in front of me.

"Ana," said Tim. "Babe."

I looked up and saw his concerned eyes.

"Where are they?" I said.

"Basement."

I pushed by him and entered, moving through the bar with rapid steps. The viewing booths were downstairs. I descended quickly and stopped at the base. The sudden stillness put my inner state into sharp contrast. My skin was clammy all over, and my chest felt tight. My breath was like a winter breeze.

There were four booths with large windows that looked onto the underground dungeon. The entrance to each one was covered top to bottom in a black velvet curtain. I sauntered by the first booth, hearing whispers and muted laughter. I pushed the curtain aside and peeked in. I found a couple seated side by side, the woman's head resting on her man's shoulder as they watched on silently.

My jaw then clamped tight and my blood became ice when I saw them through the window. Jasmin was suspended in the middle of the room like a trophy, her legs stretched like a ballerina preparing for a grand jeté. Her arms were tangled together by a straightjacket of rope, her eyes mesmerised by her captor. *My man.* His eyes reflected what was now in his heart, and it was no longer me. None of the girls over the years had even gotten close. He had captivated them while maintaining total control. Now, Jasmin was his captive, but she was the one holding the power. She had achieved what no other woman could; other than Arabella and Caroline. And me.

I wiped my cheeks and found tears, coming in waves like the water crashing on the beach where Jordan met with his betrayal by Caroline. He had felt able to share that story only once with me, and his eyes at the time revealed a sorrow I had never seen in him, before or after. Its depth unsettled me. That sorrow was now mine.

The ice seeped from my blood. It crossed my limbs and into my fingers and toes, unrelenting in its march. When it reached my heart, the tears stopped. The tunnel around me faded. Jordan sensually stroked Jasmin's cheek with the back of his hand and met her lips with his. He was utterly immersed, oblivious to the world.

I moved to the next booth, and found a young guy in a suit on the stool inside, intently watching Jordan and Jasmin's show. He had brown skin, a shaved head, and a sturdy-looking body. Perfectly groomed, and a decent enough pair of shoes. After a moment he sensed my presence and turned around. I sharpened my gaze and smiled while biting my lip. The guy was as sharp as his suit. He rose to his feet and faced me. I stepped inside the booth and he met me halfway, taking me into his embrace and kissing me passionately. I felt for his cock and found a rock. No surprises there. The kid was good to go. I unbuttoned him and took it out. Stroked it a few times while he sucked on my tongue. Then I handed him a condom and walked ahead of him. Placed my hands against the glass to get a front row view and pushed my ass out. Jordan had placed his hand between Jasmin's legs, and she bent her head up to receive him. A hand reached around from the back and unbuttoned me. My trousers came down with a single, sharp snap. An arm reached around and two fingers entered my pussy, rubbing it to get it wet. My thong was pushed to the side, and the guy's dick entered me. I maintained my attention on Jordan and Jasmin. The thrusting from behind sped up, but my focus never wavered. The guy fucked me like a rabid dog, with more power than I had anticipated, my body rocking back and forth. Jordan stroked Jasmin's hair, taking a strand of it between his fingers. He cupped her face as the guy's fucking from behind me intensified. Jordan rubbed his finger gently over Jasmin's lips. Meanwhile, the guy behind me finished and fell onto my back, out of breath. He had not gotten close to breaking me open. Not even a crack. All I saw was red, the ice inside me now frozen stiff by Jordan's betrayal, as he continued to stroke Jasmin's face in a way he had never touched mine.

JASMIN

Jordan caressed my face in a way I had never before experienced. I felt like an angel above the clouds being titillated by the devil. The only thing keeping me from plunging into the fire was a simple 'yes.' A willingness to give Jordan dominance over me. My trust was in the palm of his hand. He had only to turn his wrist, and I would be incinerated.

I trusted him. I did. But there was always the chance that he could flip. That the darkness I could so clearly see in him would take over. Even for a split second, it would be enough to leave me broken and abused.

And that was the reason I had never been so turned on in my life.

I was suspended in four places, which distributed the pressure evenly along my shoulders and hips. My every cell was at his behest, ready to receive whatever pleasure or pain he deemed fit. He had a feather in his hand, and ran it over my arm, my stomach, my pelvis, my... *Oh.* A shudder shot out of my pussy and spread to the rest of me. He flicked the feather up and down, causing ripple after ripple to pulse through me.

My outer senses dominated my perception like Jordan's presence. The heat of the light, the speed and pressure of the pulse beneath my skin, the sound of Jordan's trousers rubbing against his leg as he stalked me with the feather. His breath was like a desert breeze running over my cheek. His pupils were like stars shining down on me from the night sky. I smiled, and his eyes became supernovas. He had the gift of life, and I had him where I always hoped. I wanted him to untie me now. To embrace me with his powerful arms. For us to melt into each other like last night.

But that was not the agreement. We had come to this basement for a reason, and I was not going to lose my chance.

"This was how I pictured you when I first saw you," said Jordan. "Like a little bunny in a trap."

"That's interesting," I said. "I pictured you like this as well."

I stopped there, looking through his eyes to further expose him. He held my stare and waited.

"A boy who doesn't know how to take care of his pet," I said. "Doesn't give her what she needs."

Jordan pulled his lips to the side and chuckled. Shook his head.

"Jasmin, Jasmin," he said, carefully placing the feather back on the cloth and picking up the flat wooden spoon.

The snap on my behind came quickly, and the rope cut into me when I jumped from the pain, my pulse speeding up even more.

"I'm sorry, daddy," I said. "I didn't mean to upset you."

Another snap came, and I winced. That one hurt.

"I'll tell you when you're sorry," he said.

"You're right, daddy," I said, the excitement taking me over. "I'm not sorry."

This time I screamed out, struck by a pain worse than a thousand wasp stings.

"Fuck!" I yelled, breathing heavily while squeezing my eyes shut.

I trembled to release the adrenaline. My stubbornness was going to get me badly hurt. Jordan stared me down for a long time with absolute calmness. There was no reading him. He turned and walked out of the basement with even steps. I remained there with my razor-sharp senses and intoxicating lust, craving him like water and oxygen. Next time I was not going to yell out. I was not giving him the satisfaction.

The pressure in my hips and knees went beyond aching. I needed some relief. Jordan had the strength to steady me with his pinky finger. All I had to do was ask. Submit to him with the safe word. Yell 'daddy' three times, and it would be over. Eventually, the relief came from within. My body adapted, with the erotic pleasure of surrender making the pressure bearable.

Perfect timing. My resilience had emerged just as Jordan returned — with company. My skin lit up at the sight of the two guys from the boy band, who flanked him from both sides while he marched over. *The final piece.* Their smirks showed they meant business, so Jordan had already debriefed them. They knew what they had come for. Their presence had my pussy throbbing. I bit down on my lip to contain my excitement, but did it too hard and had to stop from the pain. Jordan picked up the magic wand vibrator and turned it on. Approached me from the front, stroked my cheek with the back of his hand, held my gaze, then disappeared behind me. The wand electrified me between my legs. I sucked in some air and invited the hot guy forward with my eyes. With the devil titillating me from behind, his willing assistant took me into his arms, answering my prayer and steadying me. The surrender became everything, above all because I did not need to ask. *My hero.* The hot guy brought his head down, still holding me in his embrace, and met my lips. His mouth movements were gentle and considerate, as though my vulnerable position demanded the holiest of touches.

The wand had lulled me in, like a frog in boiling water, and now it was almost too late. I seized up all over. I was close to climaxing when Jordan suddenly pulled it back with impeccable timing. He would never give the honour to a machine. That was what made him Jordan Rambone. I could at least trust him with that.

"Right, boys," said Jordan. "You know what the lady wants. I'd give you my condoms, but they're too big for you."

The other band boy replaced the hot guy and took out a condom. He disappeared behind me while Jordan came to my front. He stared questioningly into my eyes. I nodded, and he gave the backing vocalist the signal. The foreign cock entered me, thrilling me while I continued to hold Jordan's stare. Jordan anchored me, stroking my cheek lovingly while the final step in my ultimate fantasy came to life. The pace of the guy's fucking was as rhythmic and constant as the wand. It was too much, but I had no desire to tell them to stop. Berlin's most wanted man was serving my needs, along with two gorgeous guys, and I had no hope of containing my turn on. It sucked me into a surreal state of mind. Jordan's face gradually faded, and only his ocean-grey eyes remained. Then they too burnt out, becoming plumes of smoke dissipating. The fucking from behind flooded me with overabundant pleasure, while Jordan's breath over my face put me at ease and allowed the pleasure to roam comfortably through me.

While being taken from behind, Jordan and the hot guy surrounded me suddenly, their hands running over my entire body while taking turns steadying me. They left no place unexplored, their tongues and fingers free to roam where they pleased. Up my thighs. Across my back and over my breasts. A deluge of masculine power inundated me in the fullest, the most potent form I had ever known or could imagine. It broke me open, the overwhelm of pleasure pouring out of me.

A lifetime. For a whole lifetime I had craved it. Now I was being torn to shreds under its immensity. I trembled all over, groaning, wailing with ecstacy. Jordan took out a condom. He was the finale. The alpha and the omega. What I had been thirsting for the entire evening. Without him inside me, it would all be for nothing. As he returned, the band boy pulled out of me, leaving me gasping in ecstasy. The two boys then parted to the side like loyal servants to the king. Jordan stood looking down at me. My heart ached from the pressure of wanting him. The anticipation was so strong I grew furious. *Take me, damn you! Take me now!*

I closed my eyes, gushing with expectation. The fog of silence descended. I heard only the surrounding breathing of my three captors, along with... Clacking.

Clack. Clack. I knew what I was hearing, but I had to be imagining it? Clack. Clack. Stilettos? I opened my eyes and saw Jordan, only it was not really him. His usually laser-focussed eyes were rippling, staring doubtfully at the floor. I witnessed his proud posture slump slowly in real time. His ever steady lips were turned into a frown. Behind him was his fierce, unforgiving queen. Her determined face said it all, and struck a ferocious fear into me. She had come to reclaim her man.

With two more clacks of her stilettos, she came over to Jordan's side with her eyes directed at me. Jordan sighed, his shoulder and frown dropping further. Ana turned her neck towards him.

"Hello, darling," she said.

Jordan stayed frozen.

"You two, out," she said to the boys.

They did as she told them. I barely blamed them. The look of her gave me goosebumps, dropping the temperature of the room a few degrees. Ana waited until the boys left, then clacked over to me, circling to my side. She placed a hand on my shoulder and swung me backwards. As I went back and forth, her glassy stare was there to meet me each time.

"Beautiful," she said. "I can see now why he loves you."

"Stop it, Ana," I said, growing nauseous from motion sickness.

"Leave her," said Jordan, taking a step forward.

"So you've caught her, my love," said Ana, reaching out and stopping me. "And she's caught you. What now?"

Jordan said nothing. What was wrong with him? Why was he being so... passive?

"You leave J&A?" said Ana. "What then? You meet her parents? Get married?"

No answer.

"Live happily ever after?"

"It's just some fun," he said unconvincingly.

Fun? The word caused my stomach to violently twist a hundred-and-eighty degrees. That was all I was to him?

"Fun!" hissed Ana. "It's our anniversary!"

I flinched from the force of her fury. The red lighting in the room almost turned black. Jordan sighed, and wrinkles appeared around his eyes.

"I know," he said.

"So why are you doing this? Are you trying to punish me? After all that I did for you! Without me you wouldn't be standing here."

I watched the surreal scene unfolding before me like I was hanging tied up inside a cinema. I barely recognized Jordan the man. He had completely transformed into the little boy I caught a glimpse of at Äden.

"And you're pulling out of our biggest ever event," she continued. "Think about that. Everything you've built, tossed aside. Just like that. Your reputation. Gone. Then what?"

"Jordan," I said, hearing my heartbeat throbbing in my ears. "Let me down. Please."

"You haven't thought this through, have you Jordan?" said Ana, the power of her voice drowning mine out. "When the glow fades, and the honeymoon ends, she'll want children."

I was snatched back suddenly to that moment at La Secreta with the little boy. Ana pierced into Jordan with her stare, and his eyes fell to the floor. My rope dug deeper, while a heavy sadness washed over me.

"Out," said Ana with a snap of her finger.

Jordan hesitated, looking at me first. The doubt in his eyes was palpable. I felt terribly exposed and alone, sensing him retreating. The thought of him leaving me like this tossed open the gates of hell. I shook my head, begging him not to go. His affection for me flickered, fighting to remain alight. It instilled in me a ray of hope. He was confused, but he knew the right thing to do. He was almost at the point of coming towards me. I could sense it, from his heart to mine.

Then the flickers died, and my heart fell out of my chest. He marched away.

"Jordan," I whispered, the pain of my abandonment closing off my throat.

A ray of intoxicated power shot out of Ana's eyes as she smirked, bathing in her success, before she turned and followed him. My strength left me, and the rope dug deeper than ever. Terrified and alone, I went hurtling into an infinite pit of despair from which I had no escape, and where safe words meant nothing.

"Jordan!!" I yelled.

With him gone I dissociated, and left the room also, the gut-wrenching pain too much to handle. I left my body, and found myself elsewhere entirely. In the backyard of a big white house. There was an outdoor table with places set for four. A colourful salad. A sliced baguette. Three wine glasses. A jug of orange juice.

A young girl ran in circles on the grass, chased by her mother and father while giggling and screaming. The father pretended to be a monster while the mother played protector, encouraging the girl to run away. The mother stood defiantly in the way of the playful father, who grabbed her and nuzzled into her neck while growling. The young girl screamed and ran towards them, grappling the father before the three of them collapsed to the grass in fits of laughter. The father of the girl, I realised, was the Dutchman. He pulled his head out of the game and called me over as though he were expecting me.

"Jasmin," he said with his all-powerful, sweet smile, standing up and approaching me.

"Hi," I said, rubbing my wrist, my chin lowered.

"Darling, this is Jasmin," he said to his wife, who had come up beside him and wrapped her arm around his waist.

The wife said nothing, only stared into my eyes. Her pupils glowed green for a second, then returned to their usual brown. His daughter waved at me from a distance, wearing a cute orange dress like the one I had as a child.

"Would you like a glass of wine?" said the wife.

"Sure," I said, happy to have a minute alone with the Dutchman. The wife nodded and disappeared inside the house.

"Do you want to sit down?" said the Dutchman, directing me towards the table.

"Can't I sit on your lap?" I said, expecting him to say yes.

"Aren't you too big for that?" he replied. "You're not a child anymore."

"Why don't you sit next to me?" said the wife, having magically returned and found a seat on the other side of the table.

Two glasses were already filled with chilled white wine. *How did she do that?* I looked down embarrassed at the ground while I walked around the table and joined the Dutchman's wife. She looked regal, seated perfectly upright with her shiny, healthy brown hair tied into a bun and her hands carefully placed on her lap. Her white jumpsuit looked classy and expensive, as did her diamond wedding ring.

"I recognise your voice," I said when it dawned on me that the Dutchman's wife was *her*.

"I would expect so," she said with a slow, controlled nod. "I'm glad you've been able to hear me recently."

"What are you doing here?" I said.

"Giving my gifts, of course," she said.

"Why here?" I said.

"Because here they are needed."

"Why him?"

"Because his intentions are pure."

"Pure?" I said.

"This man is a loving father and husband, and a passionate lover. He sacrifices for his family, and so he is worthy of me."

"A man needs to be worthy?" I said.

She shook her head.

"It's not a question of worth, but of authenticity, and the willingness to protect its purity."

"Will you help me find the right man?" I said.

The Dutchman's wife chuckled heartily with her deep, calm voice.

"You don't *find* the right man," she said. "That's not what this is about."

"What do you mean?" I said, irritated and confused by her words. "Of course you *find* the right man. How else would you do it?"

"Move bravely into your own journey first," said the Dutchman's wife. "When you are ready, then the right man will meet you, but only if you are both authentic. Then I'll be there. To support you both through challenging times."

"But I need you now," I said, my eyes welling up as the dungeon slowly came back into focus, and I felt the pressure of the rope again.

"Can I sit on your lap?" asked the daughter, stealing my attention from the side.

I had no idea what authenticity looked like, but this girl seemed as close to it as anyone.

"Sure you can," I said, a tear falling down my cheek.

The little girl smiled and revealed a missing tooth, the same one I lost as a child when I tripped and hit my face. She reached out, and I lifted her by her armpits. As soon as she touched my lap, she turned into a bright golden light and entered my body. Tingles spread through me. We united in fullness and magnificence, just in time for the bottomless hurt in my chest to come roaring back as I returned to the dungeon.

My love life flashed by at light speed. It left me with a sudden realisation; no man had ever shown up for me. Nobody. Not the way *she* knew he should. As I regained my senses, through the haze came a fraught, concerned-looking face.

"Kaspar?" I wept.

15

HER ASCENDING

JASMIN

I should have known. It was there all along like a landmine, waiting for me to step on it. Jordan's darkness had exploded in my face. I looked around with blurry vision, stunned by the aftershocks.

"I'll get you down, ok?" said Kaspar.

I had nothing left. My head dropped while Kaspar gently undid my hands. My left arm came loose, then my right. I was barely able to move my stiff shoulders. I could only roll my arms in tiny circles for relief. It took Kaspar a moment, but he seemed to work out the rope situation. I descended gradually onto the cold concrete before he rolled me to the side and freed my legs. The pain in my knees was other-wordly. Kaspar guided me onto my back and got to work removing the rope from the rest of my body. It was an excruciating process for me, painstaking for Kaspar. I was too exhausted and distraught to sit up. Kaspar was forced to carefully guide me up and down and side to side while he pulled out the bound rope one revolution at a time.

The final strand finally came off. I lay there, open and raw, my body and my being agonisingly naked to his sight. Nobody had seen me so vulnerable. Not my mother. Not Thomas. Nor Michaela. Kaspar took off his black t-shirt and used it to cover my midsection. The shock began to wear off, and it all came to the surface. *Her* fury unleashed itself, manifesting in a horrifying scream which must have shaken the viewing booth windows. Kaspar's head moved back reflexively from the shock. Her shriek was like thunder. The rain came immediately after. I sobbed so hard my ribs hurt.

I collapsed onto my side while Kaspar reassured me with a hand between my shoulders, saying nothing but doing plenty with his calm, masculine presence. I pushed my face into the concrete and wailed while tumbling down a dark, fathomless hole. I called on her help. She sent me an army. A group of guardian angels appeared and accepted my grief into their keeping.

The survival of my soul had been forced into a coin flip. It was on its edge as I tumbled into the place where life and death met, where I could lose my sanity and be broken forever. The life in me began to drain. The darkness came down, and a sinister pressure tightened around me. I was hurtling into the abyss, certain I would never come out. A sound escaped me which I had never heard. The cry of someone else. A new woman, her voice deeper and fuller than mine.

I had fallen too far into my internal chaos. The army of angels would not be enough. I needed something she could not give me. *Him.* I reached my hand out. Kaspar came over and leaned his body over me, gripping me tightly, diving behind me into the pit while I neared the bottom. His energy proved formidable, and before long I sensed it surrounding me. Containing me. Grounding me. The end approached at warp speed.

I sucked in a vitalising shot of air, coming to my senses, and my body returning to me. The pain and confusion left me, and my skin tickled blissfully all over. I felt the last tears drip onto my naked legs, the air blowing between the hairs on my neck. I opened my eyes, and I saw Kaspar's sharp stare and warm smile of relief.

"Hey," he said.

My breathing returned to a restful pace.

"Hi," I said wearily.

I pushed my hands into the floor. Conjured the strength to hold myself up. We sat in silence while Kaspar allowed me to return in my own time. I rubbed my face and looked around to get my bearings. The place was a cold, ugly concrete prison. There was nothing sexy about it. I had sunk low indeed.

Kaspar helped me fetch my clothes before I got dressed again. We climbed the stairs and emerged back into the bar. The movement helped lift my spirits slightly, and we found a sofa in the back, away from everyone. I spotted a bundle of rope on our table, which caused my pulse to speed up. As the panic rose in me, I was forced to look away. Kaspar noticed and stood immediately, snatching the rope up and marching inside before coming back without it. His decisive gesture had an immediate soothing effect. Tingles of gratitude pulsed through me, and I was able to breathe deep into my body again.

"How did you know I was here?" I said to Kaspar.

"Tim texted me," he said.

I wiped my face and sighed. Ana's deathly stare was etched in my memory.

"It was so strange to see Jordan like that," I said. "He just fell apart when Ana turned up."

"There's a lot you don't know," said Kaspar.

He told me everything. Jordan's depression, where he had tried to take his life. Ana turned up just in time and nursed him to health. Lured him back into the scene and supported him as he reclaimed the throne. The obligation he felt towards her for saving him. The uneasy balance that had stood between them since. The string of young men Ana had enticed into the scene through her sex therapy practice. I had almost tipped her whole empire over.

"Why does she do all of this?" I said.

"Power," said Kaspar. "It's not complicated. Growing J&A means everything to her. She's relentless. Once she breaks a new guy in, she's off to find the next one. Thomas is her new obsession."

"I knew it," I hissed. "Why doesn't she just have children of her own and be done with it?"

"Ana doesn't play housewife," said Kaspar. "Her home is J&A. She always says how we're all her children."

"So if Thomas is her new obsession, what does she want with him?" I said.

"You don't want to know," said Kaspar.

"I do want to know," I said irritably. "Tell me."

Kaspar sighed his reluctance.

"I'm pretty sure Ana planned the whole thing," he said. "I'm guessing Jordan was supposed to distract you while she recruited Thomas for J&A. She tries that kind of thing all the time, and Jordan hates it. Now Lars and Ana want to go global. They're introducing themed parties and weird sex shows."

"How does Jordan feel about it?" I said.

"I know Jordan. As arrogant as he is, the guy has morals. The theme this weekend is 'young lovers.' They've brought in a girl for Thomas to perform with. He's apparently supposed to 'steal her innocence.'"

I scrunched my face in disbelief.

"And you didn't think to tell me this earlier?"

"I'm sorry. It's sick, I know. But Ana can be a scary woman."

"That's no excuse," I said, cutting into Kaspar with a red-hot stare.

"I know," he said. "I'm sorry." He sighed and frowned. Pondered for a moment. "Ana's clever," he continued. "She gets inside your head, finds your buttons. Makes you feel amazing. It's not an excuse, but it's the truth. I liked having my pick of people to sleep with. And she knew it."

The reality had finally dawned on me. Thomas and I had been lured into a world where one woman pulled the strings. Her puppets were happy to do her bidding. They relinquished healthy love and connection for the promise of abundant sex and ecstasy. The whole thing was insane to even think about. I was barely in any shape to stand on my own legs, let alone deal with it all. The way I was feeling, there was only one place I wanted to be. I longed to be held and taken care of, and to have someone make all of this craziness go away.

"I want to go home," I said, thinking of my mother.

"I would take you there if I could," said Kaspar. "What time is your flight?"

"In the evening."

"Ok. Do you need help with anything?"

I shook my head.

"I just want to be alone."

"I understand," he said, pausing and smiling softly while looking at me. "I'll order you a taxi."

He helped me up and walked me outside. The taxi came soon after. We hugged, and once again I felt the pull to melt into his fit body. Again he let me go at the right time, and opened the back door.

"Call me if you need anything," he said.

"Thanks, Kaspar," I said wearily.

Soon I was back at Äden. I went up the elevator and cautiously entered the room, praying that Thomas was not there. It was dark and haunted inside. His stuff was gone. I collapsed relieved onto the bed face first, and shut my eyes. Dug out a little hole in the black and hid in it. Shut myself in and hoped I would never have to come out. The tears came again soon after, as the full weight of Jordan's betrayal hit, along with the absence of Thomas. I felt so alone it hurt. The sobbing took me with it, and only released me when I was too exhausted to cry anymore. With the tiny ounce of energy I had left, I set my alarm for the flight before drifting to sleep.

Having baggage was so annoying. I carried my luggage up the stairs then dragged it behind me through the airport on its two wheels. I checked in at the counter and got through security without fuss. Marched through duty-free, barely noticing the surrounding products on display. I fetched a takeaway coffee and finally found a seat at my boarding gate, ready to fly home to London.

I yawned, my eyes heavy from the lack of sleep. I tried to forget the past and focus on the future instead. Getting cosy all weekend at my parent's place. Monday night back in Amsterdam at Michaela's. Catching up for dinner after work, filling her in on the details of my insane week. And after that? I had no idea. I tried to find a comfortable position in my metal chair, to shake off the unsettling feeling I was carrying. I wanted to be ready for whatever came. But all I could see was Jordan's ocean-grey eyes. I popped open Michaela's chat window and read her last message again:

Can't wait to you see you, my beautiful girl xx

I was going home properly single. Michaela's and my dream of having our husbands together for dinner felt planets away. The four of us chatting and laughing for hours over wine. I was never going to get that. I barely felt I deserved it. Jordan had made me cynical. He had snatched the hope out of me. I was never going to be free of the past. To top it off, he was going to haunt my dreams for months, if not years.

I tried to draw some more comfort from Michaela's text. It barely made a dent. The sadness washed over me like autumn rain. The week in Berlin had left something foreign in me. A tug. An incomplete thread. A switch I could not turn off, linked to a pacemaker in my heart which pumped pain into me with each beat. To top it all off, I missed Thomas. He was my past, Jordan of all people had been my potential future, absurd as it was. The weight of their absence was tearing me apart from both sides, leaving me with only sorrow in the present moment.

My phone began vibrating. I saw the name on my screen, and the pacemaker in my heart stopped suddenly. I held my breath, hesitated, then answered.

"Hello?" I said cautiously.

It was silent on the other end. I could hear his breathing.

"Jordan?" I said.

A long pause. A sniffle.

"Hello?"

"I'm sorry I left you like that," said Jordan with a soft, unfamiliar voice.

The pain of his betrayal shot into me as I was taken back to that moment. I was not ready to face it, let alone accept his apology.

"Where are you?" I said.

"It doesn't matter," he said. "I just wanted you to know."

"Ok," I said. "So what now?"

"Ana's threatening to shut down J&A unless I go to Lars' party tomorrow."

"So let her," I said.

"It's not that simple."

"Why?"

The line went quiet for a time.

"I feel so stuck," he said.

"Why do you feel stuck, Jordan?" I said.

"You don't get it."

"I do get it. You're not like Ana and Lars. You're different. You said it yourself — I see you. And this is what I see. A man who wants love. A man who wants to be happy. You don't need J&A for that."

Jordan sniffed.

"You don't get it," he repeated with a sob. "I'm broken. I'm never getting those things."

"Jordan, you're not broken," I said, getting a look from a guy seated across from me reading his book. "There's a way through this."

"No, there isn't," he said.

"Jordan."

"I'm sorry," he sobbed. "I'm so sorry I hurt you."

The call ended. I pulled the phone away from my face, paused in shock, then called back immediately. No answer. I texted him:

Call me.

For ten minutes no reply came while I sat there anxiously tapping my foot on the floor. The pacemaker whizzed back on at triple its usual rate. From the ashes of my dead hope I felt a sudden spark, before my flame lit up again. Who was I kidding? Jordan had hurt me irreparably, but it was never his intention. The agonised way he looked at me in the dungeon at Aschinger showed his true feelings. He cared for me, even with his wounded heart. What we had this week was still young, but it was real, and it was powerful. If I could somehow free him from Ana, there might be a chance to turn it into something more.

My ears pounded and my vision grew cloudy as Ana came into my crosshairs. She had manipulated and played games with my relationship. She had humiliated me in the cruellest way, ruining my ultimate fantasy in the process. Was I supposed to take that lying down? I recalled the smug, satisfied look she gave me at Aschinger, as I lay tied up, helpless and utterly abandoned. There was not even an ounce of feeling in them. Her sick games had to end. First Jordan, now — *Shit.* In my pain and sorrow, I had forgotten about Thomas. He was now in Ana's cunning grip, in a party scene littered with drugs. Without my intervention, he would spiral down that same hole and end up back in the hospital, all because *I* invited him here. That would be on me. I had to somehow pull Thomas and Jordan out of Ana's web once and for all. If her empire fell with Jordan, then so be it. It was the least she deserved.

I thought hard. To break Ana's spell, I had to confront her on her level. That meant going to the party. Logistics. Was I really doing this? Could I just walk out of the airport after having checked in? Probably. But how to explain to my parents that I was cancelling my trip home? I brushed my guilt aside. I would find a way. I had no choice. I looked at my phone and found a text from Michaela:

Have you boarded yet?
I texted back:
Nope. Not flying out. I have some unfinished business here.
Her reply came quickly:
Are. You. Kidding. Me?? Sure about this?
Yep:) I wrote.
It took a good minute for her reply to come:
Oh, Jazzy Jaz. What are we going to do with you? Ok my love. Good luck x

I closed my messaging app. Dialled the number of the only person I trusted to help me. There was an answer after two rings.

"Hello?" he said with a surprised tone.

"Hey Kaspar," I said. "Are you going to the party tomorrow?"

"After what Ana did to you?" he said. "No, I'm not. She's lost the plot with Lars in the picture. This whole thing is getting too fucked up."

"You're right," I said. "That's why I need to go. And I need you by my side."

"Why do you want to go?"

I fell quiet. After a moment, Kaspar sighed.

"Oh, right. Jordan. When will you stop chasing his tail, Jasmin?"

"I'm not," I said unconvincingly. "Look, will you help me?"

He exhaled loudly and went quiet.

"I can go by myself then," I said reluctantly.

"No," he pushed back. "I'll come. But not because I agree with it."

My body melted with relief.

"Thank you," I said.

"Just one problem," said Kaspar. "There's no way Ana's letting you in."

Kaspar was right. But I had already thought of that. There was one womaniser stupid enough to get me into the party without Ana knowing, just for a chance to get in my pants.

"Do you have Lars' number?" I said.

16
DIRTY THIRTY

JASMIN

Our taxi cut through the dense fog which blanketed the Brandenburg countryside. You could barely see a few metres ahead, but we sped towards Villa Salace regardless, our driver focussed on the road.

Even with the plush leather absorbing the tension in my body, my leg continued to tremble anxiously. I checked my phone for a message from Jordan for the fiftieth time. He had not responded to any of my texts. I held out an insane hope that he would find the sense to break free of Ana's spell. I wanted to forget about him. To pretend like I had never met him. But just like with my leg, I had no control over my feelings. He had marked me, for better or worse.

A hand touched my shoulder.

"You ok?" said Kaspar. "Your leg's shaking."

I took in his reflection in the window before turning to face him. I nodded. He deserved to hear something overdue.

"I'm sorry," I said.

"For what?"

"The way I treated you."

"What do you mean?" he said.

"I only went out with you to Heidegger's Katze because I was trying to get to Jordan."

Kaspar's face softened into a humbled smile.

"I wasn't much better," he said, before he momentarily shrugged and looked away. "My mind was on having sex with you again."

"If that's all you wanted, then why did you come to Aschinger?" I said.

Kaspar started picking at this lower lip.

"Because after that I realised it was about more than sex," he said. "It started when I first saw you at the J&A party. I told Tim that you didn't belong there."

"What does that mean?" I said.

"At the time I wasn't sure. There was just something. I saw it for the first time on our walk."

I furrowed my eyebrows, wondering what he meant.

"When you went with Jordan instead of me, I was so angry," Kaspar continued bitterly. "But it helped me see that I had the wrong intentions. I was glad that you didn't go home with me. It forced me to look at myself differently."

"How differently?" I said.

"I asked myself what I wanted besides just fucking," he said. "Then I found out Ana was going to Aschinger, and I became worried about you."

His words gave me a pleasant jolt.

"You wanted to help me?" I said.

"I did, and it felt so natural. Being in the kink scene makes you selfish. It's all about your desires and what *you* want. Which is great. To a point. The problem is that it makes you see people as objects. But you were something else. Nobody could figure you out. What I saw in you, I wanted to do whatever I could to help you find it. I wanted you to see what I saw. You're a special woman, Jasmin. Maybe that sounds weird, but that's how I feel."

My entire body lit up, radiating my appreciation. Kaspar's face then came into focus, and it had never looked so beautiful. It was like staring at a full moon on a clear night. He stayed with me in that space, reflecting all he saw and felt in me, before lowering his head and frowning, waning in his magnificence. I had to think about his sudden appearance in the dungeon. Having seen all that he saw in me, and then seeing me surrender all of that to Jordan. Guilt washed over me.

Every action had a ripple effect. I witnessed the result of mine in his eyes, two windows which revealed the wound he was carrying from his experience of knowing me. There was something else I had been too blind to see. The way Kaspar's gaze tracked my movements at the bar, the witty and polite way he texted with me, the vulnerability he showed during our spontaneous date. Behind the facade was a human being, caught up in the glitz and depravity of J&A. It was all innocent fun until a person's true feelings revealed themselves.

I allowed my emotions to guide me forward, and rested my head on his shoulder. I had no concept of what Kaspar and I were. That was beside the point. What we shared in that moment was real. It simply *was*. And it taught me infinitely more than any hours-long argument with Thomas ever could.

I lifted my head off Kaspar and straightened up. Our taxi had slowed right down, and was winding around a private road leading towards the fog-shrouded Villa Salace. The lush, manicured surrounding grass stretched out into the distance, stopping at the edge of a barely-visible forest. Around the side was a lake with a patio for outdoor events.

We approached the white mansion, which had an immediate impact, both with its imposing size and sheer elegance. Four Roman columns stood at the entrance, with an unearthly dome protruding from the middle. The countless windows covering the facade revealed the abundance of rooms within the mansion, where private, uninterrupted encounters might take place.

Our taxi came to a stop on the cobbled front square. Kaspar and I got out with our bags and took a moment to absorb the sight. Then Kaspar invited me to walk ahead of him. A tuxedoed woman met us at the front door, her brown hair tied slick into a bun, her posture and expression an imposing display of professionalism. Flanking her were two stone-faced bodyguards in black suits, and behind her were a group of ushers leading the party participants inside.

"Good evening," she said with a thick French accent and cold expression. "May I have madame's name?"

"Jasmin Johnson," I said, gifting her a warm smile.

She typed my name into her tablet.

"Ms. Johnson," she said, looking up from the screen. "You're in the VIP section with Mr. Lecker tonight."

The hairs on my arms and head stood suddenly at the disgusting thought of sitting next to Lars, but I had to play the game to get to Jordan.

"Thanks," I said.

"You're most welcome," said the woman, breaking her impeccable demeanour to give me her surface-level parting smile. It made my hairs stand even higher.

I stepped forward while Kaspar checked in after me. We were ushered through the front entrance and into the lobby. The mind-boggling splendour of it gave me head spins and sucked the breath from me. Every inch of all three stories was ornated in gold. Each floor was propped up by Roman columns also adorned in gold at the top. Two long staircases curved down from the top-floor balcony, with the golden railings intricately decorated in circular vines as though taken straight from the Garden of Eden. The floor was marble, the stairs were covered in thick, gorgeously decorated burgundy carpets. Gold-plated sofas and more lush carpet were carefully spaced out. A gold and white chandelier as big as five people hung from the ceiling. Its decoration aspired to inspire like the Sistine Chapel, and did a damn good job of it. *Impressive.*

"What would you like to drink?" said Kaspar with a sweet, expectant look.

I inhaled deeply and smiled.

"An old fashioned," I said.

"Coming right up," he said, and went off to the bar.

While waiting, I scanned the crowd inside the grand lobby and barely recognised anyone. This was on a different level to the J&A party. These people were wealthy and affluent, dressed for status in their designer suits and cocktail dresses. The age spread was also far wider. Powerful men in their twilight years had shown up. Many of the attendees could have been supermodels or celebrities. Everyone was perfectly groomed and even better behaved. Their movements and smiles were controlled. They owned the space with their presence. I felt none of the buzz and lightness of J&A. Here the air was thick with pomp which told you to stay in your lane. Diversity was all that could brighten the scene. A wide variety of accents struck me as people migrated past holding glasses of champagne, while servers supplied them with canapés. This thing was clearly worldwide, having drawn a crowd from all over. It felt like the prelude to something more, a grand yet gentle way to ease into the big show.

"Hey, Jasmin!" said Mimi, coming up with Kaspar wearing a light-pink evening gown.

"Hi, Mimi," I said as she hugged me, making me mindful that Ana could be around.

Kaspar handed me my drink before taking a sip of his.

"Can you believe this pretentious crap?" said Mimi, looking around bewildered at the scene. "I prefer the old J&A."

"Same," said Kaspar.

"Oh," said Mimi with a sudden hand on my arm. "Do you know what happened to Jordan? Something's off with him. Tim said he saw you with him at Aschinger?"

"No?" I lied with a spike of concern.

"He's not himself," said Mimi. "He arrived earlier all depressed looking, and nobody's seen him since."

I suddenly felt like I had ants in my pants. I sipped on my drink and zoned out from Mimi's chatter with Kaspar, my mind turning over, worrying about Jordan. Then I dropped my almost-finished glass onto a server's tray. *Enough of hors d'oeuvres and small talk.*

"Let's go see the show," I said to Kaspar, who got rid of his drink and offered me his arm.

"See you inside, Mimi," I said.

Kaspar led us through the crowd and into another room with an arched doorway. Another tuxedoed woman met us, and directed us into two of the dozens of changing rooms which lined the area on both sides. I pushed through the thick burgundy curtain and entered the marble-floored space. There was a charming white dressing table, mirror and chair on one side to prepare, and a table and hooks on the other wall to organise my stuff. I got to work, taking almost thirty minutes to put on my battle suit. Finally, I tossed the curtain aside and stepped out, the clacking of my stilettos drumming in my arrival.

The look on Kaspar said it all. He lost control of his facial muscles, while continually blinking to refresh his vision. *Believe it.* His eyes fell down to my feet to pay homage, and then ran up slowly to take me in a bit at a time. From my six-inch black heels, up to my black fishnet leggings, which stopped halfway up my thighs, capped off by black leather straps. His gaze lingered between my legs, where I had set my trap. My tight leather dress cut off just below my ass, revealing my datenight string — the only thing on me not black. Kaspar had something stuck in his throat, the poor guy. He forced his mouth shut again and gulped, somehow finding the courage to move further up. My dress had the sides cut off at the hips, covering only my pelvis and half of my ass. Only a handful of straps through the middle kept my outfit erect. Kaspar revelled at the sight of my tits, which I had held in place with invisible tape. He blinked some more, and his mouth lifted into a smile before he carried on. My lips were painted hot-red, my mascara was extra thick to sharpen my eyes — and to communicate to the world that the doe-eyed young Jasmin was long gone. I had on sophisticated make-up; polished and tasteful. Diamond earrings. My long flowing hair was gone, now tied into a high bun.

A still speechless Kaspar finally locked eyes with me.

"Coming?" I said with lifted eyebrows.

"Aha," he replied with a chuckle of disbelief.

Kaspar was topless, and had on suit trousers and polished black shoes. Poor men, no room to express themselves, I thought, just as he turned around and revealed two cutouts in the back of his trousers which revealed his shapely ass. *Nice.*

We checked in our bags and walked the length of the changing area towards the main event. I had none of the nerves from the J&A party. I was on. Focussed, and beneath that, angry. With Kaspar at my side and *her* fire igniting me further with each step, I crossed the archway into the party.

The sight of it forced us both to a halt.

"My God," said Kaspar.

The room was the most magnificent thing I had ever seen. Archways all around. The level of detail in the wall and ceiling decorations was renaissance-like. Numerous chandeliers hung down and warmly lit the room. A stone fountain protruded from the middle with water gushing into the air. The place was transcendent in its spirit and beauty. When a person crossed through any of its arched entrances, they were humbled into behaving impeccably. It was designed for royalty, where only those whose position was ordained by God could feel worthy of its grace. It was this which made the fuck-fest taking place even further beyond words.

The floor was littered with discarded leather, lace and fabric. The soft classical music playing from the surrounding speakers was barely audible over the groans, moans and screams of the two-hundred-plus crowd, almost all of them engaged in some sexual act. Boundaries of gender, race or personal values meant nothing. Left at the door. Dicks were being devoured with vigorous, up-and-down head movements. Vulvas were hungrily being sucked on. The soulless and mechanical sex on display came in all positions, angles and partner collaborations. Man-on-man. Woman-on-woman. Threesomes. Foursomes. Ten people in a community of fucking. Fucking on tables. Fucking on the carpet. Fucking against the wall. Double-fucking front and back. Furious fucking from behind. Fucking on top. Fucking from the side. Fucking in the air. Finger fucking. Face fucking. Breast fucking. Ass fucking. *Fucking, fucking, fucking. Fuck!!*

The screams and moans haunted all of my senses. The hurricane of sex trembled my foundations, leaving no part of me safe. Only I could not look away. My stomach churned, and my chest split through the middle. My body told me to get the hell out of there and never come back. I stepped forward instead, and meandered my way through the maze of debauchery. People migrated in and out, some opting for the privacy of the mansion rooms, others joining the free-for-all in the great hall. Bodies were sprawled on a mixture of plush, king-sized beds or black leather mattresses. I wandered by expensive sofas, throne chairs and chaise lounges with bodies grinding over their expensive fabrics. Some people made use of the floor. A man was on his knees with his arms and feet rope-tied together tightly behind his back. He looked at me helplessly with his bright, submissive eyes while the shadow of a woman hovered menacingly over him. I continued forward through the steamy collection of body parts while my skin responded to the fog of sheer sexual energy surrounding me. It was beyond conception, so I let go of any need to understand. Insanity was precisely that — inconceivable.

I looked up. The lunacy of the ground floor had kept me from seeing what was above the entire time. On the top-floor balcony was an entourage of men in suits, looking down on the procession. Downstairs was a rapidly moving ocean. Upstairs the energy was sharp and focussed — an all-seeing eye taking it in. In the middle was Lars on an oversized yellow and gold throne chair. Four other men with pot-bellies flanked Lars' sides on their own, smaller chairs. Two of them were bald, all had the smell of shady business.

Two security guards covered the sides. In front of the four men were... I did a double take. There were...

I flinched at the sight.

"What a pig," said Kaspar, reminding me that he had been by my side the entire time.

I moved closer to get a better view. In front of Lars and his friends were five women on all fours, acting as tables for the men's food and drinks. Lars pointed at someone on the ground floor and chuckled while nudging the guy beside him, who nodded approvingly.

There was a marble-floored stage at the base of the balcony steps, with an aristocratic king-sized bed in the middle, centrally placed for some kind of show. Stairs led from the stage directly to where Lars and his entourage were sitting. Kaspar followed me as I passed the centrepiece bed before being approached by four beefy security guards.

"Name?" said one of the men, moving between us and the way up.

"Let her through!" screamed Lars from his seat, wiping his nose.

I came forward, but the security held his palm out at Kaspar.

"Not you," he said with a headshake.

Kaspar stood in his place and looked over at me with uncertainty in his eyes.

"I'll find you," I said.

I climbed the stairs with determination, until I was standing in front of Lars. His eyes tracked me up and down before he nodded repeatedly with a sharp twinkle in his gaze. His light grey suit was sharp, but his face was pale and withered.

"Jasmin, Jasmin," he said magnanimously. "Take a seat."

He nudged the pot-bellied businessman to his right, who immediately stood and disappeared inside a room behind them. Through the door I caught a glimpse of two naked, long-legged women in heels rubbing their hands over a seated man in a suit before the door closed.

I claimed my spot in the now vacant chair and looked down at the woman acting as furniture in front of me. She was wearing a shiny golden bodysuit. Her eyes were directly forward, her expression was focussed yet empty. Lars poured a glass of champagne and returned the bottle to her back, which also had a plate of caviar on it, along with a tiny mirror for his cocaine.

"I don't have riesling," he said. "Not my style."

"I'm fine," I said, taking the bottle off the woman's back and placing it on the floor.

"Suit yourself," said Lars, watching the bottle for a long time. "Ana's not happy with you, by the way. After what you did with Jordan."

"What did I do to him?" I said, giving Lars a hard stare.

He hesitated, before giving me a slanted smile, then sniffing and cracking his neck.

"It doesn't matter," he said. "We're doing fine without him. I've got no pity for the guy. He should have seen you coming."

"Where is he?" I said impatiently. "I want to speak with him."

"It's better if you stay with me," said Lars. "If she sees you with him again, she might just pull your hair out. And mine too when she finds out I let you in."

"Not if I pull hers out first," I said.

Lars measured me up carefully, before he smirked with arousal in his eyes and rubbed my thigh.

"You see," he said. "This is why I like you. You've got the fire, Jasmin. Come. It's time to make good on our deal for letting you in. Let's go to my private room."

"Is that how you treat a lady?" I said.

I left Lars' hand where it was. Stared at it, then made eye contact with him, then stared at it again. The man must have thought I was an idiot. This time *she* made eye contact with him. His reaction was immediate. His head moved back slowly, his hand lifted off my thigh.

"Treat me like a woman first," I said firmly. "Then I might make a man out of you."

"And why would I want to treat you like a woman?" he said.

"Do you want an empty fuck, or do you want to fuck a queen?" I said.

Lars looked to be measuring my question. The mood had shifted. Darkened. I could feel an unbearable heaviness, and I knew Lars could also, the way his face suddenly appeared twenty years older. The lighting had become dimmer, the noise eerily quieter. It was not coming from me, however.

The entire grand hall had suddenly descended into actual darkness. Silence followed. A spotlight came on, and drifted towards an archway in the middle of the great hall with a red carpet running towards the stage. Everyone turned to a woman's silhouette in stilettos. The environment responded immediately and magnetically to her. Numerous people stopped mid-coitus. Others propped themselves up on their arms. A loud whistle broke the tension and stole the attention of every eyeball. The silhouette came out of the light, and Ana stood in her place. She had her hip leaned to the side, holding the crowd in her grasp, before she stepped forward and cat walked towards the stage.

Her long-legged strides were precise and powerful. The showgirl look from the J&A party had been stripped away. Tonight Ana's bright red micro g-string covered the barest minimum. The rest of her tanned, flawless skin refracted the light around the edges of her voluptuous curves. Her jet-black hair was tied into a ponytail which flicked hypnotically from side to side, mirroring her movements. At the first J&A party, Ana was the friendly and hospitable matriarch who created a nurturing space to explore your sexuality. Tonight the lovely hostess had been tossed aside by this shadow queen cutting through the place like a sword.

The lighting then came back on, revealing the entire crowd watching in awe. The sight of Ana unleashed brought back the insecure, subdued Jasmin. I lowered my chin and felt my power retreating inside.

"How does she do that?" said Lars, shaking his head then placing a finger on his left nostril and snorting air. He bent over and started chopping up another line of cocaine with his credit card while gawking at the scene below.

Ana stopped in front of a naked middle-aged man on his chair being massaged by two women. They were no match for her. The man turned his head to Ana and remained transfixed while her hips swayed in the shape of an eight. Ana called him with her index finger. He stood, and she pointed to the floor. He got down and crawled towards her before she pressed his face between her legs and continued her sexual dance. He lifted his hand to grasp her hip, but she slapped it away and marched onto the stage. He followed, first crawling, before getting to his feet. I had noticed his Viagra erection from the beginning, which did not belong on a man his age. It was standing at attention, pointed directly at his mistress.

Mid-walk, Ana snapped her fingers at a fit, spry-looking guy with a buzzcut, and pointed to the stage. She climbed up and stood beside the centrepiece bed, then turned around to find both men at her side. She pushed the young guy to the side, and the older man onto the mattress. Slipped a snug-fitted condom out of her micro string and tossed it at him. Watched him put it on. Forced the other guy to watch while she mounted the erect older man and began fucking him. Her hips glided sensually and athletically back and forth. The man tried to reach up to touch her breast, and she slapped him away again and picked up the speed. Ana's eyes were not on her sex partner. Rather they were taunting the young guy standing by the side of the bed waiting his turn. It never came. Ana's powerful and bewitching fucking emptied the older man within seconds. His torso lifted off the bed while he came, looking like an evil spirit had entered him. Ana lifted her leg and immediately got off him, her exorcism complete. She sauntered by the young guy, stroked his cheek with the back of her hand, then left him behind. The older man was still on his back, gazing in wonder at the ceiling.

The potentials came one by one, and Ana took her pick from the litter. Man after man, emptied in sixty seconds, happily offering their virility to her. Each sacrifice energised her to a higher level than the last. Her fucking was bewitching. Antagonistic. It grew rabid, her firm, curvaceous body aggressively pumping each of her victims dry. Ana's surreal, alternate reality absorbed me fully, as she stared directly at me in challenge while gyrating over one cock after another. Yet I could not look away. Nobody could. The insanity, the absurdity, the enchantment of her show had put the entire party under. When Ana was done, she left a dozen men in her wake, all of them drunk from her poison. Each of them was in a daze by the side of the stage, left seated or kneeling, struggling to find themselves again.

"What a show!" screamed Lars at the top of his lungs, lifting to his feet and clapping feverishly above his head. "Now that's a fucking queen," he added, looking down at me. "What makes you think you're better than her?"

Applause rang out from the crowd, along with laughter and amusement. Lars' taunt caused my face to burn red. Meanwhile, Ana stared directly at me. She held me there for an eternity, making me feel like a little girl. Then she dropped me like I was nothing, walking away through the crowd. It lit a fire under me which compelled me to go after her.

I hesitated, and doubt rolled into me. Ana was at the peak of her power. Could I match her? My body then jolted suddenly, and *she* shot out, bringing a sharp inhale that lit me up from inside. I blinked a few times, and my vision brightened. I kept Ana in my sight, my twenty/twenty sight illuminated by a roaring inner flame. I spotted Kaspar with his arms crossed, appearing unimpressed by the whole thing. Discussions and chatter had broken out. The excitement had an undercurrent of unrest, the crowd wanting their next fix. It left an opening, out of which an idea struck me.

"Just watch," I said to Lars and stood.

I descended the stairs quickly, and placed myself in the middle of the stage with intention. Stood tall and firm, emitting regal energy into the crowd.

"Dim the lights!" screamed Lars from above.

The lighting lowered, and the spotlight came on me. Wild applause broke out, forcing Ana to stop in her tracks and turn around. Her demented stare directed at me showed her fury at my challenge. I matched her energy, remaining firm. The crowd's eyes alternated between Ana and me. They sensed a conflict brewing, and their rapture and applause told me they welcomed this budding rivalry. But this would be no catfight. I was a lioness. And I was going to show Ana the slave master how a woman created a king.

I pointed at Kaspar and called him with a come hither motion and a smile. He chuckled with some hesitation, before he walked over and stood at my side.

"Sure you don't want to do this with Jorda—" he said.

I snatched his hand suddenly and led him with long, sharp steps towards the throne chair at the front of the stage. Invited him to sit, which he gladly did. As soon as his bare ass touched the cushion, a shift occurred. He laid his hands against the armrests, familiarising himself with his new throne. His head lifted, and his features came into focus. The tone of his muscles, the glow of his tan, the hope in his eyes. It was time for the coronation.

Kaspar took in the sway of my hips as I came towards him.

"Keep your hands right there," I said.

He gulped and nodded, and I gave *her* the floor. I stared directly at him with my cat eyes while I ran my hands over my breast and down between my legs. Kaspar bit his lower lip and tilted his head back in arousal, exposing his wide neck. I slowly turned around and bent over, almost touching my toes. Lifted my hand and sucked on my two fingers before reaching behind, sliding my datenight string to the side and entering my wet fingers into my pussy. From the side I had my eyes locked onto Kaspar the entire time. I could feel the tension in him protruding to the edges of the great hall. The lump in his trousers grew harder and bigger, as did the eyes of the crowd. I heard only the juice of my pussy sprawling from my finger action, and the odd wild reaction from the congregation. I slid my fingers out and stood straight. Turned towards Kaspar and wiped my soaking fingers over my tits before licking them clean.

The crowd reacted with uproar. Emboldened by their energy, I took another step towards Kaspar and leaned forward, so that our bodies were almost touching. I lowered myself and brought my lips towards his, stopping just short of them coming together. The energy in our mouths swelled. It was too much. Too beautiful. *Too real.* When the tension between Kaspar and me threatened to explode, I pulled back, lifted myself upright again and circled Kaspar with a sexy strut, allowing him the space to exhale his astonishment. Wolf whistles and drawn out moans from the crowd lifted my strut almost to a waltz. The crowd's frustration was at a tipping point. I had them hanging on my every move, which had me grinning ear to ear.

With Kaspar's hands remaining on the side of the throne as instructed, I invited him to lift and press them towards mine, uniting us by interlacing our fingers. We exchanged knowing smiles, feeling our combined energy flowing through each other. Kaspar slowly guided my hands around his neck, pulling me closer. I lifted my legs one foot at a time onto the sides of his throne to get into a squat. I then grinded my booty against the mountain in his trousers, feeling it get even harder. His cock swollen stiff, I leaned my face in and kissed him passionately. His energy had aligned with mine like a cobra to a snake charmer. We were in harmony. In flow. I released his lips, looked into his bedazzled eyes and winked. He raised his chin, and nodded humbly and proudly, and the crowd went berserk.

Kaspar signalled for me to stand up. I complied, sliding off him. He joined me on his feet and began clapping, encouraging the crowd to raise the roof further. I came over and planted a final kiss on his forehead, and his coronation was complete. We smiled, and laughed, and bathed in the crowd's adulation. I looked over to Ana. Somehow a crack had appeared in her spell, and in the crowd's earlier debaucherous smirks, which had morphed into warm smiles. Their eyes radiated beauty and honest appreciation. Their applause was electrifying, rumbling the floor beneath us.

It caused an enormous fissure through the middle of the room. On one side was Ana the shadow queen, frozen stiff, her only movement being her eyes feverishly scanning the space. On the other side stood Kaspar and I, divine in our mandate, and pure in intention. 'Young lovers' in our own right, shining together in equal harmony, defiant in the face of the all-seeing eye.

The shift in mood forced Lars off of his high horse, as he stomped down the stairs from the balcony, flanked by his security guards.

"You call that a spectacle?!" he yelled, challenging the rebellious crowd. Then he turned to me with fury in his eyes, his head bright-red like a cherry lollipop. "Why the hell didn't you fuck him?" he said with a hiss.

"Because I'm more than that," I said, wrapping my arm around Kaspar's shoulder.

Meanwhile, the crowd stepped up their rebellion.

"Jordan! Jordan! Jordan! Jordan!" they chanted, calling for their king.

The deafening yells went on for minutes while Lars tried unsuccessfully to shoosh the crowd back under control.

Then, there he was, standing on the balcony in front of Lars' throne. My chest seized up, and I stopped breathing. Jordan had stumbled in, wearing black suit pants and an untucked, unbuttoned white shirt. His hair was wet and plastered over his face at the front, and sticking out in all directions at the back. In his hand was a bottle of whiskey. The anguish and shock in his eyes was palpable as he looked down at the women acting as tables, before he gazed out over the scene of his corrupted empire. The noise of the crowd lessened as all eyes went on him.

"What the fuck is wrong with you all!?" he screamed at the top of his lungs.

"Jordan!" yelled Ana, who had stepped forward suddenly into the congregation. "Honey. Don't!"

Silence descended over the great hall. Jordan lifted up each of the women acting as Lars' tables, beckoning them to leave. He then turned his attention to Lars, who looked like an alien ship had arrived on Earth, his eyes transmitting fury and confusion. Silence continued to reign, Jordan holding us all captive for what felt like forever. Then he stepped forward, bent over the railing, and vomited.

The crowd came back to life, voicing their collective shock. Lars signalled to two security guards, who quickly approached Jordan and grasped him by the arms. Jordan moved like water, despite his drunkenness. In a second he had one of the security guards on the floor. The other guard stepped back cautiously, before pouncing on him.

"Where is he, Lars?" yelled Jordan as the two security guards dragged him out. "Huh?! Where's your little CK model?"

Amid the unrest, Lars spoke into the ears of his black-suited chaperone, before the chaperone urgently waved someone in from the side. Just when I thought the whole spectacle had gone beyond absurd, it went a step further. I turned my head, and was almost forced to laugh out loud when I saw them. Thomas approached the stage wearing a white kimono. Whatever Ana had done with him, it worked. My surprise quietened quickly, and I became absorbed by his fluidity, the ease in his proud, elegant posture. Holding his hand was an olive-skinned, long black-haired beauty in a flowing white dress. The guy who could barely piece together a decent five-minute session with me was about to put on a show for a crowd of hundreds.

Nobody knew what to make of the new arrivals. When Thomas saw the curious crowd he stopped, appearing hesitant. The girl let his hand go and made her way onto the stage with light steps. Her dress ran down to her ankles, and it looked like she was floating as she reached the bed and made herself comfortable. Thomas turned and marched back inside a room off to the side, while Lars came beside me.

"Stunning, isn't she?" said Lars to rub it in, seeming relaxed again now that his show could resume.

She was beyond that. I had never seen such immaculate skin, such enthralling eyes.

"The purest of the pure," added Lars, his attention completely on her.

I studied her carefully. *Pure? Not sure about that.*

"Let's go see what's wrong with your boy," said Lars before walking towards the room Thomas had disappeared into.

I hesitated, my mind turning briefly to Jordan, before I was compelled to follow Lars. I stole another glance at Thomas' girl as I passed and felt my blood boil. She was lying on her side, twirling her hair and staring innocently into the distance while waiting for her saviour. *Keep up the act, bitch.*

On the way I spotted a group congregated near the entrance archway. I recognised some of them from Äden and the first J&A event. They were putting some of their clothes back on, appearing to be abandoning the party. The rest of Lars' fickle crowd sat by eagerly awaiting the beginning of the main event, while others resumed the sex-fest with full intensity, seeming to have already forgotten about Jordan. The unnerving groans and moans followed me into the room. There I found Lars, Thomas and their boys club congregated around a stash of drugs big enough to bake a cake with. Lars had one arm over Thomas, another over a jolly-looking guy with dark stubble.

"Gentlemen, Thomas needs some courage juice," said Lars as I approached. "Giacomo. Do the honours."

The guy on Lar's left moved forward, carrying a plastic vial containing a clear liquid. He gave Thomas a heart-melting smile, then grew serious and carefully dosed some of the vial's content into a tiny bottle. Finally, he emptied the liquid into a glass of water and handed it over to Thomas. A destabilising wave of light-headedness washed over me.

"Thomas," I said reflexively, stepping forward from behind the group.

Thomas turned and appeared to be seeing me for the first time. In a way, he was. We had become strangers to each other over this week. His eyes tracked me up and down. Lars came in from the side, and signalled towards the glass in Thomas' hand.

"Drink this, and you'll fuck like a God," he said.

"Thomas, don't," I warned.

Thomas' dazzled expression remained in place for a moment. Then it hardened.

"What," said Thomas. "This?" he asked, holding up the glass. "Or that?" he added, pointing toward the girl waiting for him on the centrepiece bed. "Are we still telling each other what to do, are we?"

His words struck me like a lightning bolt well before I comprehended what he had said. Nausea washed over me, and spun my head backwards. The man in the kimono was right. The reality about my ignorance had been hanging over me for years, and it took those exact words to free it. The full weight of it collapsed right on top of my head.

"Give me an empty glass," said Thomas to Giacomo, who complied, before Thomas poured half of his drink out.

"All of it," cried Lars. "Down the hatch!"

Thomas shook his head disapprovingly at Lars, then sculled what was left of his drink. He had every right. The decision, and the consequences, were his.

"Suit yourself," said Lars. "Pussy," he added, snatching the bottle of drugs from Giacomo.

He squirted a dose far bigger than Thomas' into his own glass and drank it all. Giacomo watched on in horror but was too slow to intervene.

"Oh, fuck," Giacomo mouthed, looking at all his friends, who were fighting to hold back their shocked reactions.

Thomas' mind was elsewhere. He inhaled some more courage into his lungs and began his march towards the stage.

"Wait," I said, putting a hand on his shoulder. "Listen, I don't want to stop you from doing anything. I just want to talk."

"About what, Jasmin?" he said with an impatient sigh.

"She's not as innocent as Lars says. You know that, right?" I said.

"Yeah," said Thomas with a cynical chuckle. "I know. She's an actress. What's your point?"

"Oh," I said. "So you're still going to do it?"

"Jesus, Jaz," said Thomas. "You're unbelievable."

He pushed past me and made his way onto the stage with even steps, then gracefully crawled onto the bed. His partner played her role well, but so did he. Only he was not acting. Not since university had I seen the moment take him like that. His sexual flow was authentic, and people noticed. *I* noticed. The purity of his conviction was enough to capture even his girl's heart. The two lovers unified into a horizontal dance for the ages. He took her in missionary while she dug her nails into his back, then from the side, his face close to her's as she lifted it to the ceiling and moaned. Then he guided her on top of him, their bodies appearing as two organs of a harmonious whole. Pinned on his back, Thomas celebrated and enabled the expression of her feminine wonder with only his eyes and hands.

That woman, gushing with life, was a manifestation of celebration. She could have been me. I clenched my fists and forced my jaw shut, my teeth aching from the pressure. *She could have been me.* The crowd watched on in absolute stillness, mesmerised by the young lovers' show. Thomas' partner was a wonder to behold, free and celestial in her beauty. Her body rolled with the power of mother nature, rising and crashing, expanding and contracting according to some kind of divine plan. *Why not me?*

When the girl's energy began to fade, Thomas rolled her over and began to penetrate her with force. His bare ass moved up and down as he fucked his new-found masculine power into her, him and her both strangers before my eyes. Every passionate thrust inside her dug up more of the radiation waste of our relationship. I resisted it, and lost myself in the exploding hot rage. *Let go*, she told me. I did. With the outer shell worn away, the black sludge of grief spilled out. With it came the same relief I felt during our breakup. Only this time it was permanent.

It had not all been Thomas. It was me too. *Control, control, control.* Like two people in deep water desperately clinging to the other for safety, but only pulling each other under. We forgot that we could just float away and swim, unaided, yet side-by-side. It would have been so easy, so effortless — if only we could have learned to let go. If only *I* could have learned. Instead, I kept my focus solely on Thomas and his faults. It would have only taken one person to break the cycle, and I could have made that choice at any time. We had both grown so much over the last week. I grieved now for a *decade* of lost growth.

A lifetime of resistance melted like ice during the first sun rays of spring. My shoulders relaxed, followed by my back, stomach and legs. I felt my feet for the first time rooted into the floor, the air moving into my lungs and tingling through my blood. A part of me was still in the shadows, so I took a step backwards to feel the rising sun. A stranger's body was there to meet me, and my head smashed onto him, ending with a steely, skull-shattering shock you usually get from hard concrete.

I shook my head and found some focus. Lars' alert, overstimulated eyes were half-closed, his tight, business face was droopy. He was deathly pale, his skin blotched with shades of yellow.

"I've decided," he slurred. "I want to fuck a queen. Let's go to my private suite."

He reached out and snatched me towards him by the hip. I pushed against his chest to break away, but his grip was steel. His legs, on the other hand, were jelly, and he swayed off to the side and sent us collapsing to the floor.

"Ah!" I yelled from the sharp pain of my shoulder hitting the marble rock.

People from all around rushed over while I lay on my side nursing my upper arm.

"Jasmin, are you ok?" said Mimi, now dressed in a black thong.

Mimi helped me onto my feet, and we looked down at the pitiful heap before us. Lars stayed moaning on his back with his eyes closed. Giacomo and his friends soon came over, their eyes showing concern for me and their mouths smiling widely at Lars.

"Ok?" said Giacomo to me.

"Yes, I'm fine," I said. "What did he take?"

"Too much of something," said Giacomo. He kneeled down to turn Lars into a recovery position. "He'll be knocked out for five hours."

"Oh, God," I said, putting a hand over my mouth, trying to hold back my laughter while fighting off the guilt of my amusement. "Is he going to be ok?"

"He should be," said Giacomo. "He's a big guy."

The concerned tension of the group which had assembled around us eased off. Meanwhile, Lars' stiff body kept us on edge, until Mimi broke the ice by finishing her cocktail and placing her glass on Lars' forehead. The group broke out laughing, and each person took turns using Lars as a makeshift table. Whiskey and wine glasses were carefully stacked onto his torso.

"Jesus," I said, stepping forward.

I bent down and carefully removed the glasses and bottles from him. Mimi helped by placing them in a neat collection on the floor. Without another word, I walked away. Thomas was at the bar in the hall of fucking, his kimono resting open over his body, revealing his sweaty torso and penis. His eyes were both dreamy and resolute, his demeanour was calm.

"Still have something to say?" he said.

"Yes," I said as I approached. "That is a great cock."

Thomas smiled with his entire face and shook his head amusedly. I sat next to him, giving him time to adjust to my presence. We took a silent moment to watch Lars being carried away by the security guards.

"Happy Birthday, by the way," said Thomas.

"Thanks," I said, rubbing his shoulder.

We were done. We both knew it. For closure's sake, we got talking while looking out over the sun setting on our relationship. We discussed our first years together, and the painful years that followed. The fights that brought us to the brink, the beautiful times which brought us to the height of ecstasy. We reflected on the week that got us here. I told Thomas he could have fought for me rather than hand me over to Jordan on a plate. He meticulously explained his side, including his awakening at Passion Parade. How in that moment he saw the writing on the wall, and allowed his heart to guide him towards giving me what I wanted. I finally recognised the love behind his act. How difficult it was for him to let me go to Jordan. The excruciating pain he went through this week, as reality came knocking, ripping him to shreds and building him up again into a more mature person. Out of the two of us, he was the first to initiate the letting go process.

"You did an amazing thing," I said. "I'm proud of you."

He nodded graciously.

"You know..." he said, hesitating and measuring his words.

"What?" I said.

"I always wanted the fire in our relationship," he began. "But without the risk of getting burnt. I'm sorry, Jaz. I was a coward. You deserved better."

My heart cracked open, and forgiveness came pouring out like doves. I held my open palms up to him, and he placed his hands over them, pulling me into his embrace. The week had taken it out of me, and my strength was failing me. I felt his fullness and bathed in it. He gladly shared it with me. Sensing when I was full and steady again, he let me go.

"I remember you saying earlier this week that I made you feel inadequate," I said, holding his eye contact. "You are so fucking adequate."

He exhaled slowly and squeezed his eyes shut, and nodded.

We settled into observer mode while the sex wound down and the flow was turned up. Someone put on a slow, dark electronic set with heavy beats and moody harmonies. The lights were dimmed again, and people climbed onto the stage, turning it into a makeshift dance floor. A spontaneous, Berlin-style club party broke out. The balcony upstairs was empty, Lars' entourage having disappeared. In the rubble of Lars' downfall, the music had taken over as the sole higher power. Everyone was equal within the network of energy and vibration on the floor.

Thomas and I watched on, two people swimming side by side in an ocean of bodies grinding and swaying. Over the course of an hour, the dancing became softer, the energy fuller and more vibrant. People cuddled and moved together to the melodies. Mimi, Kaspar, Tim and the girls were there, gladly lost in the flow of the music. April, as always, was a beacon of fire, dancing seductively in the middle with bodies around her, savouring the warmth of her heat. Even the snooty crowd had thrown off their invisible shackles and fallen for the irresistible pull of the music. People of every age, gender, colour and corner of the planet had merged their energies into one and offered it to the godly sound coming from the speaker.

Suddenly I felt Ana in my veins, sensing her watching me from her dark corner. I put a hand on Thomas' shoulder.

"Take care of yourself," I said.

"You too, Jaz."

We shared a final hug and parted ways. I ambled around the makeshift dance floor, searching. I turned my neck suddenly to a candlelit room, where I spotted moving silhouettes. I allowed my instinct to guide me toward it, the hairs on my head lifting as I approached the arched entrance.

It was dimly lit and shadowy inside — a very different kind of darkroom. There were many hiding spots. Cabinets and bookshelves lined the walls, and tall throne chairs and sofas were placed throughout. A large dining table with chairs stood in front of a fireplace. The flicker of candlelight created movement in all corners. With my heart beating in my throat, I worked my way around a collection of sofas and coffee tables with dozens of lit candles. The music coming from outside had invaded the space and made it difficult to hear movement. Then I found Jordan on his ass, his head bowed over his knees, and Ana standing a few metres away from him in a black silk robe.

The boy I had caught a glimpse of at Äden lifted his tear-and-snot-covered face. When he recognised me, his eyes welled up, then closed shut as he lowered his head again and sobbed.

I came to my senses. There was no other way to describe it. Jordan, or at least the idea of Jordan that he had conjured out of pure status and arrogance, had collapsed under the weight of his own pride. He was no king of Berlin, no man above men. He was a wounded boy, hiding where nobody had thought to search.

"Amazing," said Ana. "Look at him. Nobody could break him open, not even me, until you came along. You achieved in a week what I failed to do in years. And then you barged your way into my party, and ruined it with only a lap dance."

"This is all so fucked up," I said, taking in the sight of Jordan's sorry state. "How did we get here, Ana?"

Ana's eyes shook awake and locked onto me, swelling open.

"How did we get here?" she said sharply. "You tell me, Jasmin."

I trembled from the force of her conviction, the immensity of the fire coming through her eyes. It only forced me to see the pain in them. Ana shifted her attention to her man, looking him over with concern. With his act gone, her fear of his hollowed-out heart had returned, leaving a sad emptiness where the pill of pleasure no longer had an effect. I felt compelled to take her pain into my hold, to pity it and give it love.

"You were gladly a part of it," said Ana, crouching down next to Jordan, running her fingers through his hair. "Nobody forced you to come into this world."

A knife drove into my lower chest. I was transported back to Aschinger, and felt myself tied up from head to toe in Ana's web of deceit and power. Only I had freely walked into it. I had been blind, but I had also been free to choose. The difference between now and Aschinger was that there was no rope binding me. Ana was right.

I looked Jordan over. Delved into his ocean-grey eyes, and envisioned what our potential future could be. The mind-blowing sex. The long conversations in bed. Trips to the Caribbean. Fine dining.

His powerful arms holding and steadying me during difficult times. We had the potential to be great together.

"He's all yours," I said.

Potential. That was all we were. And Ana had crossed that ocean years before. She was everything to him, and him to her. That much was clear now. J&A was there for a reason, and I had no place in it. I stared into Ana's eyes for an eternity, then smiled warmly at her like she was everything. Then I turned and walked away without looking at Jordan again. The candles flickered in slow motion, the trajectory of my entire future was irreversibly altered.

The dancing outside in the great hall was now feverish, having developed into a vortex of sheer joy. I went over to the stage and joined in, allowing the wisdom in my body to guide my sensual movements. I let it all go. Exorcised my twenties in the heat of the collective energy. Freedom alone would never solve my problems. The coming years would be difficult, challenging me in ways I could never envision. I had been captive to the past, caught in a maze of my own dysfunction. Now freedom was my captain, guiding me towards a life of purpose and meaning. On my side I had the power of choice.

In the flow of movement, I felt spacious inside. *Authenticity*. The Dutchman's wife's words reverberated in me. Then Kaspar appeared, sliding across and grooving side to side with a steady rhythm. I raised my arms and rested them on his shoulders, and he held me in place by my hips.

"Look at you," said Kaspar, tracking me up and down. "Stunning."

"Thank you," I said. "For showing up. For helping me see. I know this wasn't easy for you."

Kaspar nodded.

Authenticity. Kaspar had lacked that in the beginning. Not anymore. He was standing before me completely exposed, simply because it felt right. I embraced him with immense love, pouring it all into him as a token of my thanks. He had restored my faith in what a man could be. I prayed that I also had left him with something beautiful and enlightening. Our eyes transmitted their mutual gratitude.

"It's time for me to go," I said.

Kaspar released me, stepped back and nodded with a smile in his eyes towards the open road. I took it without hesitation. On my way out I watched Thomas dancing in the distance with his eyes closed, smiling warmly to himself, gladly lost in the groove. Giacomo approached him with a cheeky smile and opened his palm. Thomas looked down, then shook his head to refuse the offering, before returning to his bliss. Jordan, the fallen king, came stumbling out into the great hall soon after in his drunken state while people watched on with amused disgust. Only Thomas went over to him. He wrapped his arm around Berlin's former most-desired man, and spoke kind words into his ears. The sight of them together gave me tingles.

I left the party at its peak, and emerged from the mansion, heading towards the fog-covered forest. I sat for a long time on the grass by the trees, comforted by the sprawling nature behind me, and reflected into the early morning. Eventually, it was time to go. I got to my feet and slipped into the forest. The insects, birds and critters tolerated my presence long enough for me to emerge on the other side, where the first rays of the rising sun blanketed me. I stepped onto the open field as the fog began to clear, with the desire to be free an expression of my authenticity. It felt amazing. *Her* powerful energy coursed through me, preparing me for a new era.

I thought of the Dutchman's wife again and her beautiful words: *Move bravely into your own journey first.* It left me with one thought:

I was so fucking ready for my thirties.

Printed in Poland
by Amazon Fulfillment
Poland Sp. z o.o., Wrocław
05 October 2022

7326985d-2e32-42d0-ac81-b66cb1087ba0R01